New York Empires Series

Going All In
Icing The Puck

GOING ALL IN

New York Empires

CASSANDRA CARR
ISABO KELLY
STACEY AGDERN

T&D
PUBLISHING

GOING ALL IN

Published 2017 by T&D Publishing

Cover art design © 2016 Kim Miller

Interior book design © 2017 T&D Publishing

ISBN-13: 978-1-944600-03-7 (Trade Paperback edition)

First printing: June 2017

For information, contact T&D Publishing www.TandDPublishing.com

CONTENTS

GOING ALL IN

New York Empires

CASSANDRA CARR
ISABO KELLY
STACEY AGDERN

HEDGING HIS BET

Cassandra Carr

CHAPTER ONE

No me jodas! Don't fuck with me today," Annalise Alonso muttered under her breath as yet another guest stepped into her path. Cursing the fates for sticking her on this job at a Vegas Night fundraiser put on by the New York Empires hockey team, she balanced slim crystal champagne flutes on a small round tray in front of her as she wove her way around the room. This was at least her tenth trip through the crowd, and she was praying her manager George would move her to another task soon.

Her leg hurt, as it usually did when she was on her feet, but Annalise never complained. She was grateful for the work. At least she'd be able to buy groceries and maybe pay some of the electric bill with her salary from tonight. With his temper getting the best of him yet again, her younger brother Hector hadn't been able to hold down a job lately, and her salary from Creative Catering was all they had to rely on.

Annalise heard a screech and stopped to see what was going on. A woman was just getting to her feet after having taken a tumble down the stairs, and people had stopped to watch the commotion as if it were a train wreck. Shaking her head, Annalise turned away, just as a hulk of a man rose from the dealer's seat at one of the blackjack tables. As he knocked into the edge of the tray with his elbow, she threw her hand around the front of the glasses, but it was too late. Like beautiful dominoes they fell forward, onto her arm and all over him and then, when she jerked back, several fell toward her, soaking her white tuxedo shirt.

She watched in horror as the flutes crashed to the floor, sending champagne and tiny shards of crystal flying several feet around the two of them. The man made a desperate attempt to catch a couple of the glasses as they tumbled over, but once he had one in each hand he didn't seem to know what else to do. His tuxedo shirt, which undoubtedly wasn't a ten-dollar purchase from the thrift store like hers, along with his also-sodden jacket dripped the expensive bubbly steadily onto the floor.

Cursing again, Annalise grabbed a stack of beverage napkins from another waiter who'd come over to help and tried to mop some of the fizzy mess off the man. She only succeeded in making things worse though, as bits of white from the napkins clung to the wet suit coat framing his saturated shirt. Then her face flamed as her knuckles brushed his groin on one of her strokes. He looked down at her—way down, with dark eyes full of regret and embarrassment.

She dropped the wad of damp napkins on her tray. "I'm so sorry!"

"Not your fault. I wasn't watching where I was going," the man explained, his voice deep and rumbling.

George lumbered over, motioning to another staff member, who ran to get a mop. "We apologize, sir. Annalise was clearly not paying attention. If you send me the dry cleaning bill I will make sure you're reimbursed for the cost." He glared at Annalise, and she realized he'd be taking it out of her paycheck. She closed her eyes, as her hopes of actually being able to pay a bill vanished.

"Not necessary."

"The girl caused the accident and she'll pay for it," George answered. And then continued so softly Annalise almost didn't hear him, "Along with all of these broken glasses."

The man glanced at Annalise again, and his gaze moved from her flaming red face down. Annalise's eyes followed the movement and she realized her shirt had become transparent, along with her dollar-store white bra. Her nipples, which had hardened into points, were easily visible given her Puerto Rican coloring. She blushed harder. Forcing herself to raise her gaze, she saw that Mr. Tall, Dark and Built's gorgeous brown eyes had transformed, his pupils blown with heat. He touched a hand to his shaved head and blew out a breath.

"Excuse me," she said, and stepped around both of them. Fleeing to the relative safety of the kitchen area, she grabbed an apron someone had tossed on a prep table and wrapped it around her sopping wet torso. From there she ran for the bathroom, no longer caring who was cleaning up the mess or what George would say about her leaving him there to deal with the man.

Due to her heritage she definitely wasn't anyone's idea of thin, and her too-large breasts were just one of many banes of her existence. It was difficult at best to find bras that fit, especially with her nonexistent clothing budget, and many times she ended up with the kind of cheap, ill-fitting bra she was wearing today. Untying the apron, Annalise surveyed the damage in the mirror. Then burst into tears.

*****

Marcus Mitchell felt like he'd jumped into a pool in his tux. He wasn't a fan of dressing up, but the team had wanted the players to wear formal attire to their annual Vegas Night. Since he hadn't thought he'd be getting sprayed with champagne, he didn't have other clothes on him and wondered if they'd let him go home early.

Probably not.

After assuring the asshole he assumed was the catering manager that the hot little number he'd bumped into would most definitely *not* be paying for his dry cleaning bill, he excused himself, heading to the men's room to see what he could do with his clothes.

As he rounded the corner by the restrooms he spied the woman—Annalise, the manager had called her—hightailing it to the women's room. Marcus watched as her round, curvy ass and hips swayed inside pants not made for a woman's body. And she definitely had a woman's body, from the top of her straight, black hair to the small feet encased in a pair of black sneakers that looked odd with the rest of the outfit. He couldn't forget how her nipples had beaded from the cold champagne or the discernible outline of her sizeable tits as she'd unwillingly starred in her own wet t-shirt contest. His dick had hardened as soon as he'd gotten a gander at the dusky nipples, which were a few shades darker than the olive of her skin.

She was definitely of Hispanic heritage, given her coloring. At first he'd thought maybe she shared the same Native American blood he'd gotten from his mom's family, but when he'd looked at her again it was obvious from her round, light brown eyes, full lips and button nose she wasn't Native American. When he'd stood to his full height she'd only come up to his pecs, so he guessed she was only a little over five feet tall, but her chest was not in proportion to the rest of her, a fact he thanked God for. He loved tits—small ones, big ones—he wasn't picky.

He removed his jacket and then peeled off the drenched shirt. The undershirt he had on would have to do for now, but after blotting off the tuxedo jacket he decided he'd better put that back on. With all the alcohol flowing out there he didn't need any more attention from the puck bunnies than he was already getting. Being one of the few bachelors left on the team, as well as one of the most highly-paid players, meant he got more than his fair share of feminine attention. Lately he'd found himself wishing they'd all just leave him alone. Marcus much preferred a quiet evening spent at home to the craziness that was the Manhattan club scene.

As he headed back into the banquet room, he hoped Annalise wouldn't catch too much hell for this. It wasn't her fault. He went directly to the bar and got a draft, downing almost a third of it in one long pull. He didn't drink a lot, and he definitely wanted to keep control over himself, given the…quality of many of the female attendees, but he needed to calm down. Flashes of Annalise's breasts kept playing in his mind on a loop, like some sort of personal porno, and his cock refused to listen to reason.

Marcus caught glimpses of Annalise as she continued working. It looked as if she was still wearing the now-damp tuxedo shirt. Didn't they have spare uniforms around? A flare of something hot—jealousy or possessiveness—reared up in his chest as he thought about his teammates and the other men at the event checking out her rack.

He tried to catch her to tell her he'd take care of his tux himself. She shouldn't be held responsible for something that wasn't her fault. When he couldn't get a hold of her, he then tried her manager, but the man insisted Annalise make amends. Frustrated, Marcus slunk over to the bar and got himself a cola. Then an idea popped into his head.

"Hey, buddy, do you know Annalise?"

The bartender looked up. "Yeah, sure. We work together sometimes."

Marcus put on his best hangdog expression. "We had a collision tonight and my tux got wet. Your manager is blaming her and wanting her to pay for my dry cleaning. I told the guy it was as much my fault as hers, but he's insisting."

"Typical. The guy's a total bastard, if you hadn't noticed. I wouldn't even bother with this job if I didn't have student loan debt up the wazoo."

"Yeah, I caught onto his personality pretty quickly. I just feel bad. Is there any way you'd be able to get me some contact information for Annalise so I can call her and make sure she doesn't pay for my mistake? I've been trying to get her alone away from her boss tonight, but he's always hanging around."

The man reached for a glass and began drying it, his eyebrows drawn down. "I shouldn't do this…"

"Come on, man. Even if I never give that guy a receipt, which I wouldn't do in a million years, he's gonna dock her pay. You know I'm right."

The bartender glanced in Annalise's direction. "Yeah, and that's the last thing she needs." Marcus wondered where the cryptic comment came from but said nothing, lest he spook the guy. "Okay, lemme go look it up on the clipboard in the back."

Marcus reached a hand out. "I appreciate this, man. By the way, my name is Marcus Mitchell."

"I know who you are." He grinned and Marcus relaxed a little. "But swear to me you won't hurt her. A lot of people say you're one of the nice guys, but she doesn't need someone who's just looking for an excuse to go after a quick lay. If you're just gonna dick her around then I'm not gonna help you out."

"Seriously, I just wanna make sure she's okay."

The bartender assessed him for a moment before nodding. He left and Marcus turned toward the crowd. Without the buffer of the gambling tables between him and the puck bunnies it was a little harder to shake them off, but he managed. He had no interest in a one-night stand. When he'd been younger, sure. But now he was thirty-three and those days were long over.

He hadn't been lying when he'd said his intentions toward Annalise were honorable, he just hadn't been telling the whole truth. If he had a chance to get to know her better, he had a feeling he'd like her. Call it gut instinct, but Marcus's gut had never done him wrong. The bartender came back, slipping him a small piece of paper. Marcus tucked it in his pocket, tipped the guy fifty bucks, and went to see what his teammates were doing.

Chapter Two

By the time she got home and was finally able to remove her prosthesis her leg was killing her. The damn thing rubbed against her all the time and hurt like hell. She wished she had one that fit better, but beggars couldn't be choosers, and she certainly wasn't far above begging. Hector was nowhere to be found. Big surprise there. At least she'd been able to grab some leftover canapés so she'd have a meal tonight. The food was the biggest benefit of working for a caterer.

Annalise sat down on her ratty couch with the to-go box perched on a TV tray next to her and assessed the damage from the prosthesis. Angry red lines ran from the point where the prosthesis fit onto her leg to halfway up her thigh. She ran her fingers lightly over them and winced. Good thing she wasn't working again until Tuesday—it would give her a couple of days to get the soreness and inflammation down before she had to do it all again. But she was scheduled Friday and Saturday night next weekend, and though she was looking forward to the money, she definitely wasn't relishing the inherent aches.

When Annalise rose the next morning Hector still wasn't around, and she sighed. She hoped he wasn't getting into a bad crowd again. He'd been in and out of jail for the past couple of years, all for stupid stuff like trespassing and vandalism. But as she well knew, that's how the trouble started. You did some petty stuff and before you knew it found yourself driving the getaway car in an armed robbery, like her friend Flora, who was currently serving three to five years. For about the millionth time she thanked God that her own life had taken a different turn. Poor she may be, but at least she had her morals.

Annalise was just heading to the market to buy a few groceries and pay the blasted electric bill when her phone rang. She walked to it as quickly as she was able and made it just in time to avoid the answering machine picking up.

"Hello?"

"Annalise?"

"Yes."

"This is Marcus Mitchell—from last night." Annalise had no idea what he was talking about, and apparently he sensed that in her silence, because he continued. "I was the guy you collided with."

"Oh!" Her hand flew up to cover her mouth. "I'm so sorry—"

Marcus cut her off. "Don't worry about it. Actually, that's why I'm calling. I know that manager dude said he was going to make you pay for my dry cleaning bill and I wanted to tell you I'm not going to give him a receipt for it. So if he tries to make you pay for some phony bill, don't do it."

"I don't have much of a choice," she mumbled.

"Well, then, I'll give you my number and you can tell me how much he docked you and I'll reimburse you."

"Look…"

11

"Don't argue with me. I'm not letting you pay for something that wasn't even your fault."

"Um, well, thank you." Annalise wasn't used to people going out of their way to help her and couldn't help but feel a little pathetic.

"Do you have some paper? I'll give you my cell number."

A cell phone. Man, what she would give to have a cell phone. Then she could actually call home and check up on Hector while she was working and he'd have a way to get a hold of her when he got in trouble. But that was a pipe dream. She was lucky she'd kept enough ahead of the phone company to keep her landline.

Reaching over to the pad she kept on the counter in a vain effort to encourage Hector to write her a note when he left the house, she wrote down the number Marcus rattled off.

"I want you to promise you'll call me if your boss tries to cheat you. Promise me, Annalise." His tone brooked no argument and she agreed. "Good. Now just one more thing. Can I take you out for dinner sometime?" Annalise pulled the phone away from her ear and stared at it. He wanted to go out—like on a date? She realized she'd been staring so long that Marcus was repeating "Hello?" over the phone and she quickly put it back to her ear.

"Dinner?" Annalise smacked herself on the head. She sounded like a total idiot.

"Yeah. You know, that large meal typically consumed around sundown?"

She couldn't help but laugh. "I know what it is. I guess I'm just surprised."

"What? You thought Neanderthals like me didn't eat dinner?"

"I'm sure you eat dinner, I just have no idea why you'd want to eat it with *me*." Annalise was wishing for a hole to open up under her, but it didn't happen. How much less cool could she be acting right now?

"I want to take you out because you're a beautiful girl and I'd like to get to know you better."

"Okay, but—"

"No buts. You said okay and that's all I heard. So when are you free?"

Annalise bit her lip. "Um, tomorrow night? Or is that too soon? I mean, I know you guys are busy—"

"Tomorrow night is perfect. Should I pick you up?"

Glancing around her crappy apartment in a sudden panic, she said, "No, no. Don't pick me up. I'll meet you."

"How about we go to Butter?"

"Butter?"

"Yeah." Marcus chuckled and the rich sound echoed over the phone. "It's a cool restaurant in Manhattan. Very 'in' right now."

"Okay, I can do that…"

And it'll cost as much as I make in a month…I'm so out of my league here it's ridiculous.

"Awesome. Seven tomorrow night then?" She agreed and Marcus hung up.

After setting the phone back into the cradle she sat down at the small, scarred table that served as her eating area. "I have nothing to wear to a fancy place. What was I thinking? And why I am talking out loud to myself?"

She mentally flipped through her sparse closet and was ruminating on what to do about a suitable outfit for a fancy place like this Butter must be when she heard a key scrape in the lock at the front door. Her brother Hector strolled in. "Buenos dias, pobrecita!"

Annalise rolled her eyes. Her brother had been calling her "pobrecita" forever. It meant "poor little girl", but wasn't necessarily meant in a good way. "Where have you been?"

"I stayed over at Pablo's house. I thought I left you a message."

"You didn't."

And you damn well know it, chacho.

Hector shrugged. "Sorry. We got anything to eat?"

"Not much. I was just going to the store."

"You look like you're sitting, not going to the store."

Annalise felt her temper flaring and had to consciously settle herself down before she spoke again. Hector loved getting her riled up and she was loath to give him the satisfaction of knowing he'd succeeded. "I was just about to leave." She'd hauled herself up and was out the door before he could speak another word, which was something given how sore her leg was today.

On the way to the bus stop she considered her options for her date the next night. She could wear something she already had or hope there was something at the thrift store and subsequently buy less food. Just as she was mentally tallying how much food she could buy if she went to the thrift store, an idea popped into her head. Smiling, she got on the bus and sat down gratefully. Her friend Neva had offered to lend her clothes in the past. Neva's family wasn't rich by any stretch, but they weren't living hand-to-mouth like Annalise was, so maybe Neva would have something acceptable. Even better, both girls were curvy, so even a borrowed dress might look all right.

When she returned from the grocery store she called Neva, and her friend soon arrived with several choices. Annalise had a ball trying on each outfit, but ultimately decided to go with a pair of loose black pants and multi-colored blouse. She'd have to wear her work shoes, since Neva's feet were smaller than hers, but at least people wouldn't be staring and pointing since the outfit looked decent.

After profusely thanking Neva, who insisted on knowing who Annalise was going out with before she handed over the goods,

Annalise swore her friend to secrecy. All she needed was word getting out in the neighborhood that she was dating one of the Empires and she'd never hear the end of it. Despite that sobering thought, Annalise hadn't felt this on top of the world in weeks, but she made herself approach tomorrow with cautious optimism. The few times she'd gotten her hopes up that a man was interested in her, she'd been hurt. And this wasn't just any man—he was a professional athlete who was no doubt used to dating glamorous women. But she refused to be cowed by that. Her mama, God rest her soul, had taught her to be a strong woman, and she would be, even if she had to fake it.

CHAPTER THREE

Marcus dressed for his date with Annalise with more trepidation than normal. He had no idea why he felt so anxious. She was just a regular girl. Maybe it was because he usually dated women he met through friends or his teammates. That last woman, what was her name? Kristeena? Ugh, she was so boring he'd thought at one point during dinner he'd rather talk to his hockey sticks than to her.

He wondered again if he should have insisted on picking Annalise up. It didn't sit well with him to meet his date at the restaurant and expect her to find her own transportation, but Annalise had been insistent.

Marcus arrived at Butter with a few moments to spare and went to the bar to wait. He ordered a drink and had just paid the bartender when someone tapped him on the shoulder. He turned to see Annalise standing there, smiling shyly. He took in her brightly-colored blouse and black pants, but frowned slightly when he noticed the serviceable black shoes she wore. Did she not have any other shoes or was there a reason she had to wear those? He wasn't a snob and certainly not a fashion critic but he couldn't help but wonder why she would wear black sneakers with her outfit.

Before she could notice his disquiet he schooled his expression and grinned. Sliding off the stool, he offered it to her. "They said it would be a little while until our table is ready. Would you like a drink?"

"If you're having one."

He indicated the Crown and Coke sitting on the bar. "Got one. What'll you have?"

"White wine?"

"Is that a question?" She blushed and he grinned again. He found he liked teasing her, which was a departure from his usual date behavior. The girls he normally went out with didn't handle teasing well. Though Annalise blushed beautifully, she didn't seem to be offended. The bartender came over and Marcus inquired about the varieties of white available by the glass. Annalise chose a Riesling and he settled behind her as she took a delicate sip from the glass.

She half-turned in the stool to regard him. "How did you get a reservation here? My friend said it's booked for months in advance."

"There are a few advantages to being a professional athlete in this town," he answered, with a wink.

"Oh. Well, of course. I-I didn't think about that. You can probably go wherever you want, whenever you want."

"I wouldn't say that, but it does make it easier to do some things."

"Should we look at a menu so we know what we want when they seat us?"

"Are you in that much of a hurry to get rid of me?"

Annalise bit her lip and he imagined doing much more fun things to that full mouth. He shifted his weight, hoping his growing erection wouldn't be noticeable. "No, of course not. It's just…restaurants like this want to turn their tables."

"I'm guessing they'll let us stay as long as we'd like."

She blushed again and he was hit with an image from the other night after they'd collided. She'd been blushing then too, but it wasn't her lovely face he'd been paying attention to—it was her large, full breasts, nicely outlined by a sopping wet shirt. He was forced to alter his stance again.

Now is not the time, big guy…

"So, when you're not toting champagne around, what do you do?"

"Not much, really. I only have the one job right now, and the rest of my time is mostly spent at home."

He noticed she'd said 'one job' as if that wasn't natural, but decided to ignore that for the moment. "And where's home?" He knew he was being nosy, but the girl wasn't volunteering any information about herself, so what was he to do? Talk about the weather?

"Um, the Bronx."

"Wow, really? That's cool."

Annalise shook her head, staring into her wine glass. "Not really."

Okay, new topic.

"So why isn't a beautiful woman like you going out rather than staying home?" He watched as Annalise closed her eyes briefly and could've kicked himself. How did he keep saying the wrong thing?

"I just, um, prefer to stay home."

He was reminded of a phrase he'd heard as a boy: *liar, liar, pants on fire*.

"Have you lived in New York your whole life?"

"Yes. I was born in the Bronx and I'm still there. I'm guessing, based on your accent, that you aren't a native New Yorker?"

He laughed. "Not hardly. I'm from Vancouver."

"Canadian. I should've figured that out, seeing as you're a hockey player."

"A lot of players these days aren't from Canada. Only about forty percent of current players in the NHL are, I think."

"Really? Where else are they from? I don't know much about hockey." There was the blush again.

"Europe, Russia, and an ever-increasing number from here in the States."

"Huh. I had no idea. I mean, I knew there were players from Russia and stuff, but I had no idea it was so big a sport here."

A hostess came to take them to their table and Marcus blew out a breath as he watched Annalise walk ahead of him. He really liked her, but he was starting to get the feeling the two of them didn't have much in common. What could he talk about for the rest of the night?

Fortunately, they found they both loved similar movies and television shows and the rest of the evening flowed smoother than he'd originally thought it would. The only sticking point came when Annalise had opened her menu and he watched as her mouth dropped open before she was able to shut it again. She'd tried to order a small side salad, saying she wasn't hungry, but he'd watched as her gaze had wandered toward the other diners around them, her eyes round with longing. He'd basically had to force her to order something larger. Once he had and the food had been delivered, though, she'd systematically demolished every bite and he relaxed.

It was obvious she never ate in nice restaurants. He knew waitressing for a caterer couldn't pay much and New York City was by no means a cheap place to live, but he wondered what her financial situation was. It was clearly none of his business, but he found himself with a crazy desire to take care of her. And after some of the duds he'd gone out with lately, he could use a little special someone in his life.

She refused dessert, but he insisted he was still hungry and ordered a big slice of chocolate cake with two forks. When the check came he whisked it off the table and quickly threw his credit card into the holder, handing it back to the server immediately. He was happy their dinner was only interrupted twice by fans wanting to talk to him or asking for autographs. Marcus knew where his paycheck came from and made it a point to be friendly with the fans, but sometimes it was tiresome to not even be able to stop for a morning coffee without people harping on you about the power play.

When they rose from the table, he asked, "Would you like to take a walk?"

A strange expression passed over her face before she smiled and said, "I really shouldn't. I'm stuffed and I need to get home. I'm working tomorrow."

"All right, but I'd like to see you again soon. I'm going out of town to play for the next four days, but I'll be back late Friday night. Can I see you on Saturday?"

"I'm working Saturday night."

"What time? We could have a late lunch after I get done with practice."

"I need to be there at five."

"Perfect. I'll be out in Brooklyn, since that's where our arena is, so I'll come get you and you can take me somewhere in your neighborhood so you're not too far from home before you have to work."

"I'll meet you in Brooklyn. My catering job is there that night." She wouldn't meet his eyes, and he didn't know if she was lying about her catering job being there or if it was something else, but there was definitely some weirdness going on.

He turned her to face him. "Is there something you're not telling me? If you're not interested you can say so. I'm a big boy."

"No!" She bit her lip briefly before continuing. "No, it's not that."

Raising his hand to her face, he briefly stroked her cheek with his fingertips and she shuddered. "You can talk to me."

Annalise shook her head. "I really can't."

"All right. Do you still want to go out on Saturday? Or would another day be easier for you?"

"Saturday is fine."

"Then it's settled. I'll give you a call when I'm done with practice and we can get something right around the arena."

"You drive a hard bargain," she told him, with a little smile.

"As long as you don't say no." Before he lost his nerve, he leaned down and kissed her with just a light touch of his lips to hers. Initially she jerked back, but then settled in. His arm snaked around her waist as he applied a little more pressure to the kiss. Annalise put her arms around his neck and he pulled her even tighter to him, opening his mouth and running his tongue over the seam of her lips.

Her lips separated and he plunged inside, stroking over her tongue and exploring her mouth as her grip on him tightened. Marcus let out a soft growl as he changed the angle of her head with his free hand and continued the kiss. They were standing outside the restaurant, and he knew he should be more discreet, but this woman made him crazy.

Suddenly she pushed back from him and put her hand over her ravaged mouth.

"I'm sorry," he stuttered, "I—"

Annalise shook her head and turned partially away. "It's not your fault. Anyway, I gotta go." She began to walk away and he found himself chasing her, cursing himself for his lack of control.

"Annalise, wait!" She stopped and he said, "Look. I shouldn't have done that, especially not right here on the street. You're just so beautiful, and I thought we were having a good time."

She put up a hand and he stopped talking. "We were. We did. And it's fine. I just have to go."

He watched her walk away, her gait a little jerky, and again he wondered if she was hiding things from him. Sighing, he waited until she'd disappeared down into the subway before hailing a cab.

CHAPTER FOUR

Annalise sat down on the subway and put her face in her hands. *What have I done? Why did I let him kiss me? Why did I kiss him back?*

She knew the answer to the last question, at least. She'd kissed him back because he was hot and she liked him—far more than she had any right to. Once he found out who she was and the kind of life she led, never knowing where her next meal was coming from and trying desperately to keep her brother out of jail, he'd run, just like the few other men who'd shown interest in her had. One thing was for sure. She couldn't afford to like Marcus any more than she already did. She needed to concentrate on staying afloat.

But the next day as she was getting ready for work her phone rang. It was Marcus.

"Hey. I just wanted to give you a call to tell you I had a really good time last night. I'm sorry if the evening didn't end like you wanted, but I really do want to see you on Saturday."

Annalise ran a hand over her face. "Okay." She was weak and she knew it, but she'd beat herself up later when she actually had some time. Right now she needed to get to work. "Look, I need to go. You caught me on my way out the door to work."

"Not a problem. I just wanted to touch base." He paused for a beat before saying, "Will you watch me if you're free? We're playing tomorrow night and Friday night."

"I'm off tomorrow night. I'll try to catch the game." She didn't have cable on her thirty-year-old, decrepit television, but maybe she could go to a friend's house. Of course, then she'd have to explain why she had a sudden interest in the Empires. Maybe she could read the story about the game in the newspaper and hope that was good enough.

"That's all I can ask. Take care of yourself and don't work too hard. Oh, and if your boss docks your pay, tell me and I'll reimburse you. You promised."

"Fine. I really need to go, Marcus."

The next night she was able to listen to the game on an old radio Hector had gotten from who-knows-where, but it was hard to keep up with the action with how little she knew about hockey. One thing was clear, though. Marcus was one of the stars of the team. It seemed like the announcer was saying his name every other sentence. If he was one of the team's best players, what on earth was he doing hanging around with her? Slumming it for the experience? Somehow she didn't think Marcus would do that, but she really didn't know him well.

Marcus called her on Thursday while she was having cereal, something she had for lunch frequently since it was cheap and fairly nutritious. "Did you watch the game?"

"I wasn't able to watch it, but I listened to it on the radio."

"What did you think?"

"Well, I don't know a lot about hockey, but it seemed like you were a big part of the win."

"I'll get you tickets to a game if you want to go sometime. You can even bring a friend if you don't want to come alone. As long as it's a female friend." He laughed and Annalise wasn't sure what to say.

"Maybe." It was the best she could do under the circumstances. After all, she couldn't have him paying for what were undoubtedly expensive tickets after buying her dinner. When guys did things like that they usually expected something in return. Her mother had taught her that nothing in life was free, and Annalise had discovered exactly how right that statement was countless times. Again she thought about the kiss the other night and wondered what would've happened if she hadn't pulled away and left. Would he have expected her to go back to his place for sex? The thought made her feel warm all over and she wondered at her reaction to Marcus. Either she was totally blinded by his charm or it was far too easy to get her interested. Neither one boded well for her peace of mind.

On Saturday she dressed in her most decent-looking jeans and a sweater. Marcus called at one-thirty and they met at two in the afternoon in a little bistro he'd suggested that was within walking distance of the arena. Here more of the fans recognized him, but he was polite to everyone, signing autographs and even taking a picture with a little kid with an Empires jersey on. When the meal ended he insisted on paying, even though she offered to pay her own way, and after lunch was over he kissed her again. They ended up sitting outside the bistro in the early-spring chill and making out like they were teenagers. Annalise knew she shouldn't let him allow her to get so carried away, but when he held her and kissed her it felt so good she found she was powerless to resist him. Finally she pulled away with no small amount of regret and went to work. Marcus promised to call her the next day after practice, and true to his word, he did.

"So do you have some big Sunday dinner to go to tonight?" He was fishing for information again, and she sighed.

"No."

"Then you're free? Let's have dinner."

"You want to see me again?"

"Well, yeah, that's why I called. I thought after we spent twenty minutes getting hot and heavy you would've figured out how much I like you."

Annalise couldn't deny she wanted to see him again, so she agreed to dinner. "I'll come into the city."

"Come on, Annalise. I feel like a jerk meeting you all the time. I asked you out on a date. I should come pick you up and bring you back home."

"I'd really rather just take the subway in. With traffic it'll be a lot faster anyway." She heard Marcus' grunt through the phone and knew she had him.

"Fine. I'm not going to argue with you about it. At least let me meet you somewhere near your house instead of you traveling over here. Take me to your favorite place."

My favorite place? No way in hell. That's how rumors get started and I don't need everyone talking about me.

She thought for a few seconds and said, "Okay, how about Ray's? It's Italian." Ray's was a huge café in the heart of Queens that she'd been to a few times, and it was far enough away that there was a good chance none of her friends would be there.

"Sounds good. Where is it?"

She rattled off the address and heard him writing it down. "All right. I'm gonna grab a cab, so I'll see you there in about an hour if that's okay?"

"That's fine." It would give her a chance to take a shower before hitting the subway for the ride from the Bronx to Queens.

They met and had dinner and were thankfully left alone for the most part. As Marcus paid the check he asked, "Will you come into Manhattan with me? It's still early. We can go see a movie or rent one at my house. I'm not a huge fan of being out all the time."

She knew she shouldn't, but she found herself saying yes. Marcus caught another cab and took her to his apartment in the Meatpacking District. It was hard not to gape as she looked around at the high-end kitchen and expensive furnishings. They sat down on Marcus' taupe leather couch and she couldn't help but run her hand down the arm of it, noting the soft, buttery texture. Marcus picked up a remote that had more buttons than some cockpits she'd seen on planes in the movies and pressed a series of them. The lights dimmed, the television turned on, and she half-expected a steaming cup of coffee to appear.

"What are you in the mood for? I've got tons of DVDs, or we could rent something through the on-demand system."

"Whatever you want to watch is fine."

"Come on. Give me a hint at least. Drama? Comedy?"

She had enough drama in her life already. "Comedy."

Marcus picked a comedy that had been in the theater not long before and they settled back to watch. He put his arm around her and she leaned into the warmth of his solid body. It was nice to feel taken care of, even if only for a few hours before she had to go back to her lowly life.

She let him turn her head before kissing her, and when his lips touched hers she forgot he even owned a television as sensation built up inside her. He pulled away and looked at her, his eyes pools of molten desire.

Marcus touched the hem of her sweater. "Can I?"

Annalise bit her lip before nodding. Grinning, Marcus pulled her sweater over her head and she had a few seconds of mortification about her serviceable, well-worn white bra, but he just groaned and buried his face between her breasts before kissing and licking his way back up to her neck. Her head fell back and he attacked the sensitive patch of skin near her ear. A moan escaped her.

"You like that, huh?" he murmured, reaching up to push her hair behind her back before showering more kisses along her collarbone.

"Yes, so much." She arched into him and he took the opportunity to slide one arm around her and begin to lean her back. Her prosthetic leg hung off the cushions of the couch and he pushed her other one fully onto the cushions so he could slide his long, lean body between her thighs. His erection made itself at home in the juncture of her legs and he groaned as he pressed in. Wave after wave of passion washed over her as he kissed her again, deftly unhooking her bra before taking it off and dropping it on the floor beside them.

Annalise shuddered when Marcus looked up at her as he took a hard nipple into his mouth. He tugged gently with his teeth and then licked over the spot before moving to the other breast. Then he pushed both together and went back and forth between them, ravaging each with lips, teeth, and tongue, and she began to writhe underneath him. Her very limited experience with men hadn't prepared her for the onslaught of feelings she was experiencing now. Marcus was playing her body like a finely-tuned instrument and she marveled at how good she felt. Finally she began to understand what the big deal was about sex.

Marcus caught her breast in his mouth and took in more and more, pushing it between his tongue and the roof of his mouth, and she came off the couch again. She could smell her own arousal, and while it should've embarrassed her, instead it fed the carnal flame even more.

His weight was pressed into her, holding her down on the couch, and Annalise had to force herself to take deep, even breaths, afraid she'd hyperventilate from the excitement of feeling all those pounds of hard-packed muscle and sinew flexing and moving over her.

Marcus slid down, kissing his way down her belly before sliding clumsy fingers over the zipper of her pants. She panicked and pushed him away hard enough that he landed on his butt in front of the couch. He looked up at her, surprise evident in his expression. "What's wrong? Did I hurt you?"

"No." Annalise swallowed thickly. She wanted this—she wanted to have sex with him in the worst way—but she couldn't. She just couldn't. "I should go." Stumbling to her feet on shaky legs, she bent down to fumble in the dark for her bra.

"Annalise, honey, what's going on? Did I do something wrong?"

"No. It's not you, it's me."

"What does that mean? Talk to me!"

"I-I can't. I have to go."

Marcus grabbed her hand. "I'm not letting you leave like this. I'll take you home if that's what you want, but you need to tell me what happened. I thought everything was going okay."

"It was. It was great. I told you. It's not you." She found her sweater and slipped it over her head.

"Then what is it?" She could hear the note of frustration he was unable to keep out of his voice, and she spared a glance at his groin, knowing she shouldn't because it would only make her feel worse.

Marcus took hold of her face and forced her to look at him. "Don't worry about me. That's the least of my concerns. If you don't want to have sex right now, that's fine. Just say so. I can wait." Annalise turned away from him, wiping away a tear before it had a chance to fall. He pulled her back to sit on the couch and she let him. She was so weak, but feeling his arms around her, knowing he wasn't rejecting her, made her feel unbelievably warm inside. The last time she'd even allowed things to progress this far was years ago, and when she pulled away the guy had left her apartment in a huff and never called her again.

She closed her eyes, as another tear threatened to leak out, but couldn't help the sound of distress that forced its way past her lips. Marcus kissed the knuckles of her hand, whispering nonsense to her. He was too nice. He deserved better than a poor, uneducated cripple like her. Her heart breaking, she stood up. She couldn't believe how much her heart hurt. Even though they'd only gone out a couple of times, she'd gotten in deep with Marcus. Stupid. "I really need to go." He began to stand with her and she waved him off. "Don't get up. I can see myself home."

"But—"

"Really, don't worry about it." She moved as quickly as her prosthesis would allow her to and had slipped out the door before he was able to get more than a few more words out. Luckily, he didn't chase her, and she made it down to street level before the tears began in earnest. She couldn't afford to cab all the way home and was moving through the lobby, trying to figure out how many subway changes she'd need to make to get home, when the doorman stopped her with a gentle touch to her arm.

"Miss? I'll get a cab for you."

"I don't—"

"Mr. Mitchell instructed me to get you a cab and pay the fare."

"Oh." Another tear fell and she just stood there like an idiot.

The man's gave her a small smile and she wondered how often women came out Marcus' apartment in tears. Probably not often. "I'll get that cab for you."

Soon the doorman had bundled her into the cab and she was on her way back to her own life. Her walk on the other side had ended in disaster and, though she tried to convince herself it was for the best, the image of Marcus sitting there on the couch looking so confused ate at her insides. She rubbed her forehead as a monster headache made its presence known.

When she got home, Hector was there. "Annalise? *Pobrecita?* What happened? Who made you cry?"

"Nothing happened. I just had a bad day." The lie had slipped out almost without her even being aware of it. Hector's temper was famous and the last thing she needed was him finding out about Marcus and going after him. "I'm going to take a bath and then go to bed."

Her brother narrowed his eyes as he regarded her, and she had to force herself to meet his gaze. "You sure there's nothing going on?"

"I'm sure. My leg hurts and I'm tired."

"Hey, I've got some money for you."

Her eyebrow rose. "From where?"

"Don't you worry about where."

She knew better than not to worry about where Hector's money was coming from. "Is this blood money? 'Cuz if it is, I don't want it. I don't want drug money, either. It's dirty and I don't want any part of it."

"I did some odd jobs for a guy I know. Nothing illegal. Okay? Now will you take the money? You know what'll happen if you don't."

She did. He'd spend it on booze, drugs and other crap. Reluctantly she accepted the roll of bills. If she used it tomorrow to catch up on a few bills maybe it wouldn't have time to poison the house. Sadly, at this point she couldn't afford to be too picky about where the money was coming from, much as she'd like to keep Hector out of trouble.

"Thanks. I'll pay some bills with it tomorrow."

"Good. I'm trying, *pobrecita*, I really am."

She didn't believe him, but she nonetheless gave him the biggest smile she could manage. "I'm glad to hear it." He let her go without asking about her tear-streaked face again, and she thanked the heavens for small favors.

CHAPTER FIVE

Marcus sat on his couch for a good twenty minutes going over the time he and Annalise had spent there to try to figure out what the hell had happened. She'd been into it, he was sure of that, but then she'd suddenly freaked out. As he thought back, he realized it had happened when he'd started to undo her pants. But why would that cause such a reaction?

His mind flew in a million different directions. Was she a virgin? She was certainly responsive, but not in the way he thought a virgin would be. Did she have a disease? Possible, but that didn't seem likely for some reason. Then he remembered the slight limp he'd noticed a couple of times. Maybe she had a scar on her leg she didn't want him to see or something.

He thought of his own body, which was liberally decorated with scars from all his years playing hockey. If she thought a scar would gross him out, she was mistaken, but he could see where she might feel ashamed. A lot of people were self-conscious about stuff like that.

He vowed to call her tomorrow to try to see her again. Maybe he could convince her he didn't care what her leg looked like.

Marcus considered why he was pursuing Annalise so heavily. There was something about her, something that drew him in. He wanted her, yes, but he genuinely liked her a whole hell of a lot, if he was being honest with himself.

He went to bed that night sorry about how the evening had ended and resolute to set things right first thing in the morning. When he awoke the next day he found the optimism he'd had the night before had waned a little, but he was still determined to get to the bottom of whatever was bothering Annalise.

After dumping some coffee in the fancy combination coffee grinder-maker he'd been talked into by a beautiful woman in a store, he sat and put his cell phone down on the table. As the smells of the rich French roast started to fill his apartment, he went over what he planned to say, much like he went over each opponent before a game. Marcus tried to come up with possible objections Annalise would raise so he wouldn't be caught off guard. When the coffee finished perking he added cream and a little sugar and sat back down again.

Now or never...

He dialed Annalise, and one of the contingencies he hadn't even thought of made itself apparent immediately when a male voice answered.

"This is Marcus Mitchell. Can I talk to Annalise?"

"She's out right now. Who the hell are you?"

Marcus didn't like the guy's tone and was getting a real bad feeling. "Who are *you*?"

"Her brother, and she's never mentioned any Marcus to me. I know all her friends."

"Apparently not all of them," Marcus mumbled. In a louder voice, he said, "Your sister and I have gone out a couple of times. Can I leave a message for her?"

"Hold up. You guys have gone out? Like on a date?"

"Very much like a date, yes."

"Are you the reason she came home crying last night? I'm pretty protective of my sister—"

Just then Marcus heard a muffled curse and a bunch of noise on the other end of the phone. He said, "Hello? Is anyone there?"

"Marcus?"

"Annalise?"

"Yeah. Sorry about that." She must've put her hand over the mouthpiece then because he only heard snatches of what sounded like a furious conversation in Spanish. "Please forgive my nosy brother."

"No problem. Can I see you?"

"Today's not good."

"I thought you weren't working today."

He heard a sigh. "I'm not, but I need to run errands…"

It didn't surprise him she was trying to put him off and he plowed forward. "I need to do some stuff too. Let's go together and then I'll buy you lunch. We need to talk."

"I think it's better if we just forget about seeing each other."

"Today or ever?"

She paused for a few seconds and his heart beat staccato in his chest. How did this woman tie him into knots? "Forever, Marcus," she answered in a whisper.

"I won't accept that."

Her voice rose. "What do you mean, you won't accept that?"

"I mean that I have no intention of letting you off that easily." He could feel panic rising and tried to hold onto it. He didn't want to scare her, but dammit—this wasn't fair! "I know we don't know each other that well, but when I'm with you I feel something I've never felt before. And I refuse to just forget about that. Meet me and tell me to my face you aren't interested."

Annalise blew out a breath so loudly it sounded like a wind gust over the phone. Marcus knew he had her then, though. "All right. One lunch."

"Great! I'm coming to pick you up this time. What's your address?"

"I don't want you to come here, Marcus. And with Hector around, we'll never get out of here."

He raised his gaze to the ceiling and counted to three before answering. "Fine. Where should I meet you?"

"At the Latin Kitchen on Tremont in the Bronx. I'll be there at noon."

"Sounds good. I'll see you then. And honey? Don't be scared. I just want to talk."

Marcus scrambled to shower and run a few errands before grabbing a cab for the haul up to the Bronx. When he arrived he saw that the Latin Kitchen was a large bistro-style restaurant with white cloth-covered tables. Annalise arrived shortly after and they were shown to a table. Before he let her sit down he planted a kiss on her lips and then pulled away, smiling. Plopping in the chair, he perused the menu and quickly found he had no idea what any of the food was. He heard a snicker and looked up.

"What's so funny?"

"You," Annalise answered. "You look very confused."

"I am. You're going to have to explain all this stuff to me."

She turned her menu so he could see it. "This section is all seafood. Then there's pork over here, their signature dishes here…"

"Okay, but what's in the food? I don't speak Spanish, which is what I assume this is." He felt like a total goober, but after some not-so-pleasant experiences with food on the road he'd learned to ask what was in the dishes he ate.

"Puerto Rican food isn't necessarily spicy, despite what a lot of people think. There are a lot of spices used, but not all of them are hot. You might want to start out with one of the more basic dishes like *Arroz Con Pollo*, which is basically just rice and chicken."

Marcus made a face. "I eat a ton of chicken already. What about the seafood you mentioned?"

"If you like garlic there's a shrimp dish with garlic sauce."

"Maybe not garlic..." He was hoping to resolve whatever was bugging Annalise and then spend a few hours worshipping her body, so garlic didn't seem like the best option.

She rolled her eyes as if she knew what he was thinking. "One of their signature dishes is a pork dish. It's pretty popular and it doesn't have any garlic in it."

"Great. I'll try that." They ordered and he found himself leaning over the table and grabbing Annalise's hands. He released a silent breath of relief when she didn't pull away. "Now tell me what's going on with you. Why did you freak out last night?"

Her eyes shuttered and he thought for sure she was going to clam up again, but she just shook her head slightly before sticking her leg out from under the table. "Because of this." Pulling her hand out of his grip, she raised the hem of her jeans and he saw that she had a prosthetic leg.

"That's why you got so upset?"

"I'm not normal, Marcus. I lost my leg above the knee when I was a kid. I ran out into the street and a car hit me. Now I have this thing, and it doesn't fit right, and it hurts all the time, and it's not exactly something that makes me feel sexy." Marcus started to speak, but she held her hand up and he let her continue. "When things progressed last night all I could think about was you seeing my leg and being disgusted. It's happened before, and I guess I just didn't want to deal with it again."

"Did it ever occur to you that I might not care?"

"No. A lot of guys shrink away when they see I'm crippled."

"You're not crippled! You have a prosthetic leg. There's a difference."

"That's not what most people say," she muttered, and he had to resist the urge to shake her and kiss her at the same time.

"I'm not most people. Look, for years I've worked with the Canadian sledge hockey team. Those guys are missing arms, legs, whatever, and they still play hockey. I have a tremendous amount of respect for them. And now that I know about you I can only imagine how uncomfortable doing a job like waitressing must be."

"Don't feel sorry for me, Marcus." She raised her gaze and he saw so many emotions in her eyes—defiance, sorrow, and just a glimmer of hope.

"I don't feel sorry for you. I admire you." Anything else he wanted to say was put on hold when the server arrived with their meals. He took a bite and groaned in pleasure. "This is awesome!"

Annalise smiled just a little. "I'm glad you're enjoying it."

"Totally. Now, back to the topic. I don't feel sorry for you, but can I ask why you do a job that hurts you?"

"Because it pays the best of all the things I'm qualified for, which aren't very many to begin with."

"I'm sure that's not true."

"I don't have any education. I graduated from high school, but I never went to college. Mass transit is expensive. Just living in New

York is expensive. And since my brother can't hold down a job to save his damn life, it falls to me to make the money to keep a roof over our heads and food on our plates."

Marcus liked her brother less and less with everything he found out about the guy. How dare he sit around all day and expect his sister to work? "And why can't your brother keep a job?"

"It's not that he can't. It's that he doesn't." She wouldn't meet his gaze, and Marcus was sorry he'd brought it up. Obviously it was a source of pain for her.

"Okay. I won't pry anymore." He wasn't sure where to go next. Every cell in his body was screaming at him to help her, but he had a feeling his assistance would seem more like interference, and Annalise wouldn't take kindly to it. "You know, some of the sledge hockey players live in this area. Have you ever talked to someone else who wears a prosthesis to see how they handle their daily lives?"

She looked thoughtful for a moment. "Actually, no."

"Let me put you in touch with a couple of them. I know the team doctor, too. Maybe he could lend some insight."

Or help you get a better prosthesis so you aren't in pain all the time...

"That would be nice," she answered, and he watched as the cloudiness in her eyes cleared up. He wanted to be the man who made that happen for her every day.

Now where did that thought come from?

No doubt his protective instincts were making more out of the relationship than was actually there. He didn't know Annalise very well. How could he be thinking about a future with her already?

39

Chapter Six

Annalise sat there in the middle of the busy bistro, unable to believe what was happening. She'd told Marcus about her prosthetic leg and he hadn't run screaming. In fact, he'd reacted like it was no big deal. It felt too good to be true, and no doubt was. But still, she couldn't help the little kernel of hope that was blossoming in her chest.

Marcus paid the bill. She had a feeling he'd never allow her to pay for a thing, which, though it seemed sort of unfair, was a huge weight off of her, and she smiled as they walked outside.

"Can I see your place? I want to know where you come from."

"Not this time." *If* she ever had him over she'd at least give her ratty apartment a thorough cleaning. It might not make much of a difference, but it would help her feel better.

Marcus turned and gathered her in his arms.

God, he feels so good...

"Will you come back to my place then?" He began to nuzzle her neck. "I want you. I want to show you how beautiful I think you are."

Tilting her chin up, he kissed her and she luxuriated in the feel of his soft, warm lips and then his wicked tongue as he licked at her to open for him. She felt his biceps bulge and bunch even through his sweater and jacket as she ran her hands over them. An image of her running her tongue over the hard muscles came unbidden into her head and she had to stifle a moan.

"We can't do this here," she managed to choke out when he finally pulled away. Annalise felt the loss of his warmth acutely through her own thin coat and sighed internally for about the thousandth time that she didn't have something warmer.

"You're right. Come to my house. I want to make you feel good, baby."

She stopped to consider for a minute. Marcus hadn't seemed disgusted by her disability, and he seemed sincere now. She couldn't miss the erection pressing into her while he'd been kissing her, either. A man couldn't fake that, right? So maybe he really did want her. What was she waiting for? It wasn't like there was a line of gorgeous, nice, rich men just waiting to sweep her off her feet. There was only this one, and he was looking more uncomfortable by the second as she waged this internal debate.

"Okay, on one condition."

"Name it."

"Later we're going to go out to the store and then I'm going to cook you dinner."

"More Puerto Rican food?"

"If you want more, sure, but I'm a pretty good cook. I can't afford to eat out, so I've learned how to make all sorts of things."

"That's a deal. Now can we go?" Marcus grinned and she laughed. He was practically hopping from foot to foot.

41

He bundled her into a cab, and when it pulled away from the curb and into traffic he leaned over and kissed her again. She knew she should stop him since anyone could see inside in the stop-and-go traffic, but when his hands tightened on her waist and he plunged his tongue into her mouth again, all coherent thought fled. All that was left was this moment, with this man.

Marcus' lips dropped from hers to nibble at her neck, and she let out an agitated gasp. Then his teeth caught the sensitive skin of her earlobe and tugged gently, and she realized there was a direct path between there and her sex as it warmed and seemed to swell. His hand slipped underneath her bulky sweater and she felt the pad of his thumb graze over the bottom of her breast. Her breathing sped up as he began to rub ever-so-gently across her nipple. She glanced up, but the cab driver was either very good at ignoring things in his cab or wasn't interested in watching what was going on. Either way, she was grateful.

It seemed like the cab ride took forever, despite Marcus' attempts to distract her with his drugging kisses and teasing touches. Finally they reached his apartment and, after unlocking the door, he ushered her inside and then pushed her back to the wall as his head descended again. "I want you so fucking bad," he groaned. "Can we go to the bedroom? I've got a nice, big, comfy bed in there." He waggled his eyebrows and Annalise giggled. Marcus made her laugh more than she had in years.

"Okay."

He led her down the hall and into a huge, luxuriously appointed bedroom. She slid onto the king-sized bed in his bedroom and he followed. "Will it hurt you if I lay on top of you? Would you be more comfortable some other way?"

"You won't hurt me."

"If I do I want you to tell me right away. This afternoon is about pleasure." He took her chin in his big hand and turned her to face him. "Promise me, Annalise. If something hurts or if you feel uncomfortable, tell me and we'll talk about it. I don't want you running away from me again."

"I won't."

"Good." She lay down and he crawled over her, slowly easing his body down until he was between her thighs. "You feel just like a woman should—all warm and curvy. You drive me crazy."

She still couldn't believe this was happening, that a man like Marcus would be able to overlook her physical deformity and financial situation and still want her. Annalise spared a moment to pray he didn't change his mind.

"Touch me," she urged him.

"I'm going to. I'm going to touch all of you, honey. I want to be with you. I want to make you come for me again and again."

Her sweater was off and thrown to the floor almost before she realized he was moving, and then the rough stubble on his face was tickling the swells of her breasts as Marcus nipped and sucked his way to the front closure of her bra. With one hand he opened it and then fastened his mouth to her hard, distended nipple. Her back arched and he went with her, continuing to suckle.

Marcus moved to her other breast and she put her hands on his head, wishing he had some hair to grab onto and then moaning as he scraped his teeth lightly over her. "Feels so good…"

"That's it, baby. Tell me what you want."

"I want…"

He looked up at her, his brown eyes nearly black with blatant lust. Her sex clenched and she hitched her good leg around one of his muscular thighs. "What, honey?"

"I don't know. Just more."

"I can do that." He returned his attention to her breasts and her head felt like it was going to pop off her shoulders. In her limited experience with men, no one had been able to get to her so quickly and so thoroughly. After a few moments, he slid back. "I want to see you."

She blew out a harsh breath. It was now or never. Nodding, she closed her eyes so she wouldn't see the rejection in his once he saw what her leg looked like. Marcus peeled her pants down and all the way off. Her eyes flew open when she felt his tongue on her leg right above where she attached the prosthesis. He trailed it all the way up to the juncture of her thighs and then hooked his thumbs into her panties. "Oh, God," was all she could choke out.

"That's it, baby," he cooed as he removed her panties. Resettling himself between her spread thighs, he opened her with the tips of his fingers and took a long lick. That was all it took and she came, as the emotion of the moment washed over her. "Aww, honey..." she heard in the distance as her sex clenched and her back bowed. He took another lick and a sound she hardly believed she could make flowed from her mouth.

Marcus pulled back a little and inserted one finger into her. More sensation slammed through her body and her teeth clenched. Forcing herself to breathe, she implored him not to stop. She looked up and saw Marcus' brow was furrowed. "What?"

"Um..."

She started to sit up, knowing it was too good to be true and hating herself for thinking she could finally be normal. "It's okay if you don't want to—"

Marcus laughed, but there was no humor in it. "Oh, I want to. I just—"

"Spit it out." Tears threatened and she blinked them back. She'd be damned if she'd let him see her cry.

44

"I can't believe I'm even asking this, but I have to. Are you a virgin?"

"Oh." She chanced a glance at him. His jaw was set as he watched her with narrowed eyes.

"Yeah, oh. You're really tight and I don't want to hurt you. If you're a virgin you need to tell me now."

"I'm not a virgin."

"How long has it been?"

"Almost four years." She reached down to pick at an imaginary piece of lint on his bedspread; anything to avoid having to see his face when she admitted the awful truth.

Marcus swore softly under his breath. "I'm going to hurt you. I'm not porn-star material, but I'm not small either, honey."

Annalise groaned.

This isn't happening…

"Just go slow. I want this." She lay back down and held out her hand to him. He picked it up, kissing the palm, and then moved both of their hands down to her clitoris. While they rubbed gently, he inserted the first finger again and then a second, scissoring them a little. He found her G-spot and began running the tips of his fingers over that and her thighs tightened around him.

"Is that okay?"

She was writhing on the bed. It was more than okay. It felt fantastic. "Yes, yes…"

Reaching into the nightstand, Marcus extracted a bottle of lube and a condom. He quickly rolled the condom onto his erection and then applied lube. Annalise appreciated the time he was taking, but if he didn't get inside her soon she couldn't be responsible for what she said or did.

Coming back to kneel in front of her, Marcus guided himself to the entrance of her channel. "I'll go slow," he bit out through clenched teeth. She watched as his eyes followed the movement of his cock into her. His breath was coming short and fast and she knew he must be holding onto his control with intense concentration.

As he pushed a little farther in, Annalise felt a brief ripple of pain followed by an edgy, sharp pleasure. "Oh yes. God yes…"

"So tight, you're killing me, baby." He looked up at her when he was still only a few inches in. "You all right? Still with me?"

"I'm fine. I need you." She wrapped her good leg around his waist and pulled him closer. When Marcus sank in he let out an agitated gasp. "Shhh…"

"You just, man, you feel so fucking good. I can't stand it." He withdrew and slowly moved back in. His abs stood out in stark relief and, as her gaze wandered down toward the point where their bodies were joined, she noticed a tattoo of two oriental symbols, one on top of the other.

She ran her fingertips over them. "What do these mean?"

"Courage."

"Oh wow, that's cool."

He relaxed a little, pulling out most of the way again. "You should get one."

"A tattoo?" Annalise snorted. "For one thing, I can't afford it. For another, what would I do with a tattoo?"

He stopped thrusting back inside and looked at her. "You don't *do* anything with a tattoo. It's just there. I know something *I* could do with it, though." Splaying his hand over her the area right above her mound, he said, "If you put it where mine is I could lick it on my way down to the promised land."

She blushed. No one had ever spoken to her like that before. "Well, it's irrelevant, because I can't afford to do extravagant stuff like that."

He thrust in and out again a couple of times before he murmured, "I'll pay for it. We could go together and I could get another one."

Her brows furrowed. "I can't have you paying for stuff like that just because I don't have the money."

Marcus stopped again and Annalise considered screaming. She was sorry she'd brought up the subject, but her natural curiosity had gotten the better of her. "Why not? Don't worry about that. I'm one of the highest-paid players on the Empires right now. Let me do this for you," he pleaded.

She looked up at him where he was braced over her, his arms locked. "Only if you let me do something for you." He grinned and she punched him, but he hardly even flinched. "That's not what I was talking about."

"Damn..."

He moved again, quicker this time, and Annalise decided an amendment of her statement was in order. "Well, maybe not *all* I'm talking about."

"Now you're on to something."

Marcus dropped down onto his forearms and plunged both hands into her hair. Holding her head steady, he invaded her mouth with a marauding tongue and she gave herself over to him. He must've sensed her surrender, because he pushed even deeper inside her, stretching her, and Annalise couldn't stifle the moan that forced its way out of her lungs. His weight was now pressed dominantly over her, and he held her so close no space separated their sweat-slicked bodies. He began to drive into her a little harder and pleasure sizzled through her veins. She knew she was going to come again, if only she could get a little more stimulation on her already-sensitive clit.

As if he could read her mind, he said, "Touch yourself for me. Show me what you like." He lifted off of her enough so he could see.

Annalise bit her lip. She had plenty of experience masturbating, since that disastrous encounter four years ago was the only other time she'd had sex, but doing it in front of someone? That was a whole different thing.

"I-I don't know if I can."

"Yes, you can," Marcus answered, his tone brooking no argument. "I need to know what feels good to you if I'm going to satisfy you in bed."

She barked out a laugh. "I had an orgasm almost as soon as you put your mouth on me."

"Yeah, you did, didn't you?" he teased, grinning. Then she shifted and the grin fell from his face. "You feel incredible. I can't hold out much longer. Touch yourself, honey. Let me see it." Tentatively her hand moved down her belly to the spot where she and Marcus were joined. She found her distended clit and began to rub in small circles. "Oh fuck yes," Marcus got out before starting to move once more.

He sank into her again and again as Annalise worked her clit over. Finally an overwhelming barrage of sensation slammed into her and she cried out. Marcus' thrusts now jostled her entire body and after only a few more seconds he came on a long, low groan. Collapsing on top of her, Marcus took her mouth with another deep, soul-stealing kiss. His head settled next to hers on the pillow, his face turned toward hers. She breathed in his scent, one of sex and pure male, and her sex tightened in response. His breath caught.

Rolling to the side and onto his back, he flung an arm over his face. "Wake me up in four or five days."

Annalise chuckled. "You're a professional athlete. Aren't you guys supposed to have some stamina?"

He maneuvered to his side, his head propped on his hand. "That sounds like a challenge to me. Let me get rid of the condom and take a few minutes to rest and then I'll show just how much stamina I've got, baby."

"Oh, my…"

"Yeah. You didn't think once was gonna be enough, did you? There are so many more wicked things I want to do to you." She looked in his eyes and saw more than simple lust, though, and it scared the hell out of her.

She sat up in bed. "We should go to the store to get the stuff for dinner."

"Not so fast." Sitting up himself, he put his arms around her and nuzzled into her neck. "I need to be inside you at least one more time before I'll even consider letting you out of this bed."

"But—"

"But nothing. We've got plenty of time." She shifted and winced a little. He jerked his head toward her leg. "Does it hurt?"

"A little," she admitted. She couldn't think of a good reason to lie to him about it, so she didn't.

"I'm sorry, hon. Was I too rough?"

"No, you were great. It's just been a long day."

"Do you want to take it off?"

"Oh, no, I couldn't do that."

His eyebrows drew down as he frowned. "Why not?"

"Because it looks weird."

"It's a part of you, Annalise. It's not weird."

She blew out a frustrated breath. "It *is* weird. And gross. I've learned to live with it but that doesn't mean you have to."

"I don't mind, really."

"I mind! I mind, all right?" She knew she shouldn't be shouting at Marcus. He was only trying to be nice, but she couldn't help it. She didn't want his pity.

"Okay, okay." Marcus rose and disposed of the condom before kneeling in front of her on the bed. "I don't ever want to make you uncomfortable. That wasn't my intention."

"I know," Annalise admitted. She felt like the hugest bitch. She'd ruined the mood and didn't know any way to get it back. "Can we just go to the store now?"

"Of course. Whatever you want." He began to stand up and she grabbed his hand.

"I'm sorry. It's just…" She stopped to take a deep breath and he waited patiently for her to continue. "I'm kind of oversensitive since I got teased as a child and the stupid thing just gets more and more uncomfortable the older it gets. Anyway, I'm sorry I took it out on you."

Marcus smiled and reached up to run the pad of his index finger down her cheek. "Honey, I know it's hard. I wish I could make it all better for you. Don't worry about upsetting or offending me. Believe me, given the shit I hear on the ice every day, anything you could say pales by comparison." His finger trailed down until it caught on her bottom lip. "Now, I want you to understand something. I want you. And whether or not you're wearing a prosthesis won't make any difference. Yeah, it'll be a little strange the first time we have sex without you wearing it, but it's certainly not a deal breaker. I guarantee I'll still be able to get it up." He grinned and she rolled her eyes. "Of course, if at any time you'd like to help in that endeavor, I wouldn't complain." Sinking his finger into her mouth, he moved it back and forth in clear suggestion.

She knocked his hand away playfully as she shook her head. "You're incorrigible."

CHAPTER SEVEN

Marcus couldn't believe how good he felt. After they each took a quick shower, since Annalise refused to shower with him, they headed out to the store. She told him she was making a traditional Puerto Rican dish called *Carne Mechada*, which she said was basically a Puerto Rican pot roast. As they went up and down the aisles looking for the Adobo spice she needed, plus cooking wine and other ingredients, Marcus noticed Annalise was limping. She was also trying to hide the fact she was limping, which sent a jolt of annoyance through him. He wondered how much she'd allow him to do to make dinner. The thought of her standing to cook for him put a bad feeling in his belly that had nothing to do with hunger.

When Annalise was sure she had the necessary ingredients they walked the short distance back to his apartment. He deliberately kept his strides short and pretended interest in their surroundings so they wouldn't hurry and make her even sorer. Letting them into the apartment, he placed the bags on the counter and turned to Annalise.

"I'll get started preparing all the raw ingredients. I want you to at least sit down, maybe even take your prosthesis off. I don't know if it's good or bad to take it off in the middle of the day, but it's obviously bothering you and I won't be responsible for it getting even worse because you're standing at a stove for hours making me dinner." Gently he pushed her into a kitchen chair and knelt in front of her. "Would it help if I rubbed it?"

"No, that only irritates the skin." She sighed and ran her hand over her face. "It's just chafing right now."

"So take it off."

Annalise looked away. "I don't want to."

He forced her gaze to his and said, "I told you. I've seen a lot of stumps before. It's fine."

"It's not fine with me!"

"Annalise, honey, you have to let me in. Maybe you don't realize this, or maybe you're afraid or unwilling to admit it to yourself, but you and I are dating. Exclusively, if I have anything to say about it, by the way. And if you want to see gross, I'll show you my feet. They're all deformed from years on skates. If you're in pain, I want you to take care of it."

"But I have to make dinner..." Her protest came out in a half-hearted manner and he almost smiled before he was able to force a neutral expression.

"Tell me what to do and I'll do it. Look at it this way, you'll get to boss me around for a couple of hours."

A ghost of a smile played at the corners of her mouth, and he couldn't resist leaning up and kissing her. As she opened for him, he groaned, knowing he wouldn't get enough of her even if they were together for a hundred years. It was stupid to fall this far this fast, especially with Annalise being so skittish, but no matter how many times he tried to convince himself it was better to keep things casual, he couldn't. With a sigh, he stole one last kiss before rising.

"What should I do first?"

She gave him instructions and soon the roast was in a big pan, bubbling merrily on his stovetop. Annalise was still wearing that damn prosthetic, and when it looked like the meat could be left alone for a bit he went over and swept her into his arms, heading for his bedroom.

"Where are you going?"

"You're going to take that prosthesis off and then I'm going to lick you until you come for me."

"But the meat—"

"I'll keep an eye on the meat, don't you worry. The only meat you need to be concerned with is mine." He leered at her and she laughed. Hey, if he had to be a little silly to keep that smile on her beautiful face he was more than willing to make an ass of himself. "Take off your clothes and the leg. Now. I'm hungry and I want my appetizer." He turned away to give her some privacy. "I'll check on the meat while you do that. When I get back you'd better be naked or on your way there."

"Aye-aye, sir."

He smiled as he left the room. After checking the roast, he poured himself a big glass of water and downed it, trying to cool his overheating body. Marcus wanted to make her forget about her leg, and if giving her multiple orgasms worked, he was up to the task. He just hoped his cock didn't explode. Right now it was trying to make a break for it out of his jeans. Reaching down, he adjusted himself until he was as comfortable as he could be with a raging erection and then put his glass in the sink before returning to the bedroom.

Annalise was partially under the covers, and he knew she was trying to hide her stump from him. He let her, for now, and only swept the bed sheet away far enough to expose her pink, glistening sex. Moaning, he climbed between her legs and pushed both hands underneath her ass to elevate her. He took a long, slow lick and Annalise shuddered. Blowing a stream of hot air over her, he moved in again and then a third time. When his tongue began to spear her clit in short, fast licks, she grabbed the back of his head and tugged him closer.

Her nails bit into his scalp as her orgasm began. Marcus pushed one finger and then two inside her just as the rhythmic spasms began and she answered with a low, keening cry. He would've smiled or laughed in triumph if his face hadn't been buried between her legs, but with the grip she had on him he figured he wasn't going anywhere until she let him, so he just kept licking and sucking at her clit as her climax continued.

When the contractions abated she loosened her grip and he took her hands, placing them on her belly before sitting up. "Gonna go check on the roast again. Don't you dare move."

She mumbled something incoherent and now he did smile. He considered shucking his jeans for a more comfortable, less restraining set of sweats but figured as soon as his pants were off he'd be fighting the natural urge to take her, so he left them on. Padding back to the kitchen, he looked into the pot and added a little bit of water, per Annalise's earlier instructions. After forcing himself to drink another tall glass of water, he went back to the bedroom. Annalise's eyes were closed and a Mona Lisa smile played at her lips. A sudden image of those lips wrapped around his dick shot into his head and he couldn't stifle a groan of agony.

Her eyes fluttered open and she looked up at him. "What's the matter?" He watched as she glanced down, probably to see if her leg was visible, and he wanted to laugh. If only she knew that the pain had nothing to do with her leg. Would she be flattered he was having these carnal thoughts about her?

"Nothing's wrong, baby, you just looked so beautiful and peaceful lying here in my bed. I kind of like it." He sat down next to her and lifted a hand to her face, running the pads of his fingers down her cheek, over her jaw, and all the way down to skate across the generous swells of her breasts. "I thought I told you to take everything off," he whispered, gliding his hand over one breast before cupping it through her bra. "I want to taste these."

"Then take it off."

He did and bent to bury his face in her cleavage. She had the most beautiful tits he'd ever seen. Moving his face to the side, he took one puckered nipple into his mouth and drew hard on it, pinching the other between his thumb and forefinger. Annalise tried to grab hold of his head again, but he pulled her arms over her head. He stopped sucking long enough to tell her to leave them there and then went back to work, using his lips, teeth, and tongue to distend her nipple even further. Annalise was letting out little moans and groans as he delivered the erotic torture, and her sounds only served to inflame him more.

After moving to her other breast, his hand found its way to her mound and he pushed two fingers inside of her like he had before. He wanted Annalise so badly his dick was practically clawing is way out of his clothes. Even so, he deliberately kept up a slow, teasing pace. Annalise let him play for a while but then put her hands down and tugged on his arm.

He raised his head. "What?"

"I want you."

"Want me how?"

She blushed. "In my mouth."

"And how do you want me?" A shit-eating grin formed on his face and damned if he couldn't stop it.

"Um, however you want…"

The flood of images nearly choked him. "How about if we sixty-nine?"

Blushing even deeper, she replied, "I've never done that. What exactly do you do?"

Rising, he stood beside the bed and had his jeans and boxers off in record time. Then he reached behind him and pulled his shirt over his head, tossing it on the floor. He didn't miss the hungry gaze she directed his way. That gaze drifted up to his shoulders, where two large tattoos covered both of his upper arms.

"Do you like them?" he asked.

"I do. What do they mean?"

Pointing to his left bicep, he said, "This one started out as a design of Scorpio, my birth sign. I thought the scorpion thing was kinda cool." She smiled and he went on. "Eventually through the years I've added onto that one, so now the scorpion is in the middle, but there's the Japanese symbol for family, the Olympic rings from the time I played for Canada, and a few other significant little things." He turned toward her a little so she could see his right bicep. "This one started out as one of those armband tattoos, but I thought the barbed wire looked silly and added to that one too. Now it's got an image of a Celtic god named Lenus, who's a healing god to help with my injuries, an image of a goddess named Skaldi who was said to be the goddess of ice, and a bunch of random twirls to tie it all together."

When he looked up she was smiling. Before he could say anything she reached out her hand. "Come to bed and show me how do this sixty-nine thing."

"Don't have to tell me twice." Carefully he lowered himself over her and then decided that wasn't going to work. "Lie on your side, whichever side is most comfortable." When she was situated, he crooked his head into the juncture of her thighs and took a lick. Her breath caught and then she seemed to realize she hadn't taken him in her mouth yet and reached for his cock.

"I've never done this before, so you'll have to tell me if I do something wrong."

"Baby, if you've got my dick in your mouth it's almost impossible to be doing it wrong. Just don't use your teeth." She giggled and her hot breath stole over the head. He shuddered and she did it again, deliberately this time. "Tease. Two can play at that game, you know."

"Uh-oh. I'd better behave." Using both hands, she guided his erection between her lips and his eyes closed of their own volition when the head was sucked into her warm, wet mouth.

He'd had his share of blow jobs in his time, but the innocent enthusiasm Annalise displayed just about undid him. Marcus had to fight not to guide her, choosing instead to grab handfuls of the sheet in front of him. Taking a look down, he dove for her sex like a starving man. She tightened on him and he nearly lost it again before concentrating his attention on bringing her pleasure.

Her clit was peeking out from her feminine folds and he separated them with his thumbs before pulling her clit into his mouth to take little sucking pulls from it. She moaned around his cock and he swore, releasing the nub for a moment in a vain effort to process the sensation. Before long though he had it back between his teeth and was taking her ever higher, judging by the increasingly heavy breathing and little noises she was making. Annalise bent her head to take more of him inside and his eyes closed again. He knew he was getting close and that he needed to warn her, to ask her if it was all right to come in her mouth, but his thick tongue refused to form words.

He felt the familiar stirrings of his orgasm in the base of his cock and bowed his body, pulling himself out of her mouth. She looked at him in confusion. "I'm close, honey. Really fucking close. If you don't want to swallow, tell me now."

She looked down and he noticed twin spots of color on her cheeks. "I want to," she mumbled so softly he barely heard her, and he groaned, pushing back inside. Annalise sucked hard on the head and before he knew it he was coming as sharps bursts of pleasure ran from his balls up through his cock. He was letting out a series of grunts and groans as each hit, and when Annalise kept her mouth on him and sucked all the way through he started to see spots.

"Enough." He collapsed on his back and put a hand over his racing heart. "I'll get you in a minute. I'm literally seeing stars."

Annalise laughed and turned, snuggling up next to him. "Really?"

He cracked one eye open and saw the look of smug satisfaction. "Really. You keep doing stuff like that and I'll never let you out of bed."

"Mmm, that doesn't sound all bad. You have a very comfortable bed." She rolled again and sat up. "But we should look at the meat again."

"Okay. I'll go."

When he returned she said, "We should have about forty-five minutes until we need to take it off the heat, then another fifteen while it rests."

"Rests?" He raised an eyebrow and she chuckled.

"Yes. Meat needs to rest before you serve it."

"Because it's tired from being cooked?"

She slapped his thigh and he pretended to wince. "No, because if you let it sit there for a little while it seals in the juices. Trust me."

"If you say so…" He beckoned to her to lie down. "Now, where were we? Oh yes, I was about to make you scream my name."

"You have an absolutely huge ego, don't you?"

Marcus sobered. "I actually don't. A lot of what you see is an act."

"Is that right?"

"That's right," he echoed. "When I was younger, I actually got bullied even though I was one of the bigger kids in school. Humor helped me cope and I guess I still use it sometimes."

"I wish I had been able to do that. I got bullied too, because of my leg. I had a really bad limp for a long time after I got my prosthesis and kids made fun of me. I think that's one reason why Hector's temper is so bad. He always tried to defend me. So no matter how irresponsible he acts or what trouble he gets into now, it's hard to just turn my back on him."

Chapter Eight

Annalise looked down and Marcus took a gentle hold on her chin and tipped it up so she would look at her. "He's an adult. No matter what happened to you or to him when he was younger, it's his responsibility to rise above it now. I can understand you wanting to stick by him, but you have to let him be an adult."

"I know." She felt a tear rising and willed it to stop. Marcus' head dipped down and he kissed her eye, so she guessed she hadn't been successful in hiding her upset. Then he kissed the other one before trailing open-mouthed kisses along her cheek to her ear.

"I want you again," he whispered, and Annalise shivered. "But I need a little time. Maybe after dinner. Besides, it's your turn to come. I'm getting addicted to watching you fly apart in my arms."

"I want that too." She couldn't believe she'd admitted that. What kind of woman was Marcus making her into?

"Then lie back and let me take care of you." He parted her legs and pulled her so he could kneel on the floor. "You're so pretty."

"No, I'm not."

"Yes, you are. I love your body. There's your long hair that I can tangle my hands in, your gorgeous breasts that I love sucking on, this beautiful little clit I'm about to drive wild, and best of all, your face. Man, I could kiss you for hours. I'd develop a lethal case of blue balls, but I swear it would be worth it."

Before she could make a retort he'd pushed his face between her slick thighs and her back bowed off the bed. Coherent thought was impossible as he began to nibble at her with his strong, sure lips before taking little slashing licks at her clit. All at once, the sensitivity she'd been feeling before came rushing back and she moaned.

"That's it, baby, you're gonna come for me, aren't you," Marcus murmured, still busy between her legs. "Yeah, that's my girl…"

It should've sounded condescending, but she knew he didn't mean it that way. Every word he said fed her desire more—she loved his deep voice, which grew huskier as his excitement level ratcheted up. She twisted on the bed, looking for that one little action that would send her over the edge, until he put his arms around her thighs and held her down for his relentless assault.

The thrill of not being able to move while Marcus kept at her clit sent a frisson of a ecstasy down her spine. After a few minutes he moved one arm, leaving the other to anchor her, and entered her with two fingers. "That's it, that's what I want…so wet for me."

She gasped as the ends of his fingers rubbed over her G-spot. "Don't stop."

"I'm not stopping. Not until you come for me."

"Oh God…"

"Look at me." She raised her head, which felt like a lead balloon, and saw his gorgeous face slick with her juices. A blush bloomed on her face. "Yeah, you can see what you do to me. I want you to say my name when you come, all right, honey? Say my name."

Her head lolled back onto the soft sheets. "Okay."

Marcus went back at her. It took a shockingly short time before her release rolled over her, and her fingernails scrabbled for purchase in the bed sheets. "Marcus!"

He growled and continued his exquisite torment. When another wave hit she shouted his name and he pulled away from her long enough to say, "That's it…" before returning to lavish more attention. Finally she had to practically kick him away with her one good foot as the sensations became too much for her to handle. He crawled up the bed to lie down beside her. "I loved hearing you scream my name."

"I bet," was all she could manage to get out. Her brain felt like a huge plate of scrambled eggs and she was sure she'd never be the same again.

They took both a few moments to collect themselves and then Annalise insisted she put her prosthesis back on for dinner. Marcus pulled the pot roast off the stove and set the table while it rested. It was delicious, as she knew it would be, and Marcus ate a ridiculous amount. She smiled a little to herself as she considered why he was so hungry.

He insisted on doing the dishes and told her to just sit at the table and talk to him, but she couldn't do that, so finally he relented and brought the wet pots and pans over for her to dry. As they finished, his cell phone rang and when he picked it up, he smiled. After a short conversation he put his hand over the phone. "A couple of the guys and their girlfriends are getting together at one of my teammates' apartments. Do you want to go? It would be pretty casual. They had dinner and now they're just hanging out."

She looked at him and could see he wanted to. He'd said he wasn't much for going out anymore, but she reasoned this wasn't really "out", more like "in" at someone else's house. Despite huge reservations, she wanted to make him happy, so she assented and he smiled. A few more words were said and he hung up the phone.

"If you don't want to go we don't have to, but I'd kind of like to show you off."

Her mouth dropped open. "Show *me* off?"

Marcus stopped in front of her and stooped down to kiss her briefly. Standing to his full height again, he grinned. "Yeah, show you off."

"Why?"

"Because I like you and because as I told you before, far as I'm concerned, you're my girlfriend. These guys are like family to me. I want them to meet you and you to meet them."

"All right, if you're sure."

"I'm sure. I just want you to be sure. I don't want to make you uncomfortable."

"Well…"

"What, baby?"

"It's just," she wasn't sure how to put this without calling negative attention to herself, but it had to be said, "those other girls are probably beautiful and put-together and I'm, well, this." Her hand swept down her cheap outfit.

"You'll be the most beautiful girl there, at least to me."

"That's sweet. Not true, but sweet."

"The only thing that's important is I think you're the most beautiful. But like I said, I don't want to make you uncomfortable." He sat next to her and took her hands. "Look, we don't have to be there for a bit. If you feel uncomfortable I can take you shopping for something to wear. I've got a couple of ideas." He sent her an exaggerated leer, but she shook her head.

"I can't accept something like that from you. I already take way too much."

"Look, babe, here's the deal. You're my girlfriend. I want you to be happy. If it will make you happy to have a pretty outfit to meet my friends, then we'll get you a pretty outfit. It doesn't mean you owe me anything. I hope you know me enough by now that you realize I don't operate that way."

Annalise nodded. "I know you don't. I'm just not used to people throwing money around. It's not something I'm used to and it makes me feel obligated."

"I give a lot to charity and save a ton more for when I'm done playing, but I'm paid an obscene amount to begin with. Even with my donations and saving for the future I have a lot left over. Being with you makes me happy, and I want you to be as happy as I am. Hell, if you let me I'd take you on a Pretty Woman-style shopping spree, but since I'm sure you won't, let me at least do this for you."

She had to ask the question. "Are you ashamed of how I look now?"

"God, no, honey! I could never be ashamed of you."

"You're sure?"

"Positive." He grinned like a little kid in a candy store and she said yes despite her reservations. How often did a guy offer to buy you a hot outfit? "Come on, let's go."

He urged her up and together they made their way to a little boutique near his apartment. The saleswoman looked her up and down and put both of them in big, overstuffed chairs while she browsed the store looking for things to show them. Annalise sat, trying to look at ease and sophisticated and surely failing miserably as she twisted her hands in her lap and chewed the inside of her cheek. Marcus leaned over and whispered, "If you don't stop playing with your mouth I'm gonna thrust my tongue in there to give you something better to do." Her eyes went wide and he continued. "Oh, yeah, don't think I won't. I will totally make out with you right in the middle of this store."

"I've been meaning to ask you about that…"

Marcus' eyebrows drew down. "About what?"

"Well, you're pretty famous around here, right?"

"Yeah, so?"

"So we've made out in public before. Aren't you worried about your image?"

Marcus snorted. "No, for several reasons." He held his index finger up. "One—I'm known as one of the nicest guys in the NHL—true, by the way." She groaned and he smiled. "Two—I'd gotten so sick of the dating scene in New York rumors were starting about me being gay." Now she barked out a laugh. "I know, crazy, right? Anyway, people are probably thrilled to see me with a woman and are perfectly willing to let me sex her up within their view."

"I'm sure that's not true."

The saleswoman came over then and Annalise took a couple of outfits to try on. She had to admit it was a lot of fun to feel the luxurious fabrics and revel in the exquisite fits. Marcus stood right outside the dressing room, warning her not to even look at the price tags.

She modeled each piece for him and after she finished, she gave him the pair of silky lounge pants and long tunic set she'd picked, along with a comfortable pair of flats, and he paid for the items before bringing them back to her. After dressing in her new outfit, she checked her hair and bemoaned the total lack of makeup on her face. She couldn't afford to wear makeup and had given up on it years ago.

Annalise opened the door and saw Marcus deep in discussion with the saleswoman. As she approached the pair she cleared her throat and they jumped apart like they'd been hit by shrapnel. Her eyes narrowed. What was going on? Was Marcus interested in the beautiful, thin, perky saleswoman? But then he grabbed her and kissed her right in front of the woman and Annalise calmed down a little. That hardly seemed like something a guy who was trying to pick up a girl would do. Still, she was suspicious about the conversation.

She let Marcus steer her into a cab before she turned to him. "Give it up."

"Give what up?"

"You're a terrible liar. What's going on?"

Marcus rubbed a hand over his bald head and then let out a loud breath. He turned briefly to gaze outside and then swiveled to fully face her. Taking her hands, he said, "Okay, first of all, please don't get mad."

"That's never a good way to start. Spill it."

He gave her hands a quick squeeze. "I bought everything."

"What do you mean, everything?"

"Everything you tried on, plus some jewelry and lingerie and stuff."

Annalise felt her face pale. "You bought everything…" She feared if the cab kept moving she'd lose her dinner. Pulling away from Marcus, she put her hands on her stomach.

Oh my God, what did he do? How much did it cost? What would he want from her now?

"Yeah. Everything looked so good on you and you were so happy. Please don't be mad at me."

Annalise took a breath and when she felt a little more confident she wasn't going to throw up, spoke carefully. "I'm not mad." He looked dubious and she shook he head. "Really. I'm not mad. I'm not sure how to explain this to you."

"Try."

"I guess…" She bit her lip. "I guess I feel sort of like a kept woman."

"A kept woman? What does that mean?" He leaned back against the door, crossing his arms over his chest and Annalise wished he didn't look so good when he did that. It made it very hard to keep her focus, and she needed to keep her focus about this.

"How do I explain this? I feel like you'll keep me around to look good on your arm and have sex with."

She'd never seen someone do a double-take, but that was the only word for the expression on Marcus' face. "Are you serious?"

Annalise held up a hand. "I don't think that was your intention. In fact, I know it wasn't your intention. But Marcus, you have to understand. People don't just do stuff like this. Especially not for me. You know a little of my financial situation. This is all so out of my league, I can't even comprehend this really."

"Well, people should do nice stuff for you," he grumbled. "I intend to treat you like a princess as long as you'll let me."

"I don't want to be treated like a princess. I want to be treated like a woman."

He threw up his hands. "I thought that's what I was doing." The cab pulled to the curb and Marcus groaned. "Look, are we okay?"

She felt horrible. Here they'd been having a great time, having spent practically the whole day together, her stump hadn't seemed to bother him, and he does what he thinks is a nice thing and she shits all over him. When would she learn? "We're fine, and thank you for my beautiful outfit and for all the other stuff you bought, even though you shouldn't have."

"You're welcome." He gave her a quick peck on the cheek before reaching for his wallet and paying the driver.

They walked into the building and up to the apartment of his teammate hand in hand, and Marcus didn't let her go until well after she'd been introduced to everyone. After a while, though, the men got up to get another round from the kitchen, leaving her alone with the women.

"So," one of them, a petite brunette with an absolutely perfect body from head to toe, who she thought someone had called Barb, asked Annalise, "What's your deal?"

"My deal?"

"Yeah. Where did you meet Marcus?"

Annalise cleared her throat. "At the Vegas Night event the team put on."

"Oh, were you there? I didn't see you."

"I was there." She picked at an imaginary piece of lint, feeling about two inches tall. It was clear from Barb's tone that she didn't think Annalise belonged here. And from what Annalise had seen so far, Barb was right. This was an entirely different world than the one she lived in and she had no idea how to behave, what to say or do.

Barb tilted her head and Annalise vaguely wondered if she practiced doing that at home in front of a mirror. "Huh. Is he the first hockey player you've ever dated?"

Annalise sighed. She glanced toward the kitchen. What was taking the guys so long? She made her best attempt to smile sweetly. "Yes. Why do you ask?"

What's with the third degree, chica?

"You just don't look much like the type to be going out with a hockey player."

"And what type is that?" Another woman, who Annalise recalled had been introduced as Melanie, interjected loudly, glaring at the interrogator, who looked Annalise up and down before seeming to dismiss her.

Another woman, this one about six feet tall with a mess of gorgeous wavy blond hair whose name escaped her, responded, "Marcus dates models and actresses. What did you say you do?"

"I didn't," Annalise answered through clenched teeth. The woman just sat there, eyebrows raised. "I work for the caterer who did the event."

"Doing?"

"Hey, ladies, we're trying to have a good time. What's with the inquisition?" another woman, Nathalie, asked.

Barb shrugged and said, "Just trying to find out more about our new friend." She smiled at Annalise and she could swear she saw fangs. The first one who had defended her snorted, but Barb ignored her. "After all, Marcus is one of the stars of the Empires. He has a reputation to uphold."

"What reputation?" Annalise couldn't stop herself from asking.

"One that doesn't include dating waitresses." The two woman gave each other a significant look, and Annalise decided she'd had enough. She'd put up with enough bullying in school to know she shouldn't let them get to her, but she'd wanted to make a good impression on Marcus' friends. That was a joke.

CHAPTER NINE

Annalise fought back tears. She would not give these women the satisfaction of knowing they'd hurt her. Bless the girls who'd stood up for her, to no avail. She shot both of them a look that hopefully said without words how much she appreciated them coming to her defense.

Then the ringleader of this circus from hell, Barb, spoke up again. With narrowed eyes she retorted, "You'll never keep him. Never."

That was it. "Excuse me," she mumbled as she fought her way to her feet from the soft cushions of the couch and lurched toward the hall. Where she was going, she had no idea, she just knew she couldn't stay in that room anymore. As she walked past the kitchen as quickly as her prosthetic would allow, Marcus turned to her, but she waved him off and passed the door before he could say anything. The absolute last thing she wanted was to see the pity written all over his face if he saw her now tear-streaked cheeks.

But Marcus followed.

Damn him! Doesn't he know I want to be alone?

He reached out to grab her arm and she jerked out of his grip with a strength she didn't know she possessed. Turning into the first room she came across, she realized this must be Ray's bedroom and blushed.

Keeping her back to him, she said, "Leave, Marcus. Go back to the kitchen."

He kicked the door closed and she winced. "No fucking way. Tell me what's going on." He forced her to turn to face him. "What did those girls say to you?"

"Nothing. It's nothing."

"Dammit, Annalise, it's not nothing! You wouldn't have gone flying out of the room if it was nothing. You wouldn't be standing here crying if it was nothing."

"It's just—" She sighed, rubbing her suddenly throbbing temples. "I don't belong here."

"Like hell you don't. You're with me."

"I don't belong here, Marcus, here in this world. I don't belong with you—I don't know why I ever thought I did. I guess I was just hoping—"

"I'm gonna find out what those bitches said." Marcus made for the door and Annalise dove for him, her face contorting as her stump shifted in her prosthesis. He instantly stopped and steadied her. "I'm sorry, baby. Did you hurt yourself? Let me look."

"No! I just want to leave."

"We can go back to my place."

"No." She was finally able to continue in a stronger voice. "I want to go home. Alone."

"You don't mean that. Don't let those girls make you feel like you don't deserve to be here. They're petty, jealous, stupid women."

"But don't you see?" Her voice was rising and she felt sure the entire apartment could probably hear, but at this point she didn't know how to stop the tirade. She was tired and her stump hurt and her pride was trampled. She needed to get away from him before she completely lost herself. "It's not just them. I'm going to encounter this again and again. What if I'm not wearing one of the outfits you got me? Are you going to replace my entire wardrobe? Are you that ashamed to be seen with me in my other clothes? Or were you trying to avoid this from happening?"

"I was trying to make you happy," he insisted, coming closer. She took a step back and he stopped, bringing his hands up to clasp them on the back of his neck. "Look, let's just go. I'd like to talk more about this and we can't do it here."

"I told you. I want to go home." She knew she was being stubborn and that she shouldn't take her anger out on him, but she was hanging on by a very thin thread and one more wrong word would snap it. Annalise had a temper when she got going, and right now it was about to come out, if she didn't collapse on the floor in tears first.

"Fine. If that's what you want, I'll get you a cab. But this isn't over. We're leaving tomorrow for a few days, but when I get back we're gonna hash this out. I'm not losing you because my teammates are dating a couple of bitches."

She nodded, wanting nothing more than to get away from him and this place. He got their coats and said his good-byes while Annalise waited in the bedroom. Then, head held as high as she could manage, they walked out. Melanie followed them.

"Don't let them get to you. They're just jealous because neither of them has anything to recommend them besides their looks, and no amount of plastic surgery can keep that going for them."

"Thanks." Annalise could only manage a slight smile. The woman reached out and touched her arm, then went back inside. She turned back to Marcus to find him staring at her, an intense look clear in his dark eyes. If she wasn't careful she could get lost in those eyes, and then where would she be? She took a step away from him. "Look, you don't have to come down with me. I can just take the subway home."

He gave her a gentle smile and closed the space between them again. "Don't argue with me, honey." Marcus reached up and tucked a stray lock of hair behind her ear and she fought to maintain her pique. Why did he have to be so damn nice? "At the very least, I'm putting you in a cab and paying for it. If I had my way I'd be bringing you home to my apartment to talk about this, but I've never forced a woman to do anything she didn't want to do and I never will."

When he'd gotten her a cab and had given the driver the fare and an obscene tip, he pulled her to him. Wrapping his strong arms around her, he lowered his head and kissed her. She wanted to just stand there, to not react, but she found her arms weaving around his neck as he pulled her even closer, touching the tip of his tongue to her lips to urge her to open for him. When she resisted he began to lick at her, and after a few seconds she relented and his tongue drove into her mouth, plundering her depths. He was so warm…

She remembered they were standing on the sidewalk in uptown Manhattan and abruptly pushed him away. Marcus was panting. In a cracking, thick voice he warned her, "I want you. I'm not letting you go."

So he wouldn't see the tears that sprang to her eyes with his declaration, she ducked into the cab and shut the door.

*****

Marcus walked back inside his teammates' apartment building in a haze. What the hell had just happened? One minute he and his teammates had been swapping insults and a few fish stories and the next thing he knew he was putting an obviously upset Annalise in a cab. He didn't know who had said what to her, but he sure as fuck intended to find out.

As he approached the elevators, the doors swung open and the team's goaltender, Alex, stepped out with Nathalie behind him. Before he even knew what he was saying, he addressed her. "What happened up there?"

The woman frowned. "Barb and Deb got on her case. Melanie and I tried to stop them, but they just kept going on and on about what Annalise did for a living, how you only date models, blah, blah, blah until I think she just snapped."

Marcus swore viciously and Alex squeezed his shoulder briefly. "You know how those girls are," Alex said.

"I had no idea they would ever be this blatantly cruel. If I had known, I never would've brought her here."

"Look," Nathalie said, "I hate how the evening turned out for her. Do you think she might want to have lunch with me some time, make up for having such a shitty experience tonight?"

Annalise needed all the friends she could get. He nodded, smiling. "We *are* going to be gone for a couple of days and I'd prefer not to have her sitting there stewing the whole time." He pulled out his cell phone. "She doesn't have a cell, but she does have an answering machine." He gave the woman Annalise's number and pocketed the phone. "I'm gonna go back up and see if I can shake the truth out of those girls."

"Good luck, man," Alex answered. "See you tomorrow for the flight."

Marcus waved and stepped into the elevator. He was angrier than he'd been in a good long time, and he had no intention of letting those wastes of female flesh get away with what they'd done. He knew his being this mad meant he was in deep with Annalise but didn't take the time to dissect that at the moment.

Stalking back to the apartment, he opened the door and stormed in. Three girls were still there, and the guys had re-joined them. He pointed to Barb and Deb. "You two. What the fuck were you thinking?"

"What?"

"You know what you said. Now admit it to them." He indicated his two teammates, who turned to the girls with expectant expressions.

Barb spoke up first. "We didn't say anything that wasn't true." Her voice wavered toward the end as she noticed Ray's expression had turned incredulous.

"What the hell *did* you say?"

His other teammate John leaned forward and took in the both of them. "Yeah, what the fuck kind of trouble could you have gotten in? We were only gone for a few minutes!"

"I know what they said," Melanie piped up. Both girls glared at her, but she just shrugged. "Why should I keep my mouth shut?" She proceeded to relay the conversation and as she talked Marcus found himself clenching his fists at his sides. He couldn't fucking believe it. It was even worse than Annalise had said.

Ray turned to Barb. "Do you admit you said these things to her?"

Barb's chin raised a little. "She's not like us. I wanted her to know what she was up against."

Ray spoke again, enunciating his words carefully. "Did you say them? Yes or no."

"Yes."

"Get out."

"Ray!"

"Get the fuck out of my apartment now and never come back." He made to haul her to her feet but she scrambled away from him and then rose on her own.

"Fine. If you want to pick that ugly, stupid immigrant over me, fine." Ray growled and Barb scurried to the door before turning around. "You'll come crawling back when you want to get laid."

"Go!"

John turned to Deb. "You can join her. Everything he said goes for me too."

"You don't mean that. We've been together for months! Honey, we've been talking about moving in together!"

"I mean every fucking word. I don't want to be with someone who would treat another person with so little respect."

"Please, John."

John pointed to the door. "Go now before I get even angrier. I can't believe I was so stupid as to think I might be in love with you. I'll have your stuff messengered to you." Deb stood up and sent a scathing look to Melanie. "Oh, stop with the looks. This is in no way her fault. You brought this on yourself when you decided you were better than Annalise."

Deb left and Ray turned to Marcus. "Sorry about that, man." Holding up a fist, he continued. "Bros over hos." Marcus reached out for a half-hearted fist bump with both men, and then he turned to Melanie.

"Thanks for standing up for her. Nathalie mentioned she'd like to have lunch with Annalise. I can give you Annalise's number if you want to join them."

"Sure, why not?" He rattled off the number again after Melanie opened her cell phone.

Turning back to the three remaining guys, he said, "I'm sorry the evening was ruined, but I can't say I'm sorry those bitches won't be hanging on you guys anymore. Look, I'm gonna head out. I'll see you tomorrow."

Ray nodded and rose. "Okay, dude. Again, I'm sorry for the way the girls acted. Never in a million years would I have thought they'd be so blatantly malicious."

"How could you have known that? Hopefully she'll come around and forgive me."

"She's that important to you, huh?"

Marcus considered for a moment before nodding. "She really is."

CHAPTER TEN

Marcus used the time away from home well. In addition to channeling his anger into his play, which resulted in a few penalties but a lot of points, he called the sledge team's trainer and doctor and discussed Annalise's situation with them. Both men agreed she should have a better-fitting prosthesis, but when they told Marcus how much a really good leg would run he knew why she'd never done it. She'd mentioned she had no insurance and a new prosthesis cost well into five figures. He'd pay for it without a second thought, but he doubted she would go for that idea. She was a proud, independent woman—a trait he greatly admired until it interfered when he was trying to do something to make her life easier.

He also got contact information for several sledge team members. Marcus assumed she didn't have a computer if she couldn't afford a cell phone, so he made sure there was a phone number she could call for each man. For all he knew she didn't even have long-distance service, but maybe he could convince her to use his cell to make the calls. At least that would be something.

When he got back to town he debated what to do–hedge his bet and cover all the angles by going after her himself or wait for Annalise to come to him? He still didn't know where Annalise lived, but he knew where she worked. In the end he called the catering company and found out they were working a party that night in Brooklyn. They wouldn't tell him whether or not she was scheduled to work, and he didn't blame them, but he went out to Brooklyn anyway and stood outside the place for twenty minutes arguing with himself before deciding to just go in and see if she was there. He spotted her immediately. His gaze was drawn to her like a moth to a flame. Her back was to him and she was lifting a tray laden with discarded plates and glasses. Marcus forced himself to stay where he was even though his feet kept trying to run to her and take the heavy burden himself. She'd kill him if he did, he was sure of that.

He waited, standing in the shadows near the door of the banquet room. Marcus knew he'd be lucky if no one recognized him, but he'd pulled a baseball hat over his distinctive bald head when he'd left the house, and he hoped if he kept it low people would leave him alone. She came within ten feet of him and he softly called her name. Annalise turned and her eyes widened.

He tried to give her a smile but thought it might've ended up looking like a grimace. "Can I talk to you?"

"I'm working!"

"Just a minute, I promise."

"One minute." She led the way back out the door and then leaned against the wall. He noticed she was putting her weight on her good leg, and hoped she'd at least accept the information he had. "Spill. I need to get back to work. I can't afford to lose this job."

"You won't lose it. If that asshole boss of yours tries to get you in trouble I'll talk to him. I doubt he wants to lose the Empires' business."

He paused for a few seconds, and when Annalise didn't say anything he charged on. "Anyway, I have some things for you." Handing over the folder of information he'd gotten from the doctor, he said, "There's contact information for the doctor and the trainer for the sledge team in here, and both said they'd be happy to talk to you or take a look at your leg or both. I also got the phone numbers for a bunch of the guys on the team. They're all open to a call if you want to talk to some other people about how they deal with their disability."

Annalise was staring at the folder. Finally she raised her eyes and looked at him, her head tilted to the side. "Why are you doing this?"

"Why am I trying to help you? Because I care about you. I told you. We're together, whether you think so or not. I gave you some time after those bitches went after you, but there's no way in *hell* I'm going to just let you walk away from me, from this." His voice had risen as he'd spoken and he took a big breath in and then pushed it out in an effort to calm himself down. He didn't want to scare her.

"But I thought—"

"Whatever you thought, you thought wrong. I'm here for the long haul. Now take the information. If you wanna call these guys let me know. You can come over and use my phone so you don't get charged for the long distance calls."

"I don't know, Marcus…"

"Why not at least call them?" he urged, knowing he was pushing her but so desperate to help ease her pain he didn't know what else to do.

"I guess I could."

"Great! Are you working tomorrow during the day? I have a game at night but I'll be home during the afternoon. Hey, do you wanna come see me play? I could get you a ticket."

He waited with breath held while she bit her lip. Finally, she nodded. "Okay. I have some things to do early but I could be there by two. And yeah, I'd like to come see you play. Just don't get me a ticket near any of the wives or girlfriends. I'll sit by myself."

"You can bring your brother if you want."

Annalise shook her head, her lip curled in disgust. "Hector's in my doghouse right now. I'm not giving him any treats."

"Fair enough." He stepped closer and ran the pad of his index finger down the side of her face. "See you tomorrow." Before she could protest he touched his lips to hers and then stepped back. All of a sudden he felt the urge to tell her he loved her, but now wasn't the time or place. Besides, what did he know about love? He wanted to be sure before he said anything. With one final caress, he moved away and left, feeling good for the first time since that awful mess in Ray's apartment.

*****

Annalise brought the information Marcus had given her home that night and began to pore over it. Not only had he put all the guys' contact information in the folder, he'd also included their bios and their stories about how they'd become disabled. There also contact information and office hours for the trainer and doctor he'd mentioned. She put all that aside and a bunch of printed pages wafted out of the folder and onto the floor. After bending to retrieve them, she glanced at one and her mouth dropped open. It was information about free or lower-cost prosthesis for those in need. She'd had no idea such a program existed.

Annalise quickly filtered through the rest of the papers. Her mouth was opening and closing in disbelief as she read more. Not only was there one program to help people like her, there were several. It looked like Marcus had printed it all off the Internet, which would explain why she hadn't known about the programs. She didn't have a computer and waiting for one of the four measly terminals at the library usually ate up an entire afternoon. And because she had no health insurance she hadn't been anywhere but the free clinic in years.

She'd been planning to call and cancel on Marcus for the next day, but after reading this she knew she couldn't. A tear escaped and she hastily wiped it away. Was it possible she was finally catching a break? Did someone really care?

The phone rang and she glanced at the clock. Nearly one a.m. It was never good news when the phone rang at that hour. She picked up, her heart in her throat.

"May I speak with Annalise Alonso?"

"This is."

"I'm Detective Hayes, from the D precinct of the Queens Police Department." Annalise closed her eyes, suddenly exhausted. What now? "We picked up your brother Hector tonight in a warehouse over by Elmhurst Hospital. He broke a window to get in, but since he was drunk—he threw up on the way out to the squad car and he reeks of booze—he made a lot of noise doing it. There was some other damage to the property as well. We've charged him with harassment, trespassing, burglary and resisting arrest. He'll be arraigned in the morning, but with his priors I'm guessing the judge is going to impose a high bail amount. I'd expect upwards of twenty grand."

Annalise felt sick but knew she had to keep her head. "Is he all right?"

"He's a little nicked up but, besides needing to sleep off the drunk, he should be fine. Do you know where the courthouse is?"

"Unfortunately, I do. Thanks for letting me know."

"Look," the detective said. "I'm sort of familiar with your brother. I don't think he's a bad kid and he's still young. But he's gotta start walking the straight and narrow or he's gonna end up in jail again, and for real this time."

"Yes. I've been trying to keep him out of trouble, but I work…" She knew how lame it sounded, but she was doing the best she could. When it came down to it, Hector was twenty-two and an adult. She couldn't make him do anything he didn't want to do.

She hung up and debated calling Marcus. If the arraignment was at ten there was a good chance she wouldn't make it all the way into Manhattan by two. But when she glanced at the small alarm clock on her nightstand and saw it was nearly one-thirty, she decided to wait until morning.

As soon as she woke after a fitful, nightmare-filled sleep, she called Marcus.

"Hey, I need to postpone."

"Why?"

Before she thought about the wisdom of telling him her problems she'd blurted out, "My brother got arrested last night. His arraignment is in an hour."

"Where?"

"Where what?"

"Where's his arraignment?"

"Why?"

She heard his huff of breath through the phone. "Because I'm coming with you. You shouldn't have to do this alone."

"No way, Marcus. You don't have to do that. You've got a game. This isn't my first arraignment for him. I'll be fine."

"Don't argue with me. Where's the arraignment? Come on, Annalise. Let me help. Let me be there for you. It's what boyfriends do, and make no mistake. I *am* your boyfriend." Annalise hesitated, and she heard Marcus sigh. "If you don't tell me I'll call the court houses, starting in Queens, until I find out."

"Fine," she huffed out through clenched teeth. "If you really wanna see how pathetic my life is, sure, come along."

"Your life is not pathetic, baby. You've had a rough time of it and haven't gotten many breaks. So let me help you. Let me give you some of those breaks."

She told him where the arraignment would take place and then went to hunt for her most respectable-looking clothes. It probably wouldn't make a difference. It wasn't like her brother could be un-arrested, but she always felt better dealing with authority figures when she was dressed nicely.

Annalise arrived at the courthouse to find Marcus already there. He was dressed in a suit and sitting with another man who was poring over papers. She walked over and raised her eyebrows. Marcus looked up and smiled. "Hey, honey. This is Simon Summart. He's a criminal defense attorney. My lawyer recommended him."

"And what's he reading?" She jerked her head toward the papers.

"The charges against your brother."

"How did he get the information?"

"He told them he was representing Hector and they gave them to him."

Her mouth fell open and she wanted to be annoyed at Marcus just coming in and railroading the situation, but had to face the fact that with some high-powered attorney representing him, Hector's chances for leniency were much higher. She needed to swallow her pride for her brother's sake, but that didn't mean she couldn't express her feelings. "May I speak with you for a moment?"

Marcus glanced at the lawyer, who waved them away, and then Marcus tried to take her elbow to lead her to a bench. She wrenched out of his grip and he let her go, a frown pulling down the sides of his mouth. Sitting down, she crossed her legs and looked at him.

"Okay, I know you're gonna yell at me," he began, "but I swear I'm just trying to help."

Annalise rubbed her temples. "I know. It's just—" She bit her lip. "I don't know what to say." Marcus remained silent, apparently giving her time to form her thoughts. "I know if Hector has some fancy lawyer he has a better chance, but I feel like you're taking over my life, like you think I can't handle anything. I've been handling things for myself and for Hector for a long time. I can't start relying on you for everything."

"Why the hell not?" He looked genuinely confused and part of her wanted to kiss him senseless.

The other part wanted to box his ears, though, and that's what she clung to. She couldn't lose herself in him. She'd worked too hard to carve out a life for herself. Yes, it was hard and it sucked sometimes, but it was hers.

"Because what if I do and then you leave?"

Shit, I didn't mean to say it like that...

"Why would I leave? I'm sorry, you're totally confusing me, honey."

"Everybody leaves." She couldn't keep the bitter note out of her voice and watched as Marcus' eyes widened. "Why should you be different? You're a big-time famous athlete. I can't figure out for the life of me why you'd want to have anything to do with me. I'm poor, Marcus. I'm uneducated. I have a shitty job and a good-for-nothing brother. I have nothing going for me." She reached up and hastily swiped at a tear before chancing another look at Marcus.

His face softened. "Oh, baby. You have a lot going for you. First of all, I don't care if you're poor, other than that I want to help you. I have the money to help you and having it sitting in my bank account doing nothing when I could be doing stuff to make your life better doesn't sit well with me." She started to speak but he held up his hand. "Let's see, what else did you say? Oh, yes, uneducated. So am I. I assume you finished high school. So did I, but that's as far as I made it, too. I can't do much about your job, but I can help you with your brother if you'll let me. And as far as you not having anything going for you, well, that's where you're dead wrong. You've got a ton going for you. You're beautiful, and you're smart, and you're independent, and about a million other things I'd be happy to expand on when we have more time." He glanced at the lawyer, who'd stood and was waiting for them. "But right now we need to go get your brother out of jail."

Annalise chewed on the inside of her cheek for a minute and then nodded. "Okay." Marcus held out his hand and she took it. As they walked into the courtroom, she couldn't believe how good it felt to have someone else there, someone on *her* side for a change. Another tear leaked out.

"Hey, none of that. You need to be strong for your brother."

Annalise nodded, too overcome with emotion to speak. A few minutes later her brother was led into the courtroom in cuffs and she bit her lip until she tasted blood. He'd screwed up so many times, but he was all she had left. Marcus' lawyer stepped forward and Hector's head snapped around to stare at the guy and then back at her, his mouth agape. The lawyer spoke to the prosecutor and the judge for a bit and then motioned to Marcus. Annalise was afraid to breathe. Finally, after another conference the judge nodded.

"After speaking with Mr. Alonso's attorney, the state is willing to release Mr. Alonso on ten thousand dollars bail. Mr. Alonso, you are not to leave the state. Mr. Mitchell has agreed to take responsibility for you. I suggest you don't let him down."

Hector cleared his throat. "I won't." His voice was thick with emotion and Annalise put her hand over her mouth to stifle the sob. Her other hand was still wrapped up in Marcus's, and he wasn't letting go. She felt anchored for the first time in a very long time.

"Once bail is posted you're free to go, Mr. Alonso."

Annalise turned to Marcus. "I'll pay you back for this."

Marcus' eyes narrowed. "You'll do no such thing." Before she could argue he tugged on her hand. "Come on, I've got my credit card with me and Mr. Summart said I can post bail with it. Let's go get your brother." He stopped for a second and put his heavy hand on her shoulder. "You aren't alone anymore. I'm going to take care of you, whether you like it or not."

They posted bail and then waited for Hector to be released. When he was, Marcus took him aside and they went far enough away that she couldn't hear the conversation, but it mostly consisted of Marcus talking and Hector nodding. Returning to Annalise's side, Marcus said, "Now let's go look at your apartment. I want to make sure it's safe, and if it's not, I'm going to do something about it. Call me overbearing or heavy-handed, call me whatever the hell you want, but I will not have my girlfriend living somewhere I don't think is safe."

Hector still looked shell-shocked as he and Annalise followed Marcus out of the courthouse. Marcus hailed a cab and when it came, he ushered them inside before getting in himself. They arrived at the apartment and Annalise winced, looking at it from Marcus' perspective. The building was three stories high with a total of twelve tiny, run-down apartments. Graffiti colored the brick exterior and the intercom system hadn't worked the entire time Annalise had lived there. Marcus got out of the car, buttoned his suit coat, and looked at the place from roof to street, his brows drawing further down the longer he stared.

He jerked his head toward the door. "Let's go inside."

Knowing she couldn't put him off, she led the way up to the front door, then up three flights to their apartment. It was like she could read Marcus' mind. He no doubt didn't approve of a third-floor walk-up with her leg issues, but beggars couldn't be choosers. Unlocking the multiple locks on her front door, she then pushed it open and both Marcus and Hector stepped inside.

"Would you like some coffee or something?" Her heritage demanded she at least offer him a drink, though her fingers positively itched to hunt through her pantry for something to feed him.

"No, thank you, baby." Marcus turned to Hector. "Can you leave us alone for a few minutes?"

Hector glanced at her and then nodded. Once he'd left Marcus spun to face her. "You know I want you to move, right?"

"I'd suspected as much, but I can't afford to. You know that. And before you go saying you're gonna buy me a penthouse in midtown Manhattan, consider that my job is close to here, as well as my friends."

"I don't like it. I don't think you're safe."

"It's not the safest neighborhood. I'm not gonna lie to you about that. But I can't afford to move."

"Then make me a deal."

Annalise frowned. "What kind of deal?"

"If you can't move at least let me bring in some guys to make this place safer. They can install a security system, put some bars on the windows—"

"You think my landlord is gonna go for that?" She was incredulous. Her landlord had had a hissy fit when she'd wanted a peephole in the front door.

Marcus' mouth set in a straight line. "He'll go for it."

"What are you planning to do, bribe him? He's a slumlord, Marcus. If he knows who you are and that you have deep pockets he'll find reasons to keep coming to you for more."

"That's fine, as long as you're safe."

Annalise groaned. "You are the most stubborn man I have ever met."

"Like I said, as long as you're safe, I don't care what I have to do. I wish I could convince you to live somewhere else, which yes, I would pay for, but I know you won't do that. You're too independent for that, and I admire that quality in you, really, I do. But baby," he came over and took her hands, looking into her eyes, "if I don't think you're safe I'll go crazy. I need to know that the woman I'm falling in love with isn't in danger."

She felt her face flaming as her mouth dropped open. Finally she managed to croak out, "Love?"

Marcus smiled and her heart skipped a beat. "Yes, love. I'm falling in love with you and I hope you're at least falling a little bit in love with me too."

"I am," she admitted. "I shouldn't be, but I am."

He let her hands go and then plunged his into her hair, taking her mouth. Annalise melted into the hard planes of his body and his grip on her head tightened as he moved her to the angle he wanted. His tongue demanded entrance and she opened for him, moaning as he swept inside and explored her depths. Marcus was everything she wanted. Forever.

CASTING THE DIE

Isabo Kelly

CHAPTER ONE

Nathalie Jane Mendez stared at the small TV screen in her kitchen, waiting for the residuals of the vision to wear off, knowing what she had to do and hating it.

She had to warn him. She could practically hear her grandmother telling her she had a responsibility to tell Alexander Semenov, star goalie for the New York Empires, that he was going to be shot and killed. Soon.

She pushed away from the support of the counter and started taking dishes out of the drying rack and putting them away. Anything to keep her hands busy and her mind on the present, rather than that future picture of violence and blood.

There were many very good reasons not to say anything to Semenov.

"I could warn him and he'll make things happen because of the warning." She spoke aloud to her empty kitchen, adding to the sounds of the game on TV, all of which grounded her in the here-and-now. "He could think I'm involved in the shooting and have me arrested. He could have me fired for being a crazy person."

That idea stung. The possibility of being fired argued more with her sense of responsibility than any of the other excuses. She loved her job as a physical therapist. She'd worked so hard to get to this place in her life, and she didn't want to throw it away on something she wasn't involved in.

"Except *Yaya* would say you are involved now, thanks to the vision." Her grandmother and father had trained her. They wouldn't let her ignore her duty just because she was scared. No matter what excuses she came up with.

She stared at the screen, watching as Semenov blocked yet another shot on goal. The arena erupted in cheers. The man was nicknamed The Wall for a reason. He was on a streak and hadn't given away a goal in twenty-one games in the net. Not only did that make for an individual record-breaking season for Alexander, it meant the Empires were on the fast track to the playoffs. So long as nothing happened to their star goalie, they were a shoo-in.

Except Nathalie had just *seen* something happen to him. Something bad. And she knew deep down in her soul she had to warn him.

"He won't believe me," she told the color commentators discussing his latest save. "Normal people don't believe in visions."

Full of nervous energy, she wandered into the living room and set a series of candles up on her altar; green and brown to ground her, a single silver and a single gold to honor the goddess and god, and three black candles to ward against negative energy. She added some frankincense incense too, to help with the cleansing. She always felt the need for a short cleansing ritual after one of these rare but powerful visions.

Snapping her fingers over the candle wicks, she lit them one at a time, then she touched the tip of her finger to the charcoal brick inside her incense burner and slowly heated it until it glowed. When enough of the brick was red hot, she dropped the loose incense onto it and leaned back to breathe in the scented smoke.

How the hell was she going to tell him? She didn't dare bring something like this up at work. She was already risking her job just considering speaking to him about her vision. Lord and Lady help her if her boss, Joanne, overheard that conversation!

Glancing at her coffee table, she squinted at the invitation half hidden beneath other mail. The team was holding a charity event, Vegas Night, on Saturday. Because she was one of the PTs assigned to the team when they came into the private physical therapy center where she worked, she'd received an invitation. She hadn't intended to go.

She faced her altar. Alexander was a good man. She'd always admired him. He was all focus and concentration on the ice. Off, he was quiet, serious, and very, very private. Outside of the charity work he did with kids, he seemed to have no other life beyond hockey. At least no life that the newspapers could find.

Even while she massaged his teammates' sore muscles and listened quietly to the chatter, the only thing ever said about Alexander was that he was too quiet and private. As far as anyone knew, he rarely even dated. The players all respected and liked him, but no one seemed to know much about him, though he'd been with the Empires for three years.

After the many hours she'd spent working on his aches and pains, even talking to him some, she didn't know him either. His dedication to his own privacy and his self-contained confidence really drew her, though. The need for privacy echoed her own life, making it difficult for her to dismiss him as just another athlete. Despite her best efforts.

She couldn't just let him die. Not when she might be able to stop it.

"Hell," she muttered, and knelt down to try to gather the strength she was going to need, desperate for some sense of calm but afraid even the peaceful meditation she planned wouldn't bring her true balance. There was too much at stake. And, oh, so much that could go wrong.

*****

Nathalie stood a few feet from the craps table, watching while Alexander carried on a friendly patter with the gathered gamblers as he pushed the dice back to the shooter. He was hard not to watch.

A handsome man, he was tall enough to beat her five-foot-nine height by a few inches, had dark hair and blue eyes and that lean, Russian look coupled with an intensity that was impossible to resist. Tonight he seemed even more magnificent. Wearing a tuxedo did remarkably sexy things to him. And she'd seen him in nothing more than a towel. Which also did remarkably sexy things to him. But she couldn't think about that right now. If she did, she was likely to turn into one of the fawning women surrounding him, and she'd never tell him what she needed to.

She'd been watching him for more than half an hour, waiting for him to be relieved so she could have a moment of privacy to pass on her message. She couldn't very well tell him while so many people hovered around. And the women in slinky dresses flanking him didn't look interested in giving up their spots at the table.

Unfortunately, having him at the table was bringing a lot of bets, so she doubted he'd be relieved any time soon. Craps indeed, she thought with a groan. The whole night had been a lot of crap so far.

Needing something to do with her hands, she snatched a glass of wine off a circulating platter, thanking the young woman doing the serving. She took a sip, but it did nothing to stop her from continuing to consider her predicament.

The man hadn't been alone for even a minute since he'd entered the room. And she was getting desperate. The whole Vegas Night thing made her tense. All the flash and formal glamour made her feel out of place and awkward. Despite the height she'd gotten from her mother, the rest of her looks came from her dad's side of the family. And while she personally loved her curves and Spanish features, she would never consider herself in the same league with the gorgeous women sauntering through the room. She felt as if they could see through her, as if they knew she didn't belong because she was weird and different.

Shaking off the old insecurities, she focused on her reason for being in that room. To save a man's life, if she could. A good man, she reminded herself, who didn't deserve to die.

She moved in closer to the table, sipping her wine and trying to look like she belonged. Maybe if she could get close enough to him, there would be some lull or some bit of excitement when someone actually won some money, something that would pull attention away from him long enough for her to deliver her warning and be gone.

She hated this, hated exposing herself this way. To him. But also she risked this getting back to her boss. She really could lose her job, and the thought left her more than a little sad. Loving what she did and getting fired because of what she was would suck.

Moving in as close behind Alexander as she dared without calling attention to herself, she hovered there for another ten minutes, feeling more and more awkward as the seconds ticked by, hope of being able to do this thing and get out starting to fade.

Then a noise from across the room startled her and she turned in the direction of a growing scene. A woman, the romance writer Melinda Gould she realized with a start, was straightening her skirt at the bottom of the staircase and exchanging some pretty interesting words with someone else Nathalie couldn't see from her place in the crowd.

She realized quite suddenly, though, that the novelist had given her just the opportunity she needed. Every eye in the room was turned in her direction, and the crowd was edging closer to better see the action. Leaving Alexander in a very small bubble of isolation.

Moving in quickly, Nathalie stepped close to his elbow and rose up to whisper in his ear. "He's going to kill you if you're not careful. You have to watch out for yourself, do what you need to, to protect yourself. He won't just hurt you, Alexander, he'll kill you." She swallowed and without realizing what she was doing, touched his hand. "Don't let him."

He faced her, his brows drawn down, frowning fiercely. She didn't wait to hear his reaction to her warning. She spun away and lost herself in the still-milling crowds, making a beeline for the caterer's kitchen and a back door.

Damn, damn, damn. She'd hoped he wouldn't actually see her. But maybe he wouldn't recognize her. A small part of her kept hoping against hope she could do this and still keep her job. If he didn't know who delivered the warning, he wouldn't be able to ask her any more questions about it, or have her tossed out on her ass for being nuts.

She bumped into a burly man charging out the kitchen door, the catering manager she noted, and apologized, but he ignored her, rushing off somewhere himself. A quick glance over her shoulder had her heart beating triple time and another series of curses chanted through her head. Fuck, fuck, fuck! He was following her.

And he did not look happy.

Desperate, she scurried through the kitchen, practically running for the exit. If she could just make it out of the building, she could disappear into the pedestrian traffic and be back on the subway heading home before Alexander reached the street.

Unfortunately, she had never been that lucky.

CHAPTER TWO

Alexander's pulse pounded as he followed the woman through the kitchens. She glanced back again and this time he was positive he knew her. What the hell was going on?

"Nathalie," he called. "Stop."

She picked up her pace and her shoulders hunched. If she thought she was getting away without explaining what she'd said to him, she was sorely mistaken. He stretched out his stride and caught up to her just as she was about to exit the back door. He stopped her escape with a hand on her shoulder, firm but gentle—until he knew whether his favorite masseuse was in league with the bastard trying to bribe him.

He couldn't guarantee being gentle if she was.

"Where do you think you're going? After that ominous warning? Did Johnson send you?"

"Johnson?" she asked, without turning to face him.

The fact that she wouldn't looked at him pissed him off. He spun her around. "Don't play stupid. You just told me he was going to kill me. Don't pretend you don't know who I'm talking about."

"I don't know anyone named Johnson," she said, finally looking up at him.

"Then who were you warning me about?"

"I have no idea. I just know you're in danger."

"How?"

She swallowed and scanned the milling staff who were trying to pretend they weren't paying attention to the argument. "I just... It doesn't matter. Believe me, don't believe me." She looked him in the eye for a split second. "Just stay safe."

Then she spun away again, freeing herself from his hold and slipping out the door before he could stop her. Oh no, she was not going to run away now.

He slammed out after her, catching her before she'd gone far enough to disappear into the Saturday night New York City crowds. This time he grabbed her arm and held tight. "Listen, I don't know what this game is about. But you can tell the person who sent you to back the fuck off. I can't be bought."

She scowled, the expression furrowing ridges in her smooth forehead. "Mr. Semenov, I have no idea what you're talking about. Someone is trying to buy you? Another team?"

"You think the Empires would trade me now?"

A very slight smile slipped past her wary expression. "No. Not for all the money in the NHL."

He studied her closely, trying to read the lies in her story. She was warning him that someone would kill him. She had to know what was going on. But she looked so confused.

With a grunt of frustration, he dropped his hold on her and ran a hand through his hair. "You really have no idea who Johnson is?"

She shook her head.

"Then who did send you?"

"No one."

She heaved a sigh and turned to watch the traffic inching by. Horns blared despite the noise laws, and the sharp, cold scent of city wafted across his face.

"Listen," she said when the horns quieted, "I knew you wouldn't believe me. But… Well, I wouldn't be able to live with myself if you got killed and I could have stopped it." She wetted her lips with a quick flick of her tongue. "I'd appreciate it if you didn't mention this to anyone."

He focused in on her mouth, a generous mouth he'd frequently admired. "You're afraid of getting fired?"

"Among other things," she muttered, almost too quietly to hear over the traffic and shouting pedestrians. She shrugged and said, "You should get back. The women will miss you." For the first time that evening, she smiled, real and genuine.

And Alex was reminded sharply why he'd always been fascinated by this particular woman. She was beautiful, but in an earthy, natural way. Her long dark hair hung in easy, thick waves, her face was barely made-up, and her dress was almost demure with its long sleeves and high neck. So unlike the slinky numbers most of the women inside were wearing. But the red silk skimmed over her generous breasts, hugged her little waist and flared out around her curvy hips. Her heels brought her nearly to his height, and she carried herself with a casual, unconscious grace.

He'd seen her in the crowds earlier that night and had to blink back a moment of shock. At the rehab center, she wore ugly tan slacks and a baby blue polo shirt that did not accentuate her natural sex appeal at all. He'd always suspected that under her uniform her body was made for sex, but seeing her in that red dress confirmed it. She was a walking erotic dream. And the more he considered the lovely swell of her breasts, the less he remembered of their conversation.

Get a grip, Alex. She's probably lying about Johnson. She's probably the slob's girlfriend.

He clenched his jaw to keep from saying anything to send her running into the crowds. When she continued to stand there staring up at him, waiting for him to say something, he felt his pulse speed. He could lose himself in her dark eyes. So much for getting a grip. "They won't even notice I'm gone," he said, nodding back toward the kitchen door.

She snorted. "Right. Beyond the fact that the women who wouldn't leave you alone all night will notice, you're you. And everyone who paid good money to come to this event will want a picture taken with the Empires' star goalie. Go back. But be careful. Stay out of dark alleys. Or empty buildings. Or... Well to be honest, I..." She bit her lip and her eyes widen. "I mean, I'll see you next week. At the Center."

She slipped away, disappearing quickly in the crowds.

He considered the passing traffic a few minutes longer, determined not to wait until next week to continue their conversation. She didn't want him to tell anyone she'd given him a what? A message? A warning? She didn't want him to talk to anyone about this. Which meant she wouldn't be any more forthcoming at the Center than she'd been just now.

He'd have to get her outside of work, somewhere private. He wanted answers, and he had no intention of letting her slip past him so easily. He'd earned his nickname, The Wall, for a reason.

As the cold finally seeped in through his tuxedo jacket, he returned to the now-closed kitchen door and ducked back inside. Only as the chill numbing his hands and face started to thaw did he realize Nathalie hadn't been wearing a coat.

She was going to freeze on the way home, something that bothered him more than he thought it probably should. But more importantly, if she'd left a coat at the check counter, he now had an excuse to contact her and bribe her into a private meeting. No one wanted to be without a coat in February in New York.

The irony of the fact that he intended to use bribery against a woman who could be working with the man trying to bribe him was not lost on him

CHAPTER THREE

Nathalie slid into the coffee shop booth across from Alex, feeling like an idiot. Forgetting her coat at the event had been a stupid lapse, but she couldn't believe he'd noticed. She didn't actually get cold very easily. Especially when she was upset or angry. Her body temperature rose and her palms hit the heat level of boiling water if she didn't stop the process. She wore a coat to blend in and make sure no one noticed anything weird about her. But she didn't actually need it most of the time.

He handed the long, black wool coat to her, and she bundled it up on the booth seat. "Thank you," she muttered.

She knew why he'd gone to the trouble of collecting her coat. It wasn't out of some altruistic sense of chivalry. He didn't trust her, didn't believe her, and wanted to grill her on what she'd said to him last night. Her coat was an excuse.

And she couldn't have refused his offer to return the coat today because then he might bring it to the Center. There would be questions. Difficult to answer questions. So with a sense of resignation and dread, she'd agreed to meet him at this Upper East Side burger joint, hoping the crowds would keep him from asking too much. As usual, the place was packed. But the bastard had managed to get them a booth at the back of the first floor where they'd have some semblance of privacy.

"You must have been cold going home," he said, as he motioned to the waitress. "Coffee, please."

He glanced at Nathalie with raised brows. She nodded.

"Two cups," he told the waitress. She nodded, smiling at him like he was a movie star, and hurried away to get their order. "So?"

"What?" she asked, still thinking about the moony-eyed look the waitress had tossed at him. She couldn't blame the woman. Alexander Semenov was gorgeous even in the flat diner light. He was casually dressed in jeans and a sweater that managed to accent his muscular physique without actually clinging to his muscles. The purple color of the sweater sharpened his blue eyes, leaving her a little stunned as she stared at him. Yeah, she had great sympathy for the waitress. If he looked at the woman at the wrong time with those eyes, they were going to end up with laps full of hot coffee.

"So were you very cold getting home?" he repeated, calling her back to the conversation and away from an examination of his mouth.

"I was fine. Subway's warm."

"You live far from your stop?"

"Close enough. Why did you make me come here?"

"I want answers. You know that."

She slumped against the backrest. "I know. I was just hoping you'd forget all that stuff—except for the part about being safe."

"I'm not that easy."

She almost smiled, but his serious expression made her humor evaporate. The waitress chose that moment to settled thick white mugs of coffee in front of them. They didn't talk until she'd finished setting out the little metal carafe of milk and the white ceramic holder festooned with sugar and sweetener selections.

"Can I get you anything else?" the waitress asked, her full attention on Alex.

"Not just yet. Thank you." He smiled up at her briefly, long enough to be polite but not so long as to encourage her attention. Then he stared back at Nathalie.

The full force of his focus was difficult to take without fidgeting in her seat, but she managed. She cupped the coffee mug in her hands and allowed the heat building in her palms to warm the drink a few extra degrees. She liked her coffee scorching. The scent was a little dull and watered down, so she was going to need it hot to swallow it.

When they were relatively alone again, Alex said, "You need to tell me how you know I'm in danger."

No I don't. She almost said the snarky comment aloud. She didn't *need* to do anything. Except she had felt compelled to warn him. She had only herself to blame for being in this awkward situation. That and her stupid vision. But she'd stopped resenting the visions a long time ago.

"You won't believe me."

"Try me."

She looked around the crowded diner. She really didn't want to say this out loud here. "Listen," she said without facing him, "I love my job. Really, really love my job."

"You're afraid what you say will get you fired?"

"Just being here with you could be a threat to my career." She snorted and faced him. "And someone is going to see us. I'll be lucky if a picture of us together doesn't end up on the internet. Once my boss finds out…"

"She doesn't have to know about this."

"You going to keep it secret?"

"What was the last rumor you heard about me?"

She paused. "I don't really pay attention to gossip about the team."

A slight smile lifted his mouth and Nathalie was struck by just how sexy that mouth was. She swallowed back her moment of distraction to pay attention to what he had to say.

"What was the last rumor you heard about Chris Emerson?"

"You mean that stuff about him and the romance novelist last night?" she asked and then realized what she'd just admitted. "Fine. Okay. Some of the gossip gets to me. But—"

"When did you last hear anything about me?" he interrupted.

She thought about it, sipping her coffee as she considered. "I can't remember," she said finally. "The only thing I've ever heard about you has to do with your time on the ice and the children's charities you support."

"There's a reason for that. I'm private, very private."

"I know."

"And I protect that privacy. At the moment, you're included in that circle. This meeting won't get back to your boss."

She stared at him for a long minute, not immediately responding. "So no one here will report this coffee to my boss. But all it will take is one word from you." She held up a hand for silence when he started to speak. "You never said you wouldn't tell Joanne about this. If I tell you the truth, you could go to her, and I'll be fired. If I don't tell you anything, you might still go to her and have me fired. You think I'm involved in some way, and you're trying to decide what to do about that. You won't believe the truth." She shook her head. "Don't pretend you will when you don't know what I'm going to say. You won't."

She set her cup down and let out a long breath. "I risked a lot to give you that warning. Take it, don't take it. It's your choice. I would prefer you didn't get killed. That's the reason I said anything at all. But I'm not going to discuss this anymore in public where anyone can see and hear us. Good luck." She dropped a couple of dollars on the table to cover her coffee. "Thank you for returning my coat."

He reached across to grab her arm when she started to stand. "We're not done talking."

"We have to be because there's nothing left to say."

"I'm not letting you off without an explanation. I promise *not* to tell your boss anything, whether I believe you or not. If you're not involved, you have my word this conversation doesn't go beyond us."

Still crouched, halfway out of the booth, she glanced around the diner and raised her brows. "Right."

"You want privacy, this is as private as you're going to get unless you want to come back to my place."

"I'm no puck bunny, Semenov."

He actually smiled at that. His smile was lethal. "I'll be on my best behavior."

To keep from rolling her eyes, she dropped back into the seat. Her thighs were hurting from the crouch anyway.

She had to admit Alex wouldn't be hitting on her anytime soon. She wasn't exactly the gorgeous model type that the hockey players usually went out with. And she was perfectly capable of taking care of herself if he got aggressive, though she was certain he wouldn't. But despite his assurances that they were safe from observation, being seen entering and leaving his home was bound to get attention. She was *not* going back to his place, only to be kicked out when she told him she had a vision.

"If you'd feel safer, we could go to your place. I'll still be on my best behavior."

Hmm, that was something to consider. No one would think to be camped out in her neighborhood waiting for Alexander Semenov to show up. She could take him in through the side gate instead of through the main door so fewer people noticed them. And in all likelihood no one would recognize him because they wouldn't be expecting to see him.

It wouldn't matter if he learned where she lived because she couldn't imagine him venturing out her way again after this. And if he was going to have her fired, well, at least admitting the truth of her vision in her own home would keep the rest of the Upper East Side from overhearing.

She'd feel safer in her own surroundings, too. Home ice advantage. She smiled and nodded. "Fine," she said. "Get your passport. We're going to Queens."

CHAPTER FOUR

Nathalie let the Empires' star goalie into her little rent-controlled apartment and wondered at the stupidity that had gotten her to this point. She tried to remember if she'd done the dishes this morning and was relieved when she realized she had. The floor was relatively clean, no clothes tossed about. She was actually pretty tidy out of habit. She'd had to be in the past so she didn't risk sparking some random bit of household detritus into a full blown fire.

She hadn't worried about accidents like that in a long time, but the neatness habit had stayed with her. At the moment, as she led Alex into her small living room, she was grateful for that. Not that her place would live up to his, she was sure, but it was neat, it was cheap and it was all hers.

"Make yourself at home." She gestured to the cozy loveseat against one wall. "You want something to drink? I have coffee, tea, and I think some diet soda."

"Coffee would be nice but only if you're making yourself some."

"So polite," she muttered as she went into her kitchen. She glanced briefly at her altar on the way by, curious if he'd know what it was or if he'd just assume it was ordinary candles and incense. She came back out once the coffee pot was brewing. "Give it a minute."

He was sitting on her little couch, taking up most of the space with his big body. No wonder he could guard the net so well, she thought. Rather than try to squeeze onto the couch next to him and be uncomfortably aware of him, she sat in her rocking chair—a gift made by her dad for the winter solstice.

They stared at each other for long moments in silence. She was in no hurry to have this conversation. If he wanted to start things, he was going to have to ask specific questions. But when he finally spoke, his comment took her completely by surprise.

"You don't live all that close to your subway stop."

She raised her brows. "Huh?"

"You said you lived close enough that going home last night without a coat wasn't a big deal. You must have frozen making that walk in just your dress."

He sounded mad. Weird. She shrugged. "I didn't notice."

"You're lying."

"Actually, no, I'm not." She heard the coffee machine finish percolating and said, "I'll be right back with the coffee."

She pulled two mugs out of the cupboard and turned around to find Alex standing a foot away. Swallowing back her shock, she glared. "You trying to make me drop these?" She held up the cups. "Announce yourself."

"Sorry. Just wanted to see if you needed help."

"You take milk? Get it out of the fridge."

Shaking her head as her heart slowed from the momentary jolt of shock, she poured their coffee and tried to ignore him. He took up too much space in her small kitchen. She could practically feel his body heat even though they weren't close enough to touch. Her awareness of him bothered her more now than it ever had before. At work, she'd been able to concentrate and ignore her attraction to him. Or at least suppress it while she unknotted his muscles. Here, in the close confines of her home, without the buffer of other eyes, she was entirely too conscious of all his masculine appeal.

"You live here alone?" he asked.

She nodded. "You can get a lot more space in Queens for the price."

"Long commute, though. All the way to Tarrytown for work."

"Not so bad. I'm used to it." She handed him a mug. "I'm saving for someplace closer though," she blurted, then pressed her lips together. He didn't need to know that. He didn't care. "Anyway, I like the train rides. Gives me lots of time to read."

She hurried back into the living room to keep herself from babbling more. Sitting in the rocking chair again, she waited for him to resume his seat. Another long moment of silence passed before he finally broke the tension and got to the point.

"How did you know?"

She didn't bother prevaricating this time. "I had a vision." Stating it simply, plainly, and without breaking eye contact, was the only way she could get this out. "Right here, actually. In the kitchen. While I was watching that last game you guys played against Montreal."

"A vision?"

She heard the expected disbelief, and though she was prepared for it, it still hurt. "A vision."

"Of what?"

"You getting shot in the chest. The man had you at gunpoint in a place I didn't recognize—though I'm sure it was somewhere in New York."

"How do you know?"

She shrugged. "Just do."

"What else?"

"Not much more to it than that." She gulped a scalding mouthful of coffee and let the heat settle her nerves. "The man said he was tired of pussyfooting around with you. And then he shot you."

"In the chest? Not the leg or knee?"

"The chest. And then you were dead, and I was back to watching you defend the net."

He leaned against the couch and watched her. She watched him back.

"You have these…visions a lot?"

"Told you you wouldn't believe me. Not a lot. But sometimes."

"They come true?"

She nodded over her mug. The heady scent of strong, rich roast gave her something to focus on so she wouldn't have to feel the sting of his disbelief too sharply.

"Then why warn me?"

Tilting her head to one side, she let out a long sigh. "My grandmother made me."

Her response must have surprised him because he spit out a mouthful of coffee. The reaction made her laugh in a nervous burst.

"Sorry," he said. He set his mug down and went into the kitchen, returning with a handful of paper towels.

"You can leave that. I'll get it later." But he was already mopping up the slight mess off her wood floor.

"Your grandmother knows you have visions."

"My grandmother knows everything about me."

"There's more than visions?"

Yes. But he didn't need to know that part. "*Yaya* helped my dad raise me, so she's like a second mother. And she didn't actually tell me to go warn you. But she would have if she'd been there." Her grandmother and father were responsible for her moral compass. They might as well have waved the invitation to Vegas Night in her face after she'd seen Alex getting killed.

"What happened to your mother?"

Not exactly the question she'd been expecting next. "She left when I was four. Remarried an evangelical preacher, somewhere in Texas I think."

"Sorry."

She shrugged. "Long time ago." Not long enough to heal the pain of that abandonment. But again, he didn't need to know. She wasn't even sure why she'd told him about her mother. Except that she found she liked telling him the truth. For a brief moment, she could pretend he'd accept her as she was, and she'd be able to be honest with him about everything. The fantasy was short lived but pleasant while it lasted.

He settled back onto the couch and leaned forward so his forearms rested against his knees. "I don't really believe in visions."

"Yeah."

"That's why you were afraid to tell me, afraid I'd tell your boss you were delusional?"

"I'm not."

"But you're afraid that's what I think?"

"Isn't it?"

He shook his head. "I think you're too sharp and together to be delusional."

"You think I'm together?" She frowned. No one had ever called her sharp and together. His assessment felt like a compliment, especially given what she'd just told him, and that made her want to blush more than if he'd told her she was pretty.

"You've always seemed like a together, grounded kind of woman to me. I like that about you."

"Or you did until I told you I had visions?"

"No. I still like you. I'm just not sure what to think about the visions."

"Listen, you don't have to believe me. It doesn't matter to my existence if you do or don't. So long as you don't have me fired and you try to keep from getting killed, I'll consider this a win."

"It would help if you could tell me where you saw this man shoot me. I'd just never go there."

She snorted. "That would be handy. But I didn't know the location. I've never been there before."

"Would you recognize the area again if you saw it?"

"Sure." She shrugged. "But I'm not sure how that will help. I don't exactly have time to go scouring the city." She sucked her lips into her mouth for a moment, then let out a slow breath. "It was still pretty cold outside in the vision, so I think this confrontation will happen soon. Before the playoffs."

"This year? You're sure you weren't seeing something from years in the future?"

"Too much urgency. Sooner rather than later." She rocked gently in the chair as she let her mind wander back through the images of the vision. "Soon," she said more firmly. "I'm not positive how long, but this is something that will happen in the next few weeks. A month at most, if you can't avoid it." She looked right at him and said, "But I'd prefer if you avoided it."

"Me, too."

He smiled that slow, dangerous grin, and she sucked in a sharp breath. Damn the man was hot. And he probably thinks you're crazy now, she reminded herself. Except that he'd said he liked her. A treacherous little part of her heart leapt with joy at that small bit of hope.

False hope, she knew. She couldn't tell him everything, and any less than everything was nothing. He was who he was, she was who she was, and there was no way to breach the chasm that lay between them. Not that he'd want to. But the death of her illusions on that score was a hard one to take. She wasn't delusional about her visions, but she sure had harbored some illusions about her relationship with him. And she was just starting to realize how much she'd wanted more with him, even though she'd known it was impossible.

She'd been happier living with her fantasies. This reality sucked.

CHAPTER FIVE

Alex studied the woman rocking gently in her beautiful wooden rocking chair and considered that maybe she really was crazy. Which would be a damned shame because he found himself drawn to her more and more the longer they were in each other's company. He'd been telling her the truth. He'd always liked her. Seeing her outside of her work had given him more complicated ideas of what he wanted from her, too.

She was sexy as all hell, and he was pretty sure she didn't realize it. That curvy body of hers was usually hidden in her ugly work clothes, and her long dark hair was normally secured in a tight bun. Wearing simple jeans and a cashmere sweater and with her hair down, she looked soft and touchable. Her eyes were heavy-lidded, provocative and teasing. Like she knew things other people didn't.

Well, she seemed to think she did, he realized. She honestly believed she had visions. He could see that plain enough. She believed what she was saying, every damned word, and he hated it because he didn't want to think of her as crazy. She'd always seemed so grounded, so down to earth, so steady. He liked that about her. The flighty puck bunnies who surrounded him most of the time drove him nuts. Sure, they were gorgeous, and he wasn't opposed to fucking them when he needed sex. But he couldn't abide conversations with them.

Nathalie, on the other hand, was always such a pleasure to talk to.

Because she knew when not to talk, he realized. She didn't just ramble on about nonsense. She was straightforward, blunt even. But controlled and careful about what she said, all at the same time.

She reminded him of his parents that way. Quiet and dignified.

There was a seriousness to her that gave her a kind of confidence he found extremely sexy. Her confidence came from somewhere deep, not a superficial arrogance because she was pretty.

Though, she was more than pretty. He could easily imagine stripping off that soft sweater and her snug jeans and laying her out on this too-small couch while he savored every inch of her pale skin. The fantasy was vivid enough, he actually had to force his mind back to the present. Since concentration and focus weren't usually a problem, the power she had over him was worrying.

"Like I said, you don't have to believe me," she said into the quiet, startling him out of his thoughts.

He considered her dark, steady eyes. "I'm a pragmatic man, Nathalie. Whether I believe in visions or not, I'd prefer not to get killed. Which means it makes sense to take a few precautions."

"Someone is threatening you, aren't they?"

He straightened from his position leaning over his knees and decided to return some of her trust. He still wasn't sure what to believe about all this. But if she was lying to him, she was an Oscar-worthy actress, and he just didn't think that was the case. He'd always prided himself on his ability to read people, to read their body language. It was one of the things that made him so good at his job. And while

Nathalie's story was extremely farfetched, he was sure she wasn't involved with Johnson now. He would have been able to tell if she was lying. He might not believe in visions. But Nathalie did.

She was trusting him not to tell her boss about this belief of hers. He owed her something in return. "A man from my past, a guy I grew up with, Ben Johnson. I guess you could say he's fallen on hard times. He's a gambler and he's gotten himself into some trouble. He seems to think I can get him out of it."

"How? By paying off his debts for him?"

"Not exactly."

"He's a gambler, you said?" She paused. Then, "He wants you to end your streak, doesn't he? Wants you to throw a game so he can bet against the Empires and win big."

"You're very quick."

"I know. So I take it you've refused his request."

He smiled at her "I know", then confirmed her assessment of the situation.

"Have you gone to the police?"

"I talked very quietly with a friend on the force. Unfortunately, this guy hasn't done anything blatantly criminal. Yet. That I can prove. He's just tried to coerce me into helping him." He shrugged.

"Coerced how? Has he threatened you?"

"He tried. Clumsy effort. I don't have anything he can threaten me with. Not to gain my cooperation."

She frowned, so he clarified.

"I don't have any family, no wife or children. No serious girlfriend. My parents passed away years ago. I don't have any other relatives. I don't have any debts he can use against me. He knows a lot about my past since we grew up together, but there's nothing there that he can use to blackmail me. And I always hated this guy. He was a bully. I would never throw a game as a favor to him."

Alex watched her carefully when he made of point the fact that he was single, but she didn't react in any special way to that part of his story. He knew she was single. He'd quietly checked up on her before returning her coat. But if she was interested in him, she wasn't letting on.

"He was a bully? Is he still?"

"Men like him don't change. I wasn't really worried about it before this, though. As I said, I don't have anything he can use against me. And I'm not the sort of man he can push around anymore."

"But you said he was desperate. You weren't worried about him hurting you physically?"

He shrugged. "His type aren't usually brave enough to do something like that. But I figured if he really did get desperate enough, he might try to break my leg or knee, something that would keep me benched for the rest of the season. Maybe worse if he's pissed enough at me. I never considered murder as something he'd risk."

"You make it sound like his trying to break your leg would be no big deal, like you don't really care if he hurts you."

"I don't want my season to end yet. And I'd hate to be so seriously hurt my career ended already. But I have plans beyond hockey. I'd just get on with things."

Her frown deepened. "That sounds…" She snorted a half-laugh. "Very pragmatic."

"Told you so."

She laughed then, a full-throated laugh. And the sound went right to his dick. Her voice was husky and rich, calling to mind dark rooms and tangled sheets. Once again he found his concentration and focus scattered as thoughts of stripping her naked and fucking her on her little couch overwhelmed him.

He had no idea how she did this to him. He wasn't sure he liked that she could. But damned if he wasn't going to seduce her. Soon.

Because if her vision did come true, he was a dead man. And he could imagine a lot worse ways to spend his last few weeks alive than taking Nathalie Mendez to bed.

CHAPTER SIX

I have an idea."

Never had four little words filled Nathalie with such dread. "Yes?" She stilled her rocking and, after a beat, realized she was holding her breath waiting for his "idea".

"You know what this place looks like, where I'm supposed to get shot?"

"Uh huh."

"It's very possible this is somewhere I go regularly, or it's at least located somewhere along my usual daily route."

"What makes you say that?"

"During the season, I don't go to a lot of unusual places in the city. I'm too busy."

She shrugged. "Fair enough. So?"

"So you spend some time with me during my routine. When you see the location, let me know, and I'll just avoid that spot."

There was a lot wrong with that plan. She wasn't even sure where to start. "What if it's not somewhere you normally go? What if this guy tries to get you to meet him somewhere?"

"Well, that's easy. I just don't go to any meetings with him."

The incredulous look he gave her made her feel a little silly. Still. "Okay, so you don't go anywhere unusual until after the playoffs. I could just describe the location to you."

"Can you?"

She cringed. In truth, the details were a little fuzzy thanks to all the blood she'd focused on at the end of the vision. "Sort of. It's a space that's under construction. I'm pretty sure there's scaffolding and a sidewalk detour outside the building. And I think I'd remember the pattern of posters on the scaffolding if I saw it again."

"But you can't describe the posters without seeing them?"

She shook her head.

"Someplace under construction. That describes a lot of places in the city."

"Nothing jumps out at you from your routine?"

He looked into the distance and frowned, as if trying to visualize. "Actually, I can't think of any buildings being worked on anywhere around my normal haunts. That's a little strange by itself."

"But it's good, right? Just stick to the places you know and you'll be fine. End of story."

The full force of his focus swung back to her, taking her by surprise with the intensity of his stare. That focus made him very good at his job, and she suddenly had a great deal of sympathy for the teams that had to face him in goal.

"Give me two weeks," he said quietly.

She narrowed her eyes. "Two weeks for what?"

"To see all the places I go when I'm in town. Maybe you'll spot something I haven't noticed."

"Alex, people will see us together. And I have a job. I can't just follow you around for two weeks."

"After hours, I'll walk you through my routes."

"There's still that first problem." She gave him a look when he didn't react. "We'll be seen together."

He shrugged. "So we tell people we're dating."

"Whoa." She launched out of the rocking chair. "No. Absolutely not."

"Why not?"

He stayed seated but leaned back a little to look up at her. She set her coffee mug down on her little round coffee table so she didn't spill it. "I told you already, I'll get fired."

"It's not a rule that you don't date any of the players. One of the other PTs has had affairs with at least two of the guys."

She froze just as she was about to start pacing and stared at him with wide eyes. "Who?"

"If she wants to tell you, she will. But as you see, I can be discreet."

"If Joanne finds out…"

"She knows," he said, with a slight tilt of his head to the side. "So long as it doesn't interfere with your work and you keep things quiet, she looks the other way. Having something discouraged by the boss isn't the same as it being a firing offense."

That took some of the outrage out of her sails. Still, she wasn't quite ready to sit down again. "You've known this all along?"

"Dating me won't be the end of your career."

"Fake dating, you mean. And there's still the press to worry about. I can't afford to land on Page Six."

"Why? What's the big deal?"

Her mouth actually dropped open. "What's the big deal? Are you insane? I'm a witch! I have visions. Do you think if anyone in the press finds out about that, they'll leave me alone? Even after we're no longer supposedly dating? And that's just the kind of attention that *will* get me fired."

"Witch?"

She dropped her shoulders and resigned herself to giving him more than she'd ever meant to. Gesturing to her altar, she said, "I'm a practicing green witch. I don't cast spells or anything." At least not the fictionalized kind of spells people thought witches cast. "It's my religion. I pray to a goddess and god. I burn incense and candles and revere nature."

His gaze turned inward and she readied herself for his list of questions. People either got her religion or they didn't, and the ones who didn't, like her mother, tended to jump to all the wrong conclusions. But her religion wasn't even the most private thing she wanted to protect. Being a green witch wasn't something she tried to hide, even if she didn't go around shouting her beliefs to every stranger she encountered.

The pyrokinesis, however, was not something she could afford to have made public. And once the press caught a whiff of her and started to dig, she wasn't sure she could avoid her most secret of secrets getting out. Then losing her job would be the least of her problems.

"Green witch?" Alex said, his tone thoughtful. "I've never heard that term before. Is it like Wiccan?"

"Kind of. But I'm not Wiccan. There are similarities."

"You belong to a coven?"

She was surprised he got the word right. "No. I'm too private for covens. My observances aren't something I can share with others. Except occasionally my dad and grandmother."

"They're witches, too?"

"Dad is. Grandma is a Catholic with pagan leanings." She smiled at the often repeated way her *Yaya* referred to her religious philosophy.

"And I don't want their privacy invaded by the press either. Dating you will open up a can of worms, Alex. Even if it's only pretend dating." She shook her head. "No. That won't work."

"I thought I made it clear I could protect your privacy."

"You can protect your own. But you can't guarantee some nosey gossip writer won't pick me out as someone to investigate. I don't hide my religion, but I don't go around announcing it with a sign on my head either. I don't want to deal with other people's prejudices."

"I can understand that. I don't go around wearing a yarmulke or a Star of David either, though I don't try to keep it secret when I go to Temple for the high holidays."

For a moment, she was taken aback. It was common knowledge he was Jewish and, being a New Yorker, she never really thought about the fact. But she realized he was as private about his religion as she was. As private about that as he was everything in his life. Just like her.

"Guess you understand, then."

"I grew up in North Dakota with immigrant parents who were used to keeping their Judaism a personal part of their lives. We weren't exactly surrounding by a lot of other Jews. And after the treatment they got in Russia, the reason they immigrated, they were very private about their observances, even within the small Jewish community in Fargo."

"That sounds familiar." She settled back into the rocking chair, some of her worry receding. "I still think pretending to date is asking for trouble, though. But giving me a look at all the places you usually go is a good way for me to confirm the building you need to avoid."

"So long as it's not the arena or the training center, I think I can safely take the place I might get shot off my schedule until after the season is over."

She relaxed further when she realized he wasn't going to push the dating thing. Now that she'd calmed down, she knew she'd overreacted to the suggestion. He was right, they could keep her identity secret for a couple of weeks and the press probably wouldn't notice her. Though she didn't dare risk that kind of attention and got physically nauseous at the very idea of landing in the gossip pages, there was more to her rejection of the idea than just protecting her secrets.

She wasn't sure she could *pretend* to date Alex and not get so caught up in the fantasy that she got her heart broken when it was all over. Going back to just being one of his several physical therapists, chatting with him like nothing had happened. Already she was going to have trouble with that. She liked the man too damned much. And she had wanted him for a long time now—even if she did try to repress the attraction.

Spending any amount of time with him was going to risk her balance and her heart. The less personal they made that time, the better. "What other reason can we give for spending time together? Something people won't question? Hopefully something that leaves me this uninteresting side note in your life that doesn't attract attention..." She trailed off as she studied him. "Wait. Your charities."

"What about them?"

"You're involved in several. Children's and environmental causes."

He nodded.

"Maybe we could tell people I'm setting up an environmental type charity. I don't know, maybe something that involves protecting... something. And because I know you're actively involved in those types of things, I've asked you to help me set things up, maybe lend your name to it."

"You don't think your boss will object to that?"

"Any more than dating you? I doubt it so long as I don't ask you for money or bring this into work. And if she finds out, I'll tell her I intended to make sure her Center gets a lot of good press out of my efforts. She'll appreciate *that*."

"You don't want to be in front of the press," he pointed out, much too logically. "Something like that would necessitate being in front of reporters."

"Well then the whole thing falls apart before it goes too far. I don't know. I'm thinking off the cuff here."

"Easier if we just pretend to date. Your idea is pretty convoluted. Someone will figure out we're lying, and the first thing they'll assume is we were lying to cover up dating. That'll draw even more attention."

She started rocking again, tapping her foot at the same time as nervous energy jumped around her nerve endings. She made a conscious effort to keep her palms from heating while she had them on the rocking chair—even though her dad had gone to great pains to make sure the wood was treated so it was fire resistant.

"I hate this idea," she said after a minute.

"The idea of dating me?"

The tone of his voice caught her attention, and she stared at him. "We're not talking about real dating. We're talking about pretending at something and hoping not to call attention to it. I hate pretending, and I hate the thought of the possible attention this will draw."

"The attention we can control." He tilted his head to one side. "You're not embarrassed by your religion?"

"Of course not. I'm just private about it. I chose this path. I wouldn't live it if I was embarrassed by it."

"So is it really that big a deal if people find out?"

She really, really didn't want to go further into this conversation. There were a lot of reasons to maintain her privacy. Her religion was just the easiest one to explain. Except he was making it harder to use. Damn him anyway, couldn't he just accept she didn't want the attention of the press and let it go? She glanced at the clock. "I'm hungry. We skipped lunch. I'm going to order a pizza. You want some?"

"Sure. I like meat on mine."

"Don't keep kosher, then? Fine. Pepperoni it is."

"You're not vegetarian?"

"No. Not all pagans are vegetarian. Just like not all Jews keep kosher."

He nodded in acknowledgement. "Can I pay for the pizza?"

"No. I'll be right back." She escaped into the kitchen to place the call from her landline. She was avoiding and she knew it. Her grandmother would scold her for it, but she didn't like this path she was on, and she didn't know how to get off it. She didn't want to spend time with Alex and discover he was even more sexy and smart and *nice* than she already considered him.

Weren't professional athletes supposed to be womanizers and playboys? She'd be happier if he was one of those kinds of guys. Then she wouldn't have to take him very seriously and could probably even play temporary love interest without any risk to her heart at all.

Alex was different. Everything about this situation was different. And she didn't know how to make things right.

She could practically hear her grandmother reminding her she'd chosen this path, though she would be able to argue with *Yaya* about that. She hadn't chosen the vision. But she had willingly gone to Alex to give him the warning. She'd made the decision to do the right thing. And now she had to continue to do the right thing, even if it made her uncomfortable.

She just hoped it didn't leave her heartbroken and her life in complete turmoil.

Chapter Seven

"I still can't believe I agreed to this," Nathalie said, when she met Alex at the front door of her apartment building. He'd come to collect her in a Town Car, and she was surprised he could find someone willing to drive into Queens and back from Manhattan.

"You know it's the simplest solution." He held the car door for her.

"Yeah, yeah. I think you muddled my thinking with pepperoni."

"The pizza was your idea."

She settled into the back seat, fastening her seatbelt as she waited for him to come around. "So where are we going and how on earth is this part of your normal routine? Oh wait, don't tell me. You frequently come into Queens to collect strange women for dates."

"Queens is a little off my beaten track, but otherwise…"

She snorted and looked out the window so he wouldn't know she was actually charmed by his stupid humor. Ever since agreeing to his plan last night, Nathalie was regretting the decision. She'd spent her day at work massaging sore muscles and trying to figure out a way to get out of her "date" that night. Fortunately, the team hadn't come in that day, so she hadn't had to face working on Alex while anticipating a night out with him.

Her stomach churned in silly little circles that made her feel ridiculous. This wasn't a real date. He was taking her to a restaurant near his home, where he regularly went for dinner during the season. After dinner, since the weather was cooperating—cold but no snow or rain—they intended to go for a walk. This was their pretense to explore the area around his neighborhood for signs of the location Nathalie had seen in her vision. But he'd insisted on dinner first, since it wouldn't look like a date otherwise. And he'd insisted on coming to pick her up because, again, otherwise it wouldn't look like a real date.

She would much have preferred getting her own taxi in, or better yet the subway, which was both cheaper and brighter. Being stuck in the backseat of a dark car with Alex so close threw off her equilibrium.

Not a real date, NJ, not a real date, she reminded herself. But her palms were definitely edging towards hot.

Taking a deep breath, she made the effort to lower the temperature building in her hands. She hadn't had this much trouble controlling her heat levels since the pyrokinesis first manifested when she was four. She wanted very badly to blame Alex. But she knew damned well it wasn't his fault she was so attracted to him. He couldn't help being sexy and stunning and glorious.

"Where have you gone?" he asked.

The comment startled her and brought her back out of her head. "Sorry. Just thinking."

"Too much."

"Absolutely. So how was practice today?"

The white of his teeth flashed with his smile. "Good. Looking forward to the road trip tomorrow."

"Good. Good." She let silence fall again. She was not very good at small talk. Or rather, she was great at small talk when she was working on someone. She could get them to relax and ramble or she could stay silent if that's what they preferred. The problem was, this wasn't work, and he wasn't a client right now, and she was too damned nervous for small talk.

The fact that there was a driver who could overhear them meant she couldn't discuss the real issue at hand, either.

"You're nervous," he said.

Blowing out a breath that played with the tendrils of hair on her forehead, she nodded. "I don't know what to do."

"What would you normally do on a date?"

She laughed. She couldn't help it. "I wouldn't *normally* be on a date with a famous hockey player. Nothing about any of this is normal."

He reached across and took her hand, squeezing it. "Relax, have fun. This restaurant has great food. Enjoy it. And we'll deal with things as they happen."

Without trying to be too obvious, she pulled her hand from his because she could feel her skin heating and didn't want him to notice the temperature change. "I know. You're sure this isn't going to get attention?"

He shrugged. "Richard here isn't likely to call the press, are you Richard?"

"No, sir."

The driver's voice was laced with humor. And Nathalie realized the man must drive Alex regularly. No wonder he'd been willing to come all the way to Forest Hills.

"And I go to this restaurant often enough I doubt anyone is waiting to watch me eat. Especially on a Monday night. I'm not that interesting."

She dropped her chin and gave him a look. "You're one of the main reasons the Empires are headed for the playoffs. In this city, you're interesting."

"Trust me." He leaned closer and she leaned back. "I'm trusting you."

Her shoulders relaxed and she sighed. "Right. Right. Okay, fine."

His mouth ticked up in a slight smile and he grabbed her hand again, holding on this time when she tried to pull away. She scowled down at their linked fingers and wondered why he was insisting on the contact. *Pretend date!* But his driver wouldn't realize that. No one was supposed to know they weren't really dating except them. So he was probably just putting on a show for the driver.

And she needed to remember that, too.

"Your hand's very warm," he commented.

Oops. She made an effort to cool them off. Nerves weren't supposed to do this to her. She'd never had trouble controlling her heat output on other dates. What the hell was wrong with her? "Sorry." She tried to pull her hand back, but he held tight.

"Don't be. Makes you a good masseuse. You're one of the few PTs who never starts with cold hands."

"Guess I just have a fast metabolism or something," she hedged. Her ability to warm her hands without outside help *was* one of the reasons she was so good at her job. But she was surprised he'd noticed.

"What made you choose physical therapy as a career?"

She shrugged. "My grandmother is a nurse. I didn't want to do what she did, but I liked the idea of doing something in the healthcare industry. I took a few PT classes in college and it was a good fit."

He pulled up the hand he held to look more closely at her fingers. "Definitely a good fit."

She really didn't want to read any special meaning into that comment, but it was hard when he was staring at her with those sexy blue eyes. Shit. How could he possibly be such a good actor? He was a hockey player, damn it.

Why the hell was he putting on the charm so strongly? She cast a quick glance at the driver and noticed him looking into the rearview mirror. Realization dawned.

Fine. She could deal with this. She could keep in mind it was all an act and not get carried away. She could. Really. She could.

They chatted a little more about her job and then moved on to talking about his upcoming games, the road trip he was leaving on tomorrow, all harmless things that didn't lead to anymore darkly sexy looks from him. Though he held her hand all the way to the restaurant. By the time they arrived, she nearly collapsed in relief when he finally let go.

Once again, he opened the car door for her then led her up a short flight of stairs into a narrow little Italian restaurant where the maître d' knew him by name. They were seated immediately at a table near the back, far away from the front windows and the passing pedestrian traffic. The restaurant was crowded for a weeknight, but where they were sitting had a semi-private feel to it.

"Nice," she commented as she opened her menu. "Neighborhood place?"

"Mostly locals on a weeknight. Gets really busy on the weekends. But I don't usually get here then. Everything on the menu is good, by the way."

"Have you tried everything?" She smiled.

"Yes."

She ordered a small carafe of red wine—small because he was sticking to water—and they continued with the small talk, which got easier after her first few sips of wine. He asked more about her grandmother which lead to questions about her dad.

"He owns a plant nursery in Connecticut. Does pretty well."

"Really? My parents were both botanists. My dad was a professor at North Dakota State University."

"Your mom, too?"

"She was mostly a housewife, though she did some private biology tutoring. But her specialty and passion was plants. I think that's what drew them together."

She swirled the wine in her glass and decided to risk a possibly touchy question. "How did they die?"

"Car accident. Dead of winter. Head-on collision with a semi. Driver dozed off. I was a sophomore at college at the time."

"I'm very sorry. That must have been hard."

He shrugged. "It was a long time ago."

Because things had gotten too serious, she switched subjects. "I understand the recruiters tried to get you into the NHL during your junior year. Why didn't you go pro then? You could have gotten injured your senior year, ended the possibility of a pro career."

He waved that away. "My degree was more important to me. My parents wanted me to have that security. I respected their wishes. Don't get me wrong, I love hockey. I'm lucky I can make money at it. But I didn't grow up wanting to play in the NHL. I never even considered it would be possible."

"What do you want to do after?" She was very curious about this. He'd said he had a plan for when he was done with hockey. It surprised her to hear a pro athlete was even thinking about that when he was in the middle of the best season of his career. He was a little on the older side at thirty-one but not at the end of the line yet by any means. So long as he didn't get hurt or killed in the next few weeks. She shook that off to pay attention to his answer.

"I've invested in some businesses which are all doing really well despite the economy. So my money is in good shape."

"Is that what you went to college for? Investment and finance?"

"I got an economics degree. My practical Russian parents wanted me to study something that would guarantee I'd always have work. I'd intended to take the CPA exam after college."

"What happened?"

"I went to the NHL instead."

"Will you take the exam when you're done? You want to be an accountant?"

He grinned, a charming little smile that made her head spin. She really wanted to believe the wine caused that reaction but she knew better. She'd been nursing the same glass for most of the meal.

"I *was* going to be an accountant," he said. "Now, I can afford a little more whimsical path."

"Whimsical? The Wall wants to do something whimsical? I can't even begin to guess what that might be."

"Pastry chef."

She blinked, took a sip of wine, and then very carefully set her glass down. Tilting her head to one side, she said, "Pastry chef?"

"I love food. I really love the sweet stuff." He shrugged. "I thought owning my own bakery would be fun."

"You do realize that means you have to be up at five a.m. every morning, and it's really, really hard work?"

"I know. I get up early now anyway."

"Oh, no. You're not one of those?"

His eyebrows popped up. "Not an early riser I take it?"

"I've tried. I have." She shuddered. "Sunrises are lovely. But I really prefer coming at them from the back end rather than the front."

He choked on the sip of water he'd taken. "Meaning?"

"I'd rather stay up all night to see them."

"Ah. I've never heard it described that way before. So, night owl, then?"

"Very much so." She lifted her wine glass again in a silent salute to night-owl-dom.

"You realize that's one of the few things we *don't* have in common? Unless you hate sweets?"

"No! I love cake. And anything chocolate. I can't bake to save my life. Outside of a few fruit bread recipes I have for some of the Sabbaths. And I can whip up a mean cake from a box mix."

He closed his eyes and shuddered, which made she her laugh.

"But anything more complicated is beyond me," she finished.

"I'll have to make you something some time."

The idea of Alexander Semenov baking her a cake was a little too much to consider on only one glass of wine. "You really planning on becoming a pastry chef after hockey?"

He dipped his head in a slight shrug. "I'd like to."

"I would not have guessed that. Ever. Not in a million years."

"There's a lot about me people can't guess. But I'm not the only one."

He was right about that. And still so much he didn't know about her. She reined in the girly part of her that had started to think of this as a real date and went back to small talk.

After they finished dinner, he helped her into her coat. "Richard is waiting with the car at the house."

His fingers slid across her neck as she settled the coat on her shoulders and she felt the slight touch all the way to her toes. Tingling tightened her belly and started her knees wobbling. To keep from showing how severely his little touch had affected her, she stuffed her hands in her pockets and preceded him out of the restaurant. The staff wished him a goodnight, all very friendly and easy. Like they were used to having him around.

Outside, the temperature had dropped, but since there wasn't any wind, she liked the shot of cold after the warmth of the restaurant. Despite the fact she kept her hands in her coat pockets, Alex slipped a hand around her elbow, keeping her close to his side as they walked.

"Anything look familiar?" he asked, leaning his head down close to hers.

"Nothing from my vision, no."

They walked in silence for a few blocks before she said, "Maybe you should tell me a little more about your routine? I know the incident happens at night, everything was dark outside. So what do you do at night?"

"Go to and from the Brooklyn Bank Center—Richard drives me most of the time."

"When he doesn't?"

"Someone else from the car service collects us."

"Us?"

"Chris Emerson. He's my roommate."

"Oh. I didn't realize. I guess I didn't think you'd need a roommate."

"I don't. But the arrangement means we both have more money to put into other things. People don't realize it, but Chris is a genius with money. His investment advice has been invaluable."

"Wow. This is the same guy with the blue streaks in his hair? He comes across as such a playboy."

"Yeah. He has problems avoiding trouble. Actually, trouble just seems to find him no matter what he does. But he's not that guy in real life."

"Huh. Good to know." She made an effort to look around the streets they walked along. Foot traffic was quiet this time of night, but they still passed a few people. No one took any notice of them or even seemed to recognize Alex. The fact that he wore a black wool coat and a wool hat that *didn't* have the Empires' logo on it pulled low over his brow probably helped. At a glance, he just looked like any stunningly gorgeous man walking down the streets of New York.

"What else do you do at night?" she asked to keep her mind off the feel of his hand on her elbow.

"Mostly I just go to and from the arena. I don't do much during the season. Need my beauty sleep."

She snorted. "Not really. I think you're beautiful enough. How early do you get up?"

His hand flexed on her elbow. "On a training day? Five-thirty. On a day off, seven."

She groaned. "That is just so wrong."

"When do you get up?"

"Well I have to get up early on work days. My alarm goes off at six. I'm out of bed by seven. But on my days off, I sleep till at least nine or ten if I don't have plans."

"Lazy bones."

"Bet your ass. Do you leave the house before sunrise ever?" She continued to scan their surroundings, but the streets were markedly lacking in construction sites, just as he'd said.

"Sometimes to go for a run."

"Where do you run?"

"Mostly, across to Central park and then around it."

"Do you ever pass any construction on your way to the park?"

"No. Not that I've noticed recently."

"Okay, then I think that's safe. Which is good because I really don't want to get up before sunrise to follow you on a run. Plus, I don't like running. I walk. I love walking. But I don't run."

"I could always slow down and walk."

"We still have the 'before sunrise' problem with that scenario. If you don't do anything else before sunrise besides that, I think you'll be safe enough. I kind of got the impression of late night rather than early morning anyway."

Before he could ask, she clarified. "Just like I could tell it was in New York and not somewhere else. And that it was cold. Plus, there's a feel in the air at different times of night, you know? Like you can feel the sunrise coming when it's that early."

"Yeah. You can. But I've never met anyone else who noticed."

"Guess it's my witchy training." His soft snort of amusement made her smile. "Anything else you do at night? You obviously eat at that restaurant often enough they know you. Do you frequent any other places?"

"A few in the neighborhood. And one or two near the arena where a few of us players will go after a game sometimes."

"Okay, walk me past the places in the neighborhood. If I don't spot anything, I'll have to meet you after your next home game."

"Why don't you meet me there on Saturday? We're back in town late Friday night. No need to wait for our next BBC game to walk the area."

"Fair enough," she said, trying not to sound disappointed. She would have liked the excuse to go to a game.

"You still want to come to our next home game?"

She glanced at him out of the corner of her eye, wondering if he'd read her mind. "I'd love to. Not sure I can afford a ticket though."

"I can arrange one. Or do you want to bring someone with you?"

She thought of her grandmother—who loved hockey, too—but she didn't want *Yaya* involved in this thing with Alex.

"One ticket will be enough. Don't go to any trouble. I can sit in the nosebleeds. And I'll pay for it. I don't want you to feel like you have to do me any favors."

He gave her a narrow-eyed stare. "You're trying to keep me alive. You will not be paying for your ticket to the game. Or any other meals we share."

She hadn't paid tonight, but she figured he was referring to the pizza last night. "If you insist. You make more money than me, so I'm not gonna argue. I need to save my money anyway."

"What for?"

She looked up at him with her brows lowered.

"I mean do you have something specific you're saving for? Or are you just frugal?"

"Saving for something specific. Which is why I don't want to lose my job."

"You won't. What are you saving for?"

"A house," she admitted. "I want a backyard where I can grow things."

"Really? You like plants, too? Like your dad?"

She nodded. "I want my own little greenhouse where I can grow herbs, and some garden space to grow whatever I can convince to grow. I love getting my hands into the dirt. But it's hard to have that in a one bedroom apartment without a balcony."

"Why don't you work with your dad if you love that kind of thing so much?"

She shrugged. "Not my path."

He led her past a few more local restaurants, most of them small and intimate looking. When they walked by a Moroccan place, he said, "I'll take you there next. The food is superb."

Finally, he turned up his street, just off Second Avenue, heading east. The street got even quieter as they strolled by rows of beautiful brownstones. "Nice block," she commented. "Which one is yours?"

He pointed to one just two houses away. "With the green front door."

"Beautiful." She looked up and down the street. "I thought you said Richard was waiting here for us?"

"He's probably parked around the corner. Not an easy neighborhood to park in. I'll give him a call."

But when they stopped in front of his house, he didn't immediately pull out his cell phone.

"Do you want to come in for a coffee?"

Her stomach tightened again in that giddy dance that left her a little breathless. "I'd better get home." *Not a real date, NJ, not a real date.* The way he was studying her mouth argued sharply with her nagging voice of reality. "This was nice," she said. "For a fake date." *Good, girl. Remind him this isn't real. Remind your own damn self, too.*

"But you didn't see any place I should avoid?"

"Nothing. Sorry. Would have been easier if I had."

"Why?"

She lifted her shoulders. "We wouldn't have to keep up the farce of dating. My job wouldn't be in danger. And I could stop worrying."

"Ah." He glanced past her to the silent street. When he met her gaze again, he said, "Did you notice any camera happy paparazzi following us tonight?"

"No, but—"

"But you were safe enough, right?"

"You live with Chris Emerson."

He frowned at what he probably thought was a change of subject.

"Chris attracts the paparazzi. I can't come and go from your house without someone eventually noticing."

He muttered something under his breath that sounded suspiciously like "fuck" as he stuffed his hands in his coat pockets. "This really doesn't have to be an issue, you know. They look for Chris, not me."

"But if they spot you bringing a woman into your house, they'll get interested, even if it's a passing interest."

He looked her over, then took a step closer, close enough to crowd her. Because she knew he expected her to step away, she didn't. But she had to tilt her head back to look him in the face.

"There aren't any cameras here now. There won't be later. You can come in for a coffee to warm up and not risk your precious job."

"Don't dismiss my worries just because they aren't yours. You should know better."

This time she heard his "fuck" quite clearly.

"I'm warm enough," she said to try and ease the tension. "Besides, it's late. You have a big trip tomorrow. And as you said, you need your beauty sleep."

"You said I was beautiful enough," he reminded her, his gaze returning to her mouth.

"Alex…"

"I'll have a ticket for our first game back waiting for you at the Will Call," he said, and pulled out his cell phone.

As he made the call to his driver, she stepped back and took a deep breath. What the hell? Fake dates were not supposed to feel like this. She sure as hell shouldn't be thinking about kissing a man this dangerous to her peace of mind. She was here to save his life, not ruin her own.

He insisted on riding in the car with her back to her apartment, despite her best effort to dissuade him. And even though she told him in no uncertain terms he didn't need to walk her to her door, he still did.

As she unlocked her multiple locks, she could feel the solid heat of his body standing entirely too close to her back. When the door swung open, she turned to tell him goodnight and found herself practically pressed against him. "Thank you for dinner," she muttered, her throat tight.

"You're welcome." He cupped her cheek, stroking her cheekbone with his thumb.

She held her breath, not at all sure what to do because while she knew she needed to tell him to back off, she wanted to kiss him so badly she could barely think.

"Sleep well," he murmured and dropped his hand. "I'll call you when I get back into town Friday night. We can make a plan for Saturday then."

As he disappeared down the stairs, she leaned against her doorframe because her knees were shaking. She was way in over her head with him. She'd rather face the man trying to kill him. That guy she could at least slam with a fireball to make herself feel better.

CHAPTER EIGHT

Nathalie concentrated on cleaning her apartment Friday after work, pretending she wasn't waiting for Alex's phone call. He wasn't due back until very late. Getting giddy and excited about something that wasn't going to happen for hours yet wasn't productive.

But then her week hadn't been very productive. She'd spent four days trying not to think about Alex and failing. She watched the Wednesday game and wasn't remotely surprised when it was another shutout. The Wall's streak continued. She had the TV in her kitchen tuned to tonight's game, despite promising herself she wasn't going to watch.

And every time the announcer's voice rose, she ran into the kitchen to see what was happening. By the third period, she gave up pretending and sat at her counter with a glass of wine, watching as Alex managed yet another shutout and the Empires scored three goals.

Surprisingly, Alex gave an on-ice interview after, talking about his streak. He was humble and made of point of giving credit to the players who were scoring well. "You can't win games just by keeping the puck out of the home net," he said. "You still have to score on the other end. And the guys are getting that done."

She smiled and turned the TV off once he was no longer onscreen. Nice as well as sexy. A deadly combination.

She dove back into scrubbing down her home. Then she showered and changed into her meditation clothes—brown yoga pants and a green t-shirt. Finally, she settled in front of her altar. A little meditation would help her ground and center. And she needed to center before she talked to Alex again.

Touching her finger to the various candles on her wooden workspace, she let some of her nervous energy out in lighting the wicks. She lit the coal in her incense burner and dropped some sandalwood resin onto it, breathing in deeply when it started to spill heady smoke into the air.

She waited until the smoke had cleared a little, letting the calming effects of the sandalwood sink into her pores. Then, with an effort, she closed her eyes and allowed her brain to quiet. It took longer than normal to focus and release her anxiety, but she managed it, falling into that peaceful place where she felt centered, connected, and whole.

When her cell phone rang, she jumped. A quick glance at the clock told her it was a lot later than she realized.

She scrambled to the coffee table to pick it up. "Hello?"

"I didn't wake you, did I?"

The sound of his voice decimated all the progress she'd made in calming her spirit. She was giddy and nervous again instantly. "No. Night owl, remember?"

"Good. Tomorrow, do you want to meet for lunch or dinner? Or both."

"Why both?"

"Plenty of time to explore the area that way."

Spend most of the day with him? That didn't sound like a good idea. On the other hand, the quicker they located the place she'd seen him shot, the sooner she could get out of this disastrous situation. "What time for lunch?"

"How about twelve thirty? At the BBC. I can walk you around my usual routes from there."

"Okay. That won't be too early for you? You don't want to rest more?"

"I'll be up at seven."

She groaned because she'd heard the smile in his voice. "You are a crazy man, Semenov. See you tomorrow. Oh, by the way, great game tonight. And Wednesday."

"You watched?"

Since he couldn't see her, she felt free to roll her eyes. "Of course. I'm a big fan. Of the Empires. Tomorrow at twelve thirty. Sleep well."

"You, too. Try to sleep before the sun comes up."

"We'll see." She was grinning when she hung up.

*****

She woke earlier than she usually would have on a Saturday morning and spent the better part of an hour deciding what to wear. She felt ridiculous for putting in so much effort, but she justified it with the idea that—despite his best efforts—they might still end up photographed, and she didn't want to look like an idiot.

But she also didn't want him to *think* she was dressing up for him. Which was why the choice was so difficult. In the end, she went with dark-wash jeans and a fitted, patterned blouse that was relaxed enough to look like something she'd wear normally.

She met him outside the main entrance to the Brooklyn Bank Center. And because she arrived first, she took some time to study the area. Nothing immediately next to the arena jumped out at her.

She almost missed Alex approaching because she was busy considering what she knew of the area. When she did notice him, she started to return his smile of greeting but stopped. "What's wrong? You're walking funny. You got hurt last night?"

His grin turned crooked. "I thought I was hiding it well. I took one too many hard hits. Woke up kind of sore. Don't worry, I'm coming into the Center on Monday. I'll be fine."

"If you're hurt, we shouldn't be walking around until after you've been looked at. The team can't afford to have you out of commission. Not now."

"It's nothing that serious. Just a few sore muscles. The walking will be good for me. Work out the kinks."

"You're sure?"

He nodded. "Are you working on Monday?"

"I am. Why?"

"You can take care of me yourself, then. Just to be sure."

Shit. What had she just walked herself into? "If that's what Joanne thinks you need." She worked real hard to keep her voice steady, since the rest of her was anything but. Could she give him any kind of treatment with her usual detachment? Maybe her boss would assign a different PT to look after him. Worry about that on Monday, she told herself. "Okay, if you feel able, let's go to lunch. At least you'll be sitting."

To her surprise, he linked arms with her and started south, past the stadium's gated entrance. They looked like a couple. And even though she knew that was the point, having him touch her was much too dangerous.

He led her to a pub a few blocks away. It was dark, not crowded, but there were still a few people, and the woman behind the bar greeted Alex by name. Her sultry, welcoming smile dropped when she saw Nathalie.

"Brought a friend today, huh?" the bartender said. "She's cute. You here to eat or just stopping in for a drink."

Nathalie worked to keep from reacting to the "she's cute" comment, pretty sure anything she did would complicate lunch.

"Food, please, Sam," Alex said to the bartender.

"Table down the back. Great game last night."

"Thanks." He angled Nathalie in front of him and ushered her to a quiet corner booth.

After they were settled in and they'd ordered sandwiches and soup, Nathalie took a moment to glance back at the bar. The woman, Sam, flicked a look at Alex then turned back to one of the men at the bar and smiled big when he ordered another round. "Sam has a crush on you," she commented.

"She likes hockey players," he said with a shrug.

"Sleeps with a lot of them, does she?"

"She's slept with a few that I know of."

Nodding, Nathalie looked around at the pub décor. Very classic, dark wood, mirrors backing the bar, red velvet covering the seats.

"I haven't slept with Sam," he said.

"I didn't ask."

"You were curious."

She shrugged. "It's not my business. So how often do you come here after a game?"

"Couple times a month. What are you doing Monday night?"

"No plans. Are you doing something outside your routine?"

"One of the guys is having a gathering at his place here in Brooklyn. Other players, wives and girlfriends. I don't go there regularly, but I've been to his place before."

"You think Johnson might know about the party?" She considered this. Since it was a planned event, it was possible the man knew about it. Or that he stalked other players' houses. Not likely, but possible if he was as desperate as Alex seemed to think he was. It was probably safe enough for Alex to go, but she would hate to go through all this only to have him shot because she'd ignored one possible danger zone. "I should get a look at the area. I don't want to intrude on your private—"

"You're invited. No intrusion. Girlfriends and wives, remember?"

"I'm neither, though."

"You'll pass for a girlfriend."

She snorted. Then laughed. The whole idea was so ridiculous, she couldn't help it. "Fine. I'll go. What should I wear?"

"Whatever you like. The other women tend to dress up but mostly to show off for each other I think. You could go in that if you wanted to."

"I have more than one outfit. I'll change clothes."

He flashed that sexy grin of his. The bastard. "You don't dress the way I would have expected, given you're a…"

"A witch? What were you expecting, black velvet and lace?"

"Bet you look good in velvet and lace."

"I do. Look good in leather, too. But I usually wear normal clothes."

"I wouldn't mind seeing you in leather. Or lace."

"This isn't a real date, you know."

He didn't comment and she was saved from having to push the issue by the arrival of their food.

After a few bites, she forced herself to face his flirting head on. She couldn't afford to pretend to herself, and she didn't want him getting the wrong idea either. "Why are you coming on to me? Because the bartender is watching? This part of the game?"

"No. I'm coming on to you because I like you." He looked her over, the part of her he could see with the table in the way, and then met her gaze directly. "I always have, you know. Even when you're wearing that ugly uniform at work, I can't help but notice you. Hard to keep you from noticing my noticing when you're working on my muscles, though."

She shook her head, trying not to smile or be flattered. "I'm pretty sure I don't believe you, but even if I did, this isn't something that's going to happen."

"Why?"

"I've made that clear." She released a harsh breath. "More than clear. I can't afford to date you. For real."

"Even though you want to?"

"Even *if* I wanted to."

"Don't pretend. You don't think I can tell you're attracted to me?"

She lowered her brows. "Alex. Don't you pretend. What woman wouldn't be attracted to you? That's not the point."

"What is the point?"

"The point is…" She lifted her hands palms up in a kind of exasperated surrender. "The point is there's a lot about me you don't know. I'm not someone you can afford to be involved with, not given how much you like your privacy." She pushed aside her soup and folded her hands on the table. "Alex, I'm not the only one risking something here. We're better keeping this temporary and platonic."

"No, we're not." He picked up his sandwich and took a bite, looking for all the world like they were discussing nothing more serious than the weather.

She growled under her breath. "Impossible man."

They made it through the meal without another heated debate, but Nathalie couldn't stop thinking about what he'd said. She didn't want to believe he really wanted her. If this was just a game to him, a passing fancy, she could ruin her life by giving in. She'd seen the women hanging off him at Vegas Night. She wasn't his usual type.

So maybe he'd decided he wanted to get her into bed. A fun little fling for him, she was sure. But he couldn't be thinking about long term or permanent. Not after knowing her outside of work for less than a week, not after two fake dates and a pizza dinner. And with her secrets, she couldn't be in his world. He couldn't afford it any more than she could.

They wandered around the area after lunch, walking slowly in deference to his sore thigh muscle. "How bad is the bruise?" she asked when she caught him rubbing his leg.

"Not the worst I've had," he assured. "It's not pretty, though."

"Ah, poor Alex. No longer perfectly pretty?"

He laughed. "You do realize I like that you think I'm pretty, right?"

"Everyone thinks you're pretty. Except when they're facing you on the ice."

"I really like your honesty, Nathalie. You don't play games. I'm not sure I've ever met a woman who was so straightforward with me."

"I'm just glad you can take it or this walk would be very tense."

They'd been strolling side-by-side without touching, but when she smiled he took her hand and held tight when she tried to tug away.

"Your hands are warm still. Without gloves."

She made an effort to lower the temperature of her palms and changed the subject. "I don't see anything around here that looks even close to the place in my vision." Letting out a breath, she admitted something she'd been afraid to say out loud. "What if we can't find the building? What if we don't figure it out in time? What if I walk you into the place you get shot trying to find it?"

"We've got time still. Don't panic yet."

"Have you heard from him recently?"

"There was a note slipped under my door when I got back last night."

"Why didn't you tell me? What did it say?"

"Another plea for help, an offer to split the winnings of his bet. Not sure why he'd offer me money. I've got plenty."

"No threats?"

"I get the feeling from the tone of the message those are next. He's sounding more and more desperate. Whatever trouble he's in is nipping at his heels."

"Shit. Then we don't have much time."

"We have enough." He squeezed her hand. "Stop worrying. We'll keep hanging out, doing what I normally do. And, eventually, we'll spot something."

He paused, then backed them out of the pedestrian traffic and faced her. "Nathalie, I don't want you getting hurt in all this. My biggest worry is you really did have a vision, we find the building, and my old classmate finds us both there."

"Don't worry about me. I can take care of myself."

"This isn't a game."

"No. It's not. But I can handle myself. Better maybe even than you, mister pro athlete. There's still a lot you don't know about me. Trust me. I won't get myself killed."

"Good." He brushed her hair behind her ear and pulled her close enough that their bodies touched. "Because I couldn't stand it if you got hurt because of me."

And suddenly, they had a whole new set of problems.

*****

He insisted on taking her home in a taxi instead of letting her take the subway. And he walked her to her door again. She was so overly aware of him, she could barely get her keys in the different locks. Before she could push the door open, he turned her to face him.

"I want to see you tomorrow."

"Where? Where else do you go?"

He shook his head. "No, not to look. I want you to come to my house. I'll cook for you."

"No."

"Please." He cupped her cheeks in both hands and angled her head up to his. "Please." Then he kissed her.

Shivers raced across her skin at his first, soft contact. The kiss was gentle at first, just a touch of lips. His hands held her face, keeping her close even though she had no desire to move away. Angling her head, he kissed her more firmly, still gentle and coaxing. With her hands gripping his wrists, she leaned into him and kissed back, opening to the sweep of his tongue, savoring his slow tasting.

Tension tightened his muscles, she could feel it through her grip on his arms, but his kiss continued to seduce slowly, deliciously.

Nathalie's stomach clenched and her grip on his wrists flexed. She wanted to move closer but didn't want to disrupt the spell of his lazily thorough kiss. By the time he lifted his mouth from hers, barely, so she still felt his breath against her skin, she was panting with a hard-to-control need.

"Come over tomorrow," he murmured, looking her in the eyes when he asked.

When he spoke the movement of his lips brushing against hers sent yet another tremor of sensation down to her core. "I'm taking the subway."

"Just say you'll come over."

"Fine."

She felt rather than saw his smile just before he kissed her again. Still controlled, slow and drugging, still that lingering, thorough seduction. He edged her back a single step so she was leaning against the door and his body was pressed along the length of hers. The feel of all that hard muscle heavy against her was heaven.

But before she got carried away and dragged him inside, he straightened. With her face still held between his palms, he stared for a long minute. She stared back because she had no idea what to say or even if she'd be able to speak.

"Tomorrow. My place. Noon. That's not too early for you?"

She shook her head.

"See you then. Sweet dreams."

She stayed leaning against the door until well after his footsteps no longer echoed on the stairs.

CHAPTER NINE

S omewhat to Nathalie's surprise, Chris Emerson answered the door when she rang the bell at exactly noon.

"Hey, Nat. Come on in. He's in the kitchen."

"Thanks."

Chris took her coat and hung it on a wall hook next to the door, in line with other jackets. She caught a not-unpleasant but strong scent from him that seemed vaguely familiar, but she couldn't place it before he motioned her to follow him.

He led her through the beautiful, dark wood entryway, past the stairs leading up to the second floor and a narrow nook that branched off to a living room with a giant TV. Everything was so masculine and tidy. She couldn't say exactly what it was about the place, but it reminded her of Alex. It looked like the kind of place he'd live. They passed through another narrow hall to a lovely, large-for-New York kitchen which looked out onto a small backyard.

The kitchen was magnificent, all dark wood cabinets and gray and green marble. The appliances were shiny silver and the stove looked like something you'd see in an industrial kitchen. Alex had his head in the refrigerator, giving her a lovely view of his beautiful ass in fitted jeans. The long-sleeved t-shirt he wore hugged the lean muscles of his upper body, showing off the breadth of his shoulders.

She felt that stupid tightening in her lower stomach again just looking at his back, and she wanted to turn around and leave. If Chris hadn't been standing there, she might have.

"Hi," Alex said, and turned to face her with a bowl of strawberries in his hands. "Glad you could make it."

She nodded, so uncomfortable she didn't even know what to do with her hands. "I can't stay long," she blurted. She was lying. She didn't have anything else to do that afternoon. And *Yaya* would kill her for this, but… "My grandmother called this morning and wanted to have lunch. I told her I was busy, but she insisted on an early dinner." *Liar liar liar.* She couldn't believe what a coward she was, but that kiss last night had shaken her and she really didn't know what else to do.

Chris saved her from another awkward silence by saying, "He's been in here cooking all morning. You have to eat some of it."

She smiled, hoping it didn't look too forced. She'd always liked Chris. And she still had to work with these men. She didn't want that to be uncomfortable, too. "Great game Friday," she commented to Chris, as Alex approached, frowning.

"What the hell is that smell?" he asked Chris, before Chris could comment on her statement. Then Alex's brows furrowed. "You've got that shit on again, don't you? Get out of my kitchen with that smell. You'll ruin my food."

Chris shrugged, looking bashful as he waved a finger at his roommate. "Hey, now. Don't knock the Miracle ointment. The stuff is awesome in a pinch, and I have no time to do anything else today."

Nathalie suddenly recognized the menthol scent of a popular heating balm and realization hit. "You got hurt Friday?" She followed Chris back out of the kitchen. "What's bothering you?" she asked, stopping him close to the small living room with a hand on his arm.

"Chris…" Alex warned from the kitchen doorway. But she ignored him and motioned for Chris to continue.

He dumped the fleece he'd been carrying onto the floor and pointed to a spot just beyond his reach at the back of his shoulder. "There. I can't even reach it but the muscle is spasming. Needed a mirror to get the patch on."

"Let me see."

"Nat, I don't think—"

"Show me. Now," she said more firmly.

He hesitated for a long minute, staring at Alex. She squeezed Chris's elbow and nodded at his shirt. Reluctantly, he rolled up the short sleeve of his gray polo, pushing material out of the way so she could get a look at his shoulder. She removed the coated heat pad covering the bruise and gently investigated the area. The smell of the additional balm he'd used under the pad was almost overwhelming, so strong it made her eyes water.

She shook her head at his attempt at self-medication and pressed her palm over the muscle, letting heat flood her hand. "Just relax. Feels like a pretty solid knot back here. Let me see what I can do."

The focus required to heat her hands just enough and find the exact place to apply pressure took her mind off how awkward she felt in their beautiful home. She worked his muscles until she heard him groan. "That hurt?"

"No, feels great. Your hands are really warm."

"Is the muscle relaxing? Any more spasms?"

"That's helping a lot. Thanks."

After another few minutes, she stepped back and he rolled his sleeve back down. "Thanks, Nat. That really worked out the kink."

"No problem. But you should come into the Center tomorrow and have it worked on a little more. And put a hot pack on it tonight to keep the muscle from seizing up again."

"Will do." He glanced briefly at Alex, then said, "I have something I need to do, so I'll see you guys later. Enjoy lunch." He nodded to her and hurried down the hall.

When the front door closed, she faced Alex. He was scowling after Chris.

"I need to wash that balm off my hands," she said to get his attention. "Bathroom?"

He was still frowning when he nodded toward a door across from the living room. When she emerged with better smelling hands, she felt more settled. And while she couldn't say she was relaxed, at least she wasn't ready to bolt.

She went back into the kitchen and got hit once again by how gorgeous Alex looked in jeans and a t-shirt. Her calm started to slip away. She took a deep breath and said, "So what are we having for lunch?"

"Roasted chicken with a white wine sauce." He gestured to the bowl of strawberries on the central island and motioned to a chair. "Sit. I'm almost finished. Help yourself to the strawberries while you wait. You're not allergic?"

"No. Thanks." She sat and munched on a berry while she watched him work over a few pots on the stove. He looked entirely too sexy in the kitchen.

"Chris shouldn't have had you to look at his shoulder," he muttered without facing her.

"I made him, remember. And it's no big deal. It's my job."

159

"Not today. You're my guest."

"Why?"

He paused in his mixing. "Why what?"

"Why am I here?"

"I wanted to cook for you."

"But why? Alex… This is getting out of hand."

"Shut up and eat some strawberries."

His comment surprised her enough she almost laughed.

"You really having dinner with your grandmother?" he asked quietly.

"Yes," she lied.

"I'm baking a cake for dessert." He finally glanced over his shoulder. "No box mixes."

She smiled. "I'd expect nothing less from a future pastry chef."

With a nod, he turned back to the stove. "Rob wants us over around eight tomorrow night. Will that give you time to get home? Or should I pick you up from work?"

"No! Not work. I'll go home first. I'll need to change anyway. Probably not a good idea to show up in my uniform."

"So you're not going to back out, then. I was starting to worry."

"Until we find—"

"Yes, I know," he interrupted.

He leaned over to pull something delicious smelling out of the bottom of two separate, stacked ovens and gave her an equally delicious view of his backside. Damn but the man had a gorgeous ass. She'd always been a sucker for denim-encased male butts and Alex had one of the best she'd ever seen. That was not a good thing, given the tension in the room.

"I didn't invite you to this dinner tomorrow because of the stuff with Johnson, though." He plated the chicken, along with the sides of risotto and a spinach-bacon salad.

160

"Bacon, huh?" she commented. "Definitely not a kosher kitchen."

"My parents didn't push me to keep to the eating rules of Judaism. They didn't want me to stand out too much. Besides, finding kosher food in North Dakota when I was growing up wasn't really possible." He set a plate in front of her. "You want a glass of wine?"

"Water will be fine. Thank you."

She breathed in the complimentary scents of the food and hoped she could eat. Her stomach muscles were tight from nerves. As he set the water down, she regretted not accepting the offer of wine. It might relax her enough to actually enjoy the meal.

Once he was seated, she dug into the chicken. He watched her take her first bite before starting on his own lunch.

"This is really, really good," she said, her mouth still full. She swallowed. "You sure you don't want to be a regular chef?"

"I like baking better. Wait'll you taste the cake."

After eating a little more in silence, she said, "How's your leg today?"

"Sore still. You offering to work on it?"

"No. I'll look at it tomorrow. At the Center."

His eyes narrowed. "But you had no trouble taking care of Chris's shoulder?"

"Shoulders are easier than legs." Less clothes to remove.

"You afraid I won't be able to control myself if I take my pants off?"

"No." She was afraid she wouldn't be able to. "But for the purposes of this lunch, your pants have to stay on." He raised a brow and glanced down toward her lap. "My pants are staying on, too," she said dryly.

He shrugged, but the gesture didn't convey his agreement. Damn him. She was now imagining him without his pants on and that was not going to get her through this meal with her sanity intact.

As it was, she was dreading work tomorrow. If she was lucky, another one of the PTs would end up working on Alex, and she wouldn't have to worry about her errant hormones interfering.

"Chris won't be back until later tonight," he said in what felt like a change of subject.

But she had a feeling it wasn't. "Okay."

"There aren't any cameras out there right now, are there?"

"No."

"And there won't be for the rest of the afternoon."

"Fine."

"You can relax, Nathalie. You're not going to get caught here by the press. And I'm not going to attack you."

She gave him a look. "I know that." She nodded to the window at the far end of the kitchen. "How did you manage to score a backyard?"

"Happy accident. You can see it after lunch if you like."

"Thanks."

"I'll give you the full tour."

She made a point of looking around the kitchen and back down the hall. "The house is really nice, tidier than I would expect from two men who are on the road a lot."

"Maid service. I'm kind of a slob outside of the kitchen."

"I find that very hard to believe."

He looked up from his meal. "Why?"

"You're too controlled." She shrugged.

He held her gaze, and said, "Not that controlled."

Before she had a chance to react, he went back to eating and launched into chitchat that didn't make her want to squirm in her seat. His efforts worked to relax her enough that she managed to finish her lunch without trouble. When they were done, he put the dishes in the sink.

"I'll get them later," he said when she asked if she could help with the cleanup.

He turned to the top oven and pulled out a glorious smelling chocolate cake. "It'll take a while to cool. Let's do that tour, and then I'll come back and make the frosting."

"Real frosting? Not the stuff in those little plastic containers?"

He actually glared at her. "Not in my kitchen."

With a laugh, she followed him into the hall. He gave her a general tour, leading her upstairs to the second floor and showing her a larger living room with an equally large TV, bookshelves which were full of actual books and not random knick knacks, and comfortable looking furniture. There was a small bar near the large windows that looked out over the back of the house, but it looked a little neglected. The gaming equipment set up next to the TV surprised her. "You guys have time for video games?"

"They're good for the reflexes," he said, completely unrepentant.

He led her on up to the third floor and pointed out his room, Chris's room, and the main bathroom. But to her relief, he didn't linger on that floor or even open the door to his bedroom. For some reason, that eased a worry she hadn't realized she'd carried with her on the tour. And on the way down the stairs, she felt like an idiot. Confusion did not mix well with her lust, and it was playing havoc with her logic.

Back in the entryway, he grabbed her coat off the hook where Chris had hung it. He held it for her so she could slip it on.

"I'll show you the yard. It's pretty tiny, but we have a bench and a few very stubborn plants."

He grabbed his own coat and gestured her back toward the kitchen. From the backdoor, he led her down a narrow set of wrought iron steps to a small space paved with gray stones and circled by a brick fence. The neighboring houses, both to the sides and the back, could easily see into the space, but enough sun hit the area even in the afternoon to give it an open feel.

Alex had been right about there not being much to it. She stood in the center, taking in the worn wooden bench and the three pots of ragged-looking plants, the bare dirt along two sides, and the stems from ivy covering the back fence. "Lot you could do back here," she said, already imagining the plants and flowers she'd use to fill in the dirt spaces.

"I'd do more, but we really don't have the time."

"You'd rather be in the kitchen," she guessed. "Or playing video games?"

He shrugged good naturedly at her ribbing. "My parents were botanists. I'm not."

"Why the tree of life tattoo, then?" He had a large and very detailed tree inked onto his upper right shoulder which she'd always liked. But she'd never been brave enough to ask him about it. It was his only tattoo—at least that she'd ever seen. And since she'd seen him in as little as a towel, she knew he didn't have any others in any obvious places. If there were any in the less obvious places, she didn't want to know about it because she wouldn't be able to think ever again.

"I got that my sophomore year in college. A few months after my parents died."

"Tree of life because of the botany or the Judaism?"

"Both."

She smiled. "I like that. My dad would like the image. You had good work done."

"Thanks." He gestured around the little yard. "So what would you do to this place? If it was yours?"

"Oh, lots. I'd have to plot and plan. Probably get my dad in to help me diagram. But I'd definitely put an herb garden over there." She pointed to the dirt closest to the stairs. "The light seems to be good in that area. And you could easily come down and pick fresh herbs for whatever you were making. At least in the spring and summer. You'd have to either bring them inside or cover them well in the winter."

"Does your dad do landscaping? Maybe I should hire him."

"You're a little out of his way here. But because you're who you are, he'd probably make an exception. He's a big Empires fan, too."

Alex's smile made her forget for just a minute that they weren't really friends, or lovers, or anything other than sometime-colleagues who were forced together by her stupid vision. Then reality returned.

"We should get back inside," he said when she wandered to the far end of the yard, only a few feet away. "Time for cake."

"I could eat some cake," she said to cover her lapse.

He followed her back up the stairs, and she pretended he wasn't looking at her ass.

In the kitchen, he dropped his coat over a hook near the backdoor and went straight to the large mixing bowl on the counter. "Hang up your coat. I'll have the frosting mixed up in a few minutes. Then you can help me frost."

"You're putting me to work?"

"It's good for you."

She rolled her eyes but was secretly happy to have something to do with her hands that didn't involve stripping Alex naked.

To her surprise, he kept her entertained while he mixed up a chocolate buttercream, detailing the process like he was the host of a cooking show. She relaxed and laughed and enjoyed herself so much she really did forget about the strangeness of the situation. She realized that here, in his home, without any possibility that someone would spot them or snap a picture or otherwise make her life difficult, she really could just enjoy his company. And she did. Being around him made her feel…happy.

It was a happiness she knew would lead her right to heartbreak.

The cake was one of the most delicious things she'd ever had the pleasure to eat. And wicked thoughts of licking that chocolate frosting off Alex's gorgeous body ensured she'd never look at chocolate cake quite the same way again.

*****

He refused to send her home on the subway, so she had to wait for the car to arrive. She'd stuck to her story of having an early dinner with her grandmother because if she admitted to the lie, she wasn't sure he'd let her leave. And she needed to get away, soon, before she completely lost her senses. He was too much. Too sexy, too fun, too nice, too everything that was right when he was absolutely wrong for her.

She stood with him in the entryway, her hands vice-like on her purse, sweating because she'd insisted on putting her coat on already, and wondering if he'd kiss her goodbye. Afraid he would. But equally afraid he wouldn't.

"I'll pick you up at seven-thirty tomorrow night," he said before gripping her coat pockets and tugging her close.

She wanted to resist but for some reason didn't. "I'm dressing up, right?"

"Whatever you want to wear will be fine."

"Dinner? I mean, they're serving dinner?"

"Yes." He leaned in close and settled the question of would he or wouldn't he. He did. And she gave in to the kiss like this was how all their time together should end.

He held her in place with his hands in her coat pockets, not actually holding her in any other way. Their mouths were the only skin-on-skin contact, but it was enough to leave her dizzy and aware that his bedroom was only two stories above them. His slow, firm, sensuous assault did more to turn her on and rob her of balance than anything else he could possibly have done. It was like he'd uncovered the key to destroying her resolve, but it was a key she hadn't known existed until now.

When the doorbell rang, announcing the arrival of the driver, her relief was as great as her disappointment, and neither made her particularly happy.

"I'll see you tomorrow," he murmured as he let go of her coat and reached for the door. "Enjoy dinner with your grandmother."

"Thanks. And thanks for lunch."

"Anytime."

She really wished he didn't mean that but was absolutely certain he did.

CHAPTER TEN

The next morning at work, when Alex arrived to have his leg looked after, Nathalie tried very hard to look like she was busy with other things. But Joanne insisted she work on loosening the knot that had gotten worse since Friday. Alex was actually limping when he came in.

She felt bad as she watched him ease into the lifted chair that gave her easy access to his leg. He was wearing loose shorts that were easy to push out of the way so she could work. She focused on assessing the bruise, which was yellowing now, and the tightness in his right quadriceps. If not for her lack of self-control, she could have helped him with this on Sunday.

Warming her hands until they would feel good against the sore muscles, she set them gently on either side of his thigh and began a measured probe for the knot. When she found it, she actually cursed under her breath. "You should have told me your leg was this bad," she muttered as she worked.

"I did. You thought I was faking to get you into bed."

"Shut up. My boss will hear you."

He glanced behind her. "She's on the opposite side of the building. No one is listening to us. Relax."

Oh sure, relax. Like that would be a simple thing to do. She sent a little more heat into her palms, just enough to aid the massage, and moved her fingers and palms over the patch of muscle. "How's that feel?"

"Your hands feel like magic. My leg feels like crap." He grunted when she hit a particularly tight spot.

She snorted. "It's not permanent, big guy. Don't worry. You'll be ready for this next road trip."

"You checked our schedule?"

"I'm a fan, remember. I know your schedule."

"You going to miss me?"

The teasing in his tone made more than her hands warm. "Shut up." But she smiled. Damn. She hadn't meant to smile. "I'm trying to concentrate here. Or do you want me to hit a wrong nerve?"

"No, no. You just keep working that magic." He paused as he scanned the area again. The Center was quiet this early on a Monday morning, only a few clients were scattered around the large main therapy room. And none of them were close enough to catch their conversation. "Funny calling your hands magic when you're a witch."

"Funny." If only he knew.

"I was looking forward to seeing you today."

"Stop," she said, before he could continue down that conversational path. "Working here. No personal talk."

"Can I get personal tonight?"

She shook her head but didn't actually answer because her stomach was doing that fluttery dance again, and she was a little too excited about the prospect of Alex getting personal with her.

"What kind of oil do you use?" he asked, breaking into her concentration.

"Hmm?"

"Massage oil, what kind do you use? It always has a lot of good heat. But none of the other PTs seemed to get that much out of it."

"My already warm hands help." Yet another problem with getting this close to him. He was going to uncover her last secret whether she liked it or not.

"You really are the best here, Nathalie," he said quietly. "Thank you for not avoiding working on me today."

She snorted. "Joanne wouldn't let me." She gave him a sideways look and half-smiled. "But you're welcome."

He left after she'd finished with his leg, promising to see her at exactly 7:30 at her place. She hid in the back room so she wouldn't actually have to watch him leave, though she noticed he wasn't limping as he walked to the locker room. Pride in her work was quickly overshadowed by worry.

She was in the middle of a dangerous game she had no business playing. She didn't need this. She didn't want the risks. Yet, she was afraid it wasn't the uncovering of her secrets that would end up the real problem. The real problem was the fact that she was falling hard for Alex. Maybe even love. Which would suck.

But how to get out before it was too late?

*****

The dinner that night actually started out pretty well. Nathalie had to contain herself from turning into a squeeing fan girl when Chris introduced her to his date. She *loved* Melanie Gould's novels almost as much as she loved her defense of the Romance genre.

After dinner, Marcus Mitchell arrived with his date, a really sweet woman she recognized as one of the wait staff from Vegas Night. Annalise Alonso. The poor woman looked more uncomfortable in that setting than Nathalie, so she immediately felt a kinship with her. She noticed her slight limp as Annalise and Marcus walked into the living room and wondered if there was something she might be able to do for her. Maybe if they got a chance to chat and build up a little trust, she could broach the subject.

Nathalie tried to pay attention to the various conversations going on around her, but every word made her nerves tightened. One woman started discussing a reality show she and her Empire boyfriend were courting. Another one brought up having her name splashed across Page Six. All the exact kinds of attention Nathalie didn't want. Yet these women were glowing with excitement over the possibilities. The woman who'd landed on Page Six was *bragging* about it.

She didn't belong with these people. She didn't belong in Alex's world. Not if she wanted to maintain any privacy.

After a few minutes of conversation, the men all disappeared into the kitchen to get more drinks.

"Do you want something else?" Alex leaned in to ask.

"If Rob has a Scotch in there, I will love him forever."

"If I bring you the Scotch will you love me, too?"

"I'll consider not killing you for leaving me alone with all these *ladies*," she said with a snarly smile. To be fair, they weren't all bad. But they made her uncomfortably aware of her differences.

She felt like such an imposter. She wasn't Alex's wife or girlfriend, she wasn't his real date. And to top that off, she'd done some sort of PT work on every man here, though she wasn't sure any of the women realized it. Given the attitudes of a few of the flashier broads, she had

171

a feeling if they found out what she did, they wouldn't be entirely pleased at having her there.

To confirm her fears, as soon as the men left, one of the women, Barb, started in on Marcus's date. Annalise got hit by insults that made Nathalie's hands heat.

"Hey," she said, when Barb started grilling Annalise about her job. "What's with the inquisition?"

Barb shrugged and continued to lay into Annalise. Nathalie growled. Barb was joined by another bully, Deb, and before she could say more, they'd driven Annalise from the room.

The women laughed and launched into another conversation involving courting the attention of the press. Nathalie's stomach rolled. Disgusted with them, she rose to go see if Annalise was okay. By the time she got into the hall outside the kitchen, though, she didn't see Annalise anywhere. But Chris stopped her on his way back to the living room.

"What happened in there?" he murmured quietly.

She shook her head. "Ask Melanie. She'll explain." She wasn't sure she could go into the details without losing her temper. At least not before she'd had her Scotch.

She went into the kitchen, took the drink Alex handed her, and downed it in a gulp.

"What the hell happened with Marcus's date?" he asked.

She breathed down the soothing effects of the alcohol and set her glass back on the counter. Glancing at Rob, she motioned Alex outside the kitchen. Quietly, she said, "Couple of the women insulted Annalise, made the poor thing feel like she wasn't good enough for Marcus. I got to tell you, Alex, if this is the crowd you normally hang with, I'm glad we're not really dating. I'm not sure I'd be able to deal with those women without..." She was going to say setting their hair on fire but stopped herself and amended it to, "Damaging one of their pretty faces."

Alex raised his brows. "I don't hang with the women. But the guys I play with wouldn't put up with that from their girlfriends."

"Yeah, well their girlfriends have a different perspective." She shook her head, still upset about the way Annalise had been treated but also tight with anxiety about the talk of Page Six and reality shows.

"I think I need another drink," she told Alex, and he obliged. As they leaned against a kitchen counter while a few of the guys who were still in the room chatted, she tried to calm her nerves. But even the excellent Scotch and the more soothing company of the players didn't help.

This life, Alex's life, drew public attention and gossip reporters. And those *women* in there loved it, wanted it. She would never be able to be a part of that world. Not safely, not with any kind of peace of mind.

But he was. Which meant this fake dating that felt suspiciously like real dating had to end.

Marcus came into the kitchen a short time later to say he was putting Annalise in a taxi. Nathalie's anger inched up again at the thought that those women had driven Annalise away. She couldn't blame Marcus's date, though. She didn't want to go back into the room with the bitches either.

She finished the last few sips of her drink slowly, then with a great deal of care, set the glass into the nearby sink. "I need to leave," she said to Alex quietly. "Let's get the walk around the area over with, okay?"

"Okay." He took her arm and led her to the closet with their coats.

As he held her coat for her, helping her into it, she asked, "Do you know what's wrong with Annalise's leg? You think she needs some help with it?"

"You'll have to ask her." He pulled his own coat from the closet. "Or Marcus. I've never met her before this."

"Maybe she'd like to have lunch sometime. A little camaraderie after that debacle."

"Bet Marcus would love for you to do that. I get the impression this one is special to him. He's gonna be pissed when he finds out what really happened in that room after we left."

As they came out of the elevator, they ran into the very Empire in question. And he asked her what had gone on. She told him exactly what was said.

Marcus swore and Alex squeezed his shoulder in support.

"I had no idea they would ever be this blatantly cruel," Marcus said. "If I had known, I never would've brought her here."

"Look," she said. "I hate how the evening turned out for her. Do you think she might want to have lunch with me some time, make up for having such a shitty experience tonight?"

After a moment, he nodded, smiling. He gave her Annalise's phone number and details on getting in touch with her before heading back upstairs.

"Good luck," Alex said to him as he got into the elevator. "See you tomorrow for the flight."

When the elevator door closed, she said, "I hope he rips the bitches a new one."

She stuffed her hands into her coat pockets as they walked away from Rob's building. She was still concentrating on keeping her palms from sparking too hot, and she didn't want Alex to notice how warm they were in the cold night air. The fact that she was assuming he'd take hold of her hand during this walk was yet another confirmation she was losing sight of the reality of their relationship.

"I'm not sure I can keep this up," she muttered.

"What?"

"This pretend dating business."

"Then stop pretending we're pretending."

CHAPTER ELEVEN

Nathalie heartbeat quickened. If only it were that easy. If only she could let go and accept this thing between them as real. But it couldn't work and she was going to get hurt if she allowed herself to think otherwise.

"That's not what I meant," she said, walking faster to get away from the conflicting emotions he was forcing her to feel.

"Nathalie." He pulled her up with a hand on her shoulder and turned her to face him. "I didn't invite you over yesterday because of your vision. I'm not desperate to kiss you right now because I'm worried about being shot. I'm not out here with you because I seriously think we're going to find this building we're looking for."

She lifted her chin. "Why are we out here then?"

"Because you wanted to leave, and I want you happy."

"But why?"

"Because I want you, damn it." His grip on her shoulder tightened. "Why the hell does this have to be so difficult?"

"Because it is."

"Do you want me?"

"Alex…"

"Do you want me?"

She growled under her breath. "You know I do. That's not the point."

"But it'll do for now." He pulled her close and kissed her, a hard kiss this time, with a lot less restraint than he'd shown before. So hot and hard her knees went weak.

Nathalie kissed back. Forgetting to leave her hands in her pockets, she snaked her arms around his neck and held him in place. A small part of her was screaming that this was stupid, idiotic. They were out in the open! Anyone could snap a shot of this.

Her only consolation was that her face was probably well hidden in the depths of his passion. He devoured her, savored her. And any sense of logic or self-preservation melted under his assault.

"Come home with me," he said against her mouth.

"No."

"Please."

His please got her every time. She was trembling with need, desperate for the privacy of his home, his bed, desperate for him. "Bad idea."

"Good idea," he assured. He eased back, grabbed her hand and fast walked to the busier cross street a block away, where he could flag a cab.

"We haven't finished looking around the area."

"I won't come back to Rob's again until after the season is over." He waved a yellow cab to the curb in record time and practically shoved her inside.

She giggled as she settled and fastened her seatbelt. "So much for your control," she commented.

"I warned you." He took her face in his hands and kissed her again.

She gripped his wrists and eased back. "Alex, we are not alone yet."

"I don't care."

He stopped her from protesting again by kissing her and making her forget why she was trying to protest.

She got lost in the feel of his hands, his mouth, his tongue. He didn't touch her anywhere below the shoulders, which only served to heighten her need to have his hands everywhere. And she wasn't very comfortable straining against the seatbelt. But that didn't stop her from gripping his coat lapels in a tight hold to keep him close and kissing him with all the pent up desire she'd been denying for months.

When the cab pulled up in front of his home, she had a moment to wallow in embarrassment as he paid the driver. Though, being New York, the man probably saw this kind of thing a lot, but she wasn't the kind of woman who typically made out in the back of a taxi.

Alex didn't give her long to feel the embarrassment, though. He ushered her up the stairs to his front door, unlocked it with shaking hands and pulled her into the entryway before the cab reached the end of the block. When he'd closed the door, darkness enveloped them, and Nathalie felt all the tension drain away to be replaced by need and heat and want.

She tossed her purse against the wall and let him strip her coat off before helping him with his own jacket. Then he pulled her into his arms and kissed her with that same demand he'd started on the street in Brooklyn.

He moved his mouth from hers to run his lips down her neck, kissing and sucking the sensitive skin over her pulse. "You've been driving me crazy since Vegas Night," he muttered against her skin. "Before then. For months now."

"Liar."

"You've wanted me, too. That's made it all worse."

She couldn't even pretend to deny him when her body would have made a liar out of her, too. "Why didn't you…why didn't you ever say anything?"

"You kept your distance, made it clear you'd refuse if I asked you out."

"I did not." In truth, she'd never guessed he wanted to ask her out. She probably would have said no, but she hadn't realized there was a question to be answered.

He returned to her mouth and kissed her again, which was a relief. She didn't want to talk. She didn't want to think about everything this might cost her. With his mouth doing such wickedly wonderful things to her, she embraced the privacy they had now because she wanted him too much to refuse this chance.

"Upstairs," he growled and grabbed her hand. He paused on the third step. "I love how hot your hands are." He started walking again. "You have no idea how many times I've imagined these hot little hands of yours on my cock."

She tripped on a step. He held her until she got her balance, then he eased her around and pressed her against the wall, one leg between her thighs, one leg on the step above them.

The position pressed his erection firmly against her hip. He cupped her cheeks in his palms. "Avoiding getting hard while you were working on me took a lot of effort."

"Not bothering with the effort anymore," she commented and rubbed against him.

"Mmmm, do that with your hand."

She obliged, more than happy to get her hands on him. Through the material of his slacks she stroked his hardness. He groaned and dropped his head to her shoulder as his hips bucked against her palm. She took advantage of his position to nibble his earlobe, biting gently and then sucking as she continued to rub his cock. She even let a little heat build in her palm, just enough to pleasure.

He jerked back suddenly, startling her, took hold of the hand she'd been stroking him with and pulled her up the stairs. The door to his room was open when they stumbled through and he slammed it shut behind him as he dragged her to the bed.

"Chris coming home tonight?"

"Probably not for a while." He kissed her again as he unbuttoned her jeans.

"Don't you guys have to leave early tomorrow?"

"We do." He pulled back to lift her shirt over her head.

The silky material slithered over her skin in a delicious caress, revealing her simple black bra, which he wasted no time in removing and tossing across the foot of the bed. His hands replaced the material as he cupped her. "Beautiful," he said. And took one of her nipples into his mouth.

She held his head in place because she had never felt anything quite so sexy. He was still dressed, she still had her jeans on, and they were standing beside the bed in a room she'd barely glanced at while he took control of her body. She'd never wanted a man more.

"You need to be more naked," she groaned as she dropped her head back and savored the feel of his mouth sucking her other nipple.

"Yes. You too."

"Absolutely."

She went to work on her jeans and shoes while he shucked first his dress shirt, shoes then his pants. Despite the fact that she'd seen a good deal of his body before, seeing him completely naked took her breath. He was all hard, lean muscle and bone. His stomach muscles tensed and flexed as she stared. The thick corded muscle over his hip drew her attention and she reached out to stroke her fingers lightly along the line. He shuddered and closed his eyes.

His cock was thick and full and perfect, and she had to stroke that next. Even his many scars turned an already beautiful body into a work of art.

"You're not naked yet," he growled.

She was nearly naked, only her panties were still in place. "I got distracted," she said as she played with his length, spreading the moisture that beaded at the tip up and down his shaft.

His breathing sped up as she worked him and she smiled, watching The Wall lose control.

"God, your hand is hot," he muttered.

"Does this feel good?"

"Too good." He finally stopped her, gripping her wrist. "My turn."

He stripped her panties down her legs, dropping to his knees in front of her as he did so. She was the one breathing hard as he leaned forward and licked along her hot, slick entrance. A sound somewhere between a groan and a squeak escaped and she fell backward onto the bed. He followed, spreading her thighs to make more room before continuing to lick over and into her.

The tension in her core tightened until she no longer felt in control of her own body. Thrashing and moaning, she fisted the sheets with one hand and gripped his hair with the other, knowing she'd scream if he moved away now.

When he took her clit into his mouth and sucked hard, Nathalie came, her back arching off the mattress. She thought she might have screamed.

He continued to lick her gently as she came down, then he crawled up over her. She opened her eyes to look up at him. "I think I made that too easy on you." Her voice was breathy and deeper than usual.

"I like that about you."

She snorted and pulled him down for a kiss. He moved them farther up on the mattress without relinquishing his hold on her mouth. He rolled away long enough to pull a condom out of his bedside table and slip it on before returning to her. Stretching over her, he settled himself between her bent legs, his cock nudging gently at her entrance. He fingered her, rubbing moisture around her as well as onto his erection, then he slipped a finger inside as if testing.

"You are so damned hot. Sweet and hot and wet."

She actually purred under his touch, her nerves sparking with tension and excitement. "Alex, if you were to fuck me right this very minute, it would make me a very happy woman."

"You want my cock right here?" He rubbed over that hard-to-reach spot on the top of her passage and her hips jerked.

"Yes."

"More than you wanted that Scotch earlier?"

"Infinitely more. Please."

He replaced his fingers with his cock in one long, solid stroke that filled her completely. She couldn't form a coherent word after that, not even to tease him. He set a rhythm that was slow, steady and pounding, doing more to make her body sing than a frantic pace ever could have. He went deep and hard but measured, and she went moaning into another, longer orgasm that left her limp and shaking.

She clenched and shuddered around him as he moved a few strokes faster, harder until he threw his head back and groaned her name.

She cradled him close as he rested his full weight on her for a few minutes. Her brain was content and quiet, her body tired and sated. She kissed his temple and hugged him.

"Stay the night," he murmured into her neck.

"You have to get up too early. And I have work tomorrow." She would love to spend the night with him, to hold on to this peace for a bit longer, but she didn't want to send him on his road trip exhausted. "Do you know how much flak I'll get if The Wall is too tired to play well Wednesday night?"

"I can sleep on Tuesday. Stay."

"No. But if you don't mind, I will stay for a little bit longer."

"Good. That'll give me time to convince you to stay the night."

She shook her head. "Stubborn man."

"Obstinate woman." He rose up onto one elbow and traced her cheek with his free hand before kissing her. Then he rolled out of bed and left for the bathroom to clean up.

She admired his beautiful ass on the way out of the room and his full frontal nudity on the way back in. When he climbed back into bed next to her, he pulled her into his arms and kissed the top of her head.

"Can I call you while I'm away?"

"You want to?"

He nodded.

"Sure." She couldn't fool herself into thinking this wasn't real anymore, not when they were still naked and the room around them smelled like sweat and sex. This wasn't pretending or playacting. This was serious, whatever was happening between them. Everything had changed.

And she had no idea where to go from here.

But she knew one thing. She couldn't let things go any farther without being completely honest with him.

She never told the men she dated the full truth about herself, even the couple of pagan men she'd gone out with. Alex was different, though. The way she felt about him, the life he lived, everything. If whatever was happening between them had a hope of continuing past tonight, he needed to know the full truth.

A truth she was sure would put an end to things anyway.

Chapter Twelve

Alex watched her eyes grow distant as she pulled out of his arms. He knew he was going to hate the next words out of her mouth so he tried to distract her with another kiss. She refused to be diverted, though.

"I need to tell you something. The real reason I can't afford public attention. The reason my mother left us. The truth."

He sat up against the headboard and nodded. Truth between them was good. It proved she'd started to trust him. Finally. He doubted there was anything she could tell him that would change his mind about what he wanted from her, but laying all their cards on the table would only help things between them.

"Go ahead." He gestured for her to continue.

Sitting up next to him, she pulled a sheet up to her chest, covering her breasts, which was a damn shame. She took a deep breath and set her palm against his shoulder.

"Feel this?"

"Very much so. Though I'd prefer if you moved your hand a little lower." He waggled his brows, trying to draw her out of her seriousness. His attempts failed.

"Just wait. Feel that now?"

The heat coming from her hands had actually increased, warming against his shoulder in a very pleasant way. "Your hand is getting hotter." At first he thought it was just the physical contact making her palm feel warmer. But then the heat increased more and more. Enough that he noticed. "Your hand is getting a lot hotter. How are you doing that?"

She didn't answer and, after another moment, the temperature of her hand was hot enough to hurt. He sucked in a hissing breath and she pulled away. Holding it up in front of them, she stared at her hand rather than looking at him. As he watched, bright blue flames erupted along her skin, engulfing her entire hand.

"Fuck!" He pressed back against the headboard, his heart slamming against his chest.

She closed her hand into a fist and the flame went out, leaving her skin unmarred. "It's called pyrokinesis," she said. "It was the final straw for my mother. She left when she saw what I could do. Called me devil spawn and never looked back."

He watched her throat work as she swallowed hard. He looked back at her hand, afraid to get too close to her. His brain couldn't comprehend what she'd just done right there in front of him.

When he didn't speak, she nodded and climbed out of bed. He didn't stop her. But he watched as she got dressed and slowly his brain started working again.

"What are you doing?"

"Going home. You have an early morning." She met his gaze. "And I've given you a lot to think about."

"Does that hurt? The fire?"

"No. And I have a lot of control over it. It's been with me since I was four. Don't worry, I won't accidentally burn your house down on the way out."

"That's not what I was thinking."

She paused after finishing with her jeans. "Alex, this is why we can't work. You can't afford to have people find out about this."

He started to shake his head but she held up a hand for silence.

"Listen, tonight was wonderful. Fantastic. But this thing between us... If it has any hope, you need to take some time to think about what I've just shown you. To really consider if you can deal with this. With me."

She sat down on a chair near his closet and pulled on her shoes. "I don't expect declarations of love or promises of forever. But we've been honest with each other up to now. I can't continue without being honest about why I didn't want to start this to begin with."

"This is what you think will get out." He understood now. Why she'd been so resistant, why she'd made this so difficult, why she'd been pretending the attraction between them wasn't powerful and serious.

"Don't feel bad if you can't see me anymore. I understand. I do."

When he didn't say anything because he didn't have any idea what to say, she headed for the door.

"Have a good trip."

"Nathalie, wait."

She paused without turning.

He still didn't know what to say, though. He wasn't even sure why he'd stopped her except that he couldn't stand to watch her walk out his door. Even after what she'd revealed. But she was right. He needed to think about this more, to really decide if he could take this risk. He'd never shied away from risks before. The fact that he was hesitating now didn't make him happy. He just didn't know what else to do.

When he didn't say anything, he watched her shoulders rise and fall as if she'd sighed, then she opened the door and walked out without another word.

He only realized he'd left her to find her own way home ten minutes after he heard the front door close. More than anything else, that left him feeling like an ass.

CHAPTER THIRTEEN

Nathalie tried not to regret telling Alex the truth. She spent the time he was out of town convincing herself she wasn't waiting for a phone call and moving through her days as if nothing was bothering her. She knew, deep down, she'd had to be honest with him, just as she'd known she had to warn him about her vision even though she risked a lot to do it.

She didn't regret either decision. But she missed him. More than she ever thought she should. And by Thursday she knew her heart was the problem. She'd fallen hard for Alex, and it was going to take a long time to get over him. Accepting that she had to get over him because he wasn't going to be in touch ever again was a given. He hadn't made a scene and told her boss, so she would probably keep her job. But she doubted he'd let her touch him again.

Knowing he'd be back in town on Friday, and she'd have to truly face his rejection when he didn't get in touch, she made plans to have drinks with a girlfriend that night. And she turned her cell phone off after work. Less temptation to keep checking for a message if the phone wasn't on to check.

She kept the phone off after she got home, too, because she wasn't sure she'd sleep well knowing there was no message waiting for her. She didn't have voicemail on her landline, so she didn't have to worry about ignoring that phone.

At least until early the next morning when it started ringing. She was sure it wasn't her grandmother or dad because they were doing a special pre-spring sale at the nursery this weekend and would be too busy to call. None of her friends were likely to phone this early, and her boss never called on the weekends.

She lay in bed and listened to the phone ring ten times before it stopped. Telesales, she assured herself. Some poor person trying to get her to buy something she didn't want or need. Not him. Because he wasn't going to call her again. He'd asked to call her during the week and then hadn't. He'd made his decision clear.

The phone rang again at ten, twelve and two. She continued to ignore it as she tidy her apartment and did some laundry. At three, she finally decided to turn on her cell phone. Ten waiting voicemails made her stomach dance and her heart pound. Hope and dread tightened her throat. She checked who had called and each message was from Alex. More of that hope and dread snaked through her gut. She was about to play the first message when her cell phone rang again, surprising her so much she almost dropped it.

The caller id confirmed it was Alex. Sucking in a deep breath, she answered.

"Where the hell have you been?" he asked, not even attempting to start with friendly conversation.

"Around. Why?"

"I've been trying to reach you since last night."

"I was out."

There was a pause. "A date?"

She considered lying but decided there was no reason. It would only complicate things. "Drinks with a girlfriend."

Another pause had her staring at the phone to make sure it was still connected. Finally, he said, "Why have you been avoiding my call?"

"Why didn't you call during the week like you said you would?"

"You told me to think about what you'd shown me. I was thinking."

"Uh-oh."

She heard humor in his voice when he said, "Just doing what you told me to."

She waited for him to say more, and when he didn't, she flopped down on the couch in frustration. "Listen, Alex, you didn't have to call to tell me we couldn't see each other again. I would have gotten the hint. It's okay. Really."

"No. No, it's not. That's not why I'm calling."

"Then just spit it out. I have things to do today."

"What?"

She rubbed her hand over her forehead. "Alex, you're stalling."

"I want to see you. Now. As soon as you can get here."

"No."

"Please."

"Damn it." She made a face at the empty room. "It's not fair. You should really have to beg more after not calling."

"Please is begging." Again humor threaded through his voice, which had also deepened.

"Not nearly enough begging. A couple of 'pleases' and I jump to do as you asked. That's just wrong."

"You have never jumped to do as I asked."

She didn't say anything because she didn't know how to respond.

"Come over," he said quietly into the silence. "We have a lot to talk about."

"I'd rather you dumped me over the phone."

"I'm not dumping you. Come over. Please. I need to see you."

Her jaw tightened as she tried to stomp down on her unruly emotions.

"If you don't come to me, I'll come out to you."

"Fine. Fine."

"I'll see you in an hour. Nathalie. I've missed you."

She hung up before she blurted out something ridiculously inappropriate like "I love you." Then hurried to her bedroom to decide what to wear.

*****

Two hours after hanging up with Nathalie, Alex paced his kitchen like a caged animal, trying to decide if he was more pissed or worried. Had she changed her mind and decided not to come? If so, she had to know he'd come to her place and find her. Or he'd corner her at the Center, which was exactly what she didn't want him to do.

He checked the clock again. She should have been here by now. Even if she had trouble on the subway, it wouldn't take this long. He continued to pace, barely acknowledging when Chris waved goodbye on the way out to meet his lady.

When another forty-five minutes ticked by and she still hadn't arrived or even called to explain, he cursed and went to get his wallet and coat. Damn the woman anyway. If she wouldn't come to him, he'd go to her. He was hunting for his keys when his cell phone rang.

"Damn it, Nathalie," he barked as he answered her call. "Where the hell are you?"

A male voice said, "She's taken a little detour."

"Johnson? Where is she? What have you done?" Alex's palm hurt, and he looked down to see he was gripping his keys so tightly, one had cut him.

"She's safe," the bastard said, his tone managing to be both whiney and mean. "For now. But if you don't want to see this pretty face get messed up, you need to meet me. I tried to be nice. I just needed your help. But you, you can't even help an old friend? You're too high and mighty? Well, you'll help me now or your lady's gonna get hurt."

"How do I know you didn't just steal her phone?"

Nathalie came onto the line. "Don't come," she said, her voice deep and steady. "Don't come. I'm fine—" She was cut off abruptly.

"Nathalie?"

Johnson came back on. "Now, Semenov, as you can see, I'm telling the truth." He rambled off an address in Long Island City. "You've got an hour to get here. No cops or I'll kill her. Don't be late. Or your pretty girlfriend and I will have to find ways to entertain ourselves."

He hung up before Alex could say anything. Cursing roundly, he slammed out the door and went hunting for a cab.

When he arrived at the address, he realized immediately that it bore a good resemblance to the place Nathalie had described from her vision, the place he was going to be killed.

CHAPTER FOURTEEN

When Nathalie saw Alex walk into the gutted second floor of the building, she wanted to cry. "Why didn't you stay away?"

"You know why." He nodded to the gun Johnson held to her temple.

"This is the place, damn it. This is it." She gestured at the open ceiling, the bundles of wires and wood, the bare support columns and concrete floor. The only light in the room came from a single florescent bulb blinking irritatingly behind where she and Johnson stood. The scent of construction dirt and unwashed, sweating male made her stomach turn.

"I know," Alex acknowledged her warning.

"Fuck!"

Johnson laughed, the sound nervous and jumpy. "Not a delicate little thing is she?" he said to Alex. "But a pretty one. I can see why you want her. With this body? Bet she's wild in bed."

"You wish you knew that," Nathalie said, as Alex's eyes narrowed dangerously. She could get out of this. But with Alex here now, she was terrified he'd be killed or hurt before Johnson gave her a chance to escape. The bastard had taken her by surprise right outside her own apartment building, giving her no chance to act. She'd been waiting for the right moment since he'd taken her, and finally, he was close enough she could do something. But now she had to worry about Alex. Knowing this was the exact location where she'd seen him killed in her vision made the whole thing a surreal nightmare.

"Alex, get out. Don't worry about me."

"Oh, no, Alex. Worry. Worry," Johnson said. "Cause if you don't do what I tell you, I'm going to hurt this yummy girlfriend of yours. You kept telling me you had no reason to do me any favors? Well now you do. I tried to be reasonable, just asking an old friend for help. You're the one that pushed things this far. I got nothing to lose now. I either pay them back or they're going to cut me up. I got nothing left to lose," he repeated, and Nathalie heard the resolve and desperation in his voice. "But you do have something to lose now."

Johnson sniffed the side of her neck, a move that made Nathalie snarl in disgust and Alex take a step closer. Johnson pushed her head sideways, pressing the gun harder against her temple. Alex froze.

"What do you want?" Alex asked Johnson, but kept his gaze steady on her face.

"You're going to let a few pucks in during your next game. Let the other side win and end your streak. You're gonna give me the seed money I need to make the bet. And I'm going to clean up."

"What makes you think I won't call the cops?"

The gun butted her temple again. "I'm gonna keep pretty here with me until after I collect my money. You do anything I don't like, she's dead. And I won't kill her quickly, Semenov. I'll play with her first."

"What the hell happened to you, Ben?" Alex asked, as he took a single step toward them.

"Hey, desperate times, man. Guys gotta do what he's gotta do. Right?"

Nathalie rolled her eyes, but kept her mouth shut as she waited for the break she needed.

"And after you've collected your money?"

"You two can go on your way."

"You aren't worried about the police then?"

"Na. I don't think you want the police digging into your affairs anymore, do you? Not when pretty here is a witch. Not after they find out you gave me the money to place the bet. You'll want all this kept nice and quiet."

"I don't care if people know I'm a witch," Nathalie said because she wanted to make sure Alex realized that. But most of her concentration was on the movements of Johnson's body and the gun against her head. He had an arm around her waist but he hadn't bothered to bind her arms or hands. He had the gun, why would he?

She let one hand, the one opposite the gun, hang down near his thigh and waited for him to return his attention to Alex. When Alex stepped closer, she got her chance.

"Let her go, and we'll talk."

"We can talk like this. I'm tired of pussyfooting around with you, Semenov."

Nathalie's stomach clenched. The words from her vision echoed in the open, empty space, sending panic through her. Alex cursed and threatened Johnson in a way that was probably anatomically impossible. Johnson threatened back, throwing in a few anti-Semitic slurs just to charge the atmosphere more. And the two men got so caught up in their verbal fight, she got her opening.

She let heat spark on her fingertips then set them gently against Johnson's leg. The spark was hot enough to burn.

"Fuck, what the hell?" he grunted and looked down at his leg.

The movement shifted the gun a very small bit, but it was enough. She pinched the edge of the barrel with her other hand, which was already glowing with heat. She didn't dare apply heat to the chamber or magazine, but she could make the gun unusable. Her hand was hot enough that it only took a moment to collapse the very tip of the barrel, but a moment was all she had before Johnson tightened his hold on the weapon and tried to turn it to her head again.

"Wouldn't fire that if I were you," she said. "It'll blow your hand off now." She took a risk and dropped her hold so he could see the melted metal.

"What the fuck?" He pulled the gun away from her completely and she used that action to turn and thrust her broiling hand against his chest.

He screamed and launched back, but she didn't move away fast enough. He slammed the now useless gun into the side of her head. Pain exploded through her temple and cheek in the second before blackness swallowed her whole.

CHAPTER FIFTEEN

Nathalie woke suddenly and tried to sit up, panic shooting into her bloodstream. Spots jumped in front of her eyes and pain sent her retching sideways, as her stomach threatened to send her last meal back up again. Fortunately, she'd eaten ages ago and nothing came but a little bile into her throat.

She groaned and opened her eyes, panic still pushing her to see where she was and what had happened.

Before the spots cleared, she realized someone had their hands on her shoulders and was steadying her.

"Shhh," Alex murmured, "take it easy."

"Johnson?" Her voice sounded hoarse and rough.

"We're safe. Settle down and let the wooziness pass first."

She eased back onto her butt and found herself in Alex's arms. Because her head was pounding, she let it drop back against his shoulder. As her vision cleared, she realized they were still in the gutted second story of the building in Long Island City. Johnson was nowhere to be seen.

"Are you hurt?" she asked.

"Nothing that won't heal."

She turned in his arms and looked at his chest. "You're alive. There's no bullet hole."

"You did a very good job of ruining his gun. Thanks for that."

She lifted a hand and waved it. "Handy hands. Har-har-har. What happened after the bastard cold-cocked me?"

Alex fingered her temple, scowling. "You're going to have a serious lump here. And a bruise. I think we should take you to the hospital."

"And tell them what? I'll get my grandmother to look at me and make sure I'm not damaged."

"I'm going to stay with you in case you have a concussion. Your place if you'll be more comfortable. But I'm not leaving you alone until I know you're okay."

He touched her cheek and she hissed in a breath. That part of her face was starting to throb.

"My heart stopped when you went down," he said.

"What happened after that?"

"I beat the ever-loving crap out of him, until he bled. A lot."

She raised her brows. "You never fight on the ice. I didn't know you could."

"Team won't let me. Don't want to have me sent off. But I know how to throw a punch."

"A pugilist, are you?" She smiled because he looked so fierce and angry. And he wasn't dead. They were sitting in the middle of her worst nightmare and the worst hadn't happened. Relief was actually making her head hurt more, but she didn't mind that kind of pain.

"Bet your ass," he said.

To her surprise, he dropped his hand to her butt and caressed her. The feeling was almost nice enough to distract her from the ache in her face. "So after you made him bleed—thanks for that, by the way. Bastard. I can't believe he hit me with the fucking gun. Anyway, what happened after you kicked his stupid ass?"

"He threatened to go to the cops, which made me laugh."

"He didn't?"

Alex shrugged. "He's a dumb ass. He always has been, though. Which is why he got into trouble in the first place. Then he threatened you again. But he still had your handprint on his chest, so I reminded him what a bad idea that was. And I told him he needed to leave me and you and everyone else on the Empires alone, or I was going to let you turn him into a spontaneous combustion mystery. I think he's actually more afraid of you than he is of the men after him."

She snorted, then grinned big. "You know, I could probably do that. *Yaya* told me early in my training that one in every hundred cases of supposed spontaneous combustion was actually a pyrokinetic accident."

"Seriously?"

"*Yaya* could have been telling stories. She does that sometimes." She reached up and cupped his face. When he didn't flinch or pull away, she let out a slow breath. "Not afraid to have me touch you anymore?"

"I love your touch. I always have."

"Not so much right before I left that last time."

"You took me by surprise, Nathalie. People don't light their own hands on fire every day. But I'm not your mother."

She rolled her eyes. "I knew that already. I've seen you naked."

He didn't even smile at her stupid joke. "I'm not turning my back on you because of this. I don't think you're devil spawn. I actually think you're the bravest woman I've ever met."

She pulled back a little to get a better look at his face. "Brave? Me? Why?"

"Outside of taking on a desperate and corrupt scumbag without fear?"

She waved that away. "He was an idiot. His plan was never going to work. I was only really worried about him shooting you."

Taking her face very gently in his hands, he set his lips against hers in a soft, tender kiss. "You're brave," he said against her mouth, "because you live your life on your own terms without excuses or apologies for who and what you are. Another kind of woman would bow under the pressure of carrying this secret around, of the responsibility required to control this. You don't. You just get on with things."

"I'm not sure that's brave. I don't know what else to do but get on with life."

"And that's what makes you brave."

She started to shake her head but he stilled her with the hands still cupped around her jaw.

"Don't argue with me while I'm complimenting you," he said, his brows lowered.

"Fine." She nibbled her lip as she reached up to wrap her hands around his shoulders. "Where does this leave us?"

"Safe from Johnson and dating without the pretense."

"The problem hasn't gone away, Alex. This is a secret I can't afford to let out. Not if I want to live comfortably. And that asshole knows now, what if he talks? He needs money. He could go to the tabloids. Or what if someone else finds out? I can't…" She sucked in a breath. Saying this was harder now somehow. "I don't want you to risk this kind of attention either."

"I can take it. I'm not afraid of that. And Ben Johnson isn't going to be a problem now. He knows what will happen to him if he says anything."

"My job…"

"Isn't an issue either. I've already talked to your boss."

"What? When?"

"While I was away, I called her."

"What did you say?"

"I told her you and I were seeing each other, that I intended for us to see each other for a while—if I could get you to speak to me again—and that, after some time, I had every intention of things between us getting to the moving-in-together and getting-married stage. In the meantime, I would take it as a personal favor if she left you alone about our relationship."

Her eyes had widened with each sentence. All she could manage was an inarticulate grunt she'd meant to be a "What?"

"I also told her that if any gossip about us came out of the Center, even a hint of gossip about you or our relationship, I would make sure the owner found us another therapy center to use."

"Can you do that?" she breathed.

"This year I can. I have a lot of clout while this streak is happening."

She made a face she thought might have been a smile but was pretty sure it didn't look like one. "And she said?"

"Congratulations. And no rumors would come out of her Center or the gossip in question was out of a job."

"She said congratulations?"

"After a few long moments of silence."

"I'll bet." She licked her lips, then blew out a breath, her brain spinning. "You called my boss before we'd even talked. Pretty ballsy of you."

"My plan was to eliminate all the obstacles you kept throwing in our way. Your job is safe." He looked around the shadowed, empty floor and shrugged. "Johnson isn't an issue now, though I suppose that was more my obstacle than yours." He met her gaze again. "As for the rest, we'll control the information that gets out, distract and deflect attention so the press doesn't think to dig deeper. And then we'll keep to ourselves. I have no intentions of courting a reality show."

She shivered at the very idea. "How do we control the information?"

"The team's official blogger. She'll help. Write up a little piece on us dating. She'll out you as a witch, if that's okay?"

"I don't really mind that part. I'm not a secret pagan."

"And given that bit of information released willingly on our part, what else could anyone possibly think you had to hide? Fire-starters who have psychic visions are not exactly common."

"What if they contact my mother? What if she tells the press?"

"We'll calmly say your mother is crazy and get on with things. Who do you think people are more likely to believe?"

"Alex, I don't know."

He wrapped his arms around her waist, pulling her closer against the wall of his chest. "I do. I'm willing to risk this, Nathalie. For what we have. For what this can become. The only question now is, are you?"

She swallowed and looked away for a long moment. "Did you really tell my boss you thought we might end up getting married?"

"I did."

"I'm not Jewish. Wouldn't that disappoint your mother?"

"The chances of my finding a nice Jewish girl in North Dakota were very slim. She just wanted me to marry a nice American girl and build a life here."

His palm slid down her spine and back up again, and her stomach danced in reaction.

"I've got the life," he murmured. "Now I just need the girl."

"And you want me?" The idea was just mind-boggling.

"I want you. Very much."

He gave her another soft kiss, but this one had the tingling in her stomach turning into something a lot more serious.

"Be with me, Nathalie. See where this thing between us can go. Please."

She groaned and set her forehead very gently against his. "I just can't seem to refuse that please."

"I intend to keep that in mind the next time we're in bed."

"I'm looking forward to it." She laughed. She was giddy with excitement about her future, their future. And for the first time since that damned vision, she felt the risks she'd taken, the risks she would continue to take to be with him, would be easy to face. Her nightmare had become a dream.

"Come home with me tonight," he murmured, his mouth brushing against hers.

She didn't hesitate. "Yes."

Nathalie had a feeling she was going to be saying "yes" a lot to Alex from now on.

PLAYING HER GAME

Stacey Agdern

CHAPTER ONE

Even though it was an off day, even though it was only a few hours before the start of Vegas Night, Chris Emerson found himself sitting in front of Coach Peter Michaels's desk as the man himself continued to pace behind it.

"You should know why you're in here."

Chris knew damn well there was no good answer to Coach Michaels's question, so he didn't say anything. Instead, he prepared himself for the beginning of the inevitable lecture.

"You're a magnet for trouble, Emerson. I can't fathom why it is you continue to act so immaturely that you get attention from the media. " Michaels suddenly stopped pacing, choosing instead to stand directly in front of the chair Chris was sitting in. "Even worse than that, you not only find yourself in the spotlight, but relish it. At the expense of everything else, streak or no streak."

Everything else. Once again, the crux of the problem. The coach didn't like him. Some said the coach saw himself in him, but Chris didn't buy that, not for a second. The coach might see himself in the face he projected, but not in what existed behind the mask.

Because, in truth, there was nothing *else*, except the fact that he did the books for a bunch of small businesses in the village, but nobody had actually picked up on *that*. Unfortunately, as it stood, the spotlight had a nasty tendency to find him. Or, rather more importantly, it had a tendency to find those he cared about. So he played for the cameras sometimes, drawing the glare away from his brother, his roommate—the most private man in hockey—or his sister, like he had been doing the night before. It wasn't his fault the paparazzo had taken pictures of him dancing along with the crowd when his sister's quartet started playing a bit of salsa.

"Emerson!"

He shook his head, annoyed that he'd gotten lost in an answer he wasn't going to give Michaels anyway. Instead, he played it diplomatically. He had no choice. He was only on the team because Arnie Dawes, the owner, liked him. "Sorry, coach."

Michaels threw his hands out, as if he'd had enough. "Just do me one favor for the rest of the season? Will you?"

He focused on Michaels. "Yes? Absolutely."

"Stay out of the spotlight. Behave. Take lessons from Semenov… or Miller for fuck's sake."

There was only one thing he could say to that. "Yes, sir."

"Good." And then Coach looked down at his paperwork, signaling the meeting was over. And, as far as Chris was concerned, it couldn't be too soon.

Chris was so disgusted by the outcome of the meeting with his coach that he headed down to 'Razor's Ink.' He'd taken care of the shop's accounting issues for the month, didn't need another tattoo, but he wanted…something. Maybe he'd have Al take out the streaks in his hair to make himself look more presentable for one night.

Thankfully he'd driven to this meeting, so all he had to do was get into his car and drive from Brooklyn into Manhattan and the tiny part of the West Village where the shop was. Yet another village hole-in-the-wall on the outside, but twice the size on the inside. Camouflage.

The group of people assembled in the barber chairs or the waiting area of the shop welcomed him, and the dude with the Mohawk who worked behind the desk immediately changed the flat screen TVs from the sports channels to the music assortment so he didn't have to hear sports broadcasters talking about the "Quest for the Cup".

"Well, Christopher," Al boomed, emerging from the back of the space. He was the shop's owner, a tattoo artist who had his barber's license. He was also the prototypical New York punk, a living legend from the time the village was a mess and the Unbearables had just started to make trouble in New York's downtown scene. His dark eyes never missed a thing and, today, Chris felt those eyes give him the once over. "What the fuck are you doin' here today? You did the books last week, and you said no more ink."

Chris grinned in spite of himself, shook his head and held his hands up as if he were surrendering. "I know. I know. No more financials to take care of and no more ink. But…" He gestured towards the top of his head, at the blue tips which stood out against the black of his hair. "Gotta look all penguin-like tonight, and I kinda want to go low key."

Al raised a bushy eyebrow. "You? Low key?" Al laughed, one of those belly laughs that shook the walls. "You're fuckin' kidding me." But he sighed heavily and gestured towards one of the barber chairs anyway. "Never thought I'd see the day."

Chris shrugged as he sat in the chair and Al's assistant put the cape on. "Yeah, well. Times change."

In the mirror Chris watched as Al shook his head, before the man leaned down to look closer at the blue streaks on the tips of his hair. "Nah. People do. They try to hide who they are, but it never works."

Chris didn't say anything. Too many thoughts were pouring through his head to even make sense of any of them. "As long as I can stay out of trouble, I'll be fine."

Al laughed again. "You? Staying out of trouble? This I gotta see."

*****

"Mel? Are you listening to me?"

She was listening all right. Melanie Gould, romance writer, public advocate for romance readers everywhere, could probably recite her sister's cautionary speech by heart at this point. But she loved Emily and understood her concerns. Emily was the official blogger for the New York Empires and she was bringing Mark-Francis Smythe, her boyfriend and the star center of the New Jersey Palisades, to Vegas Night for the first time. She clearly had enough to worry about.

And so instead of taking refuge in sarcasm, Melanie stood up from where she'd been sitting on the living room couch and went over to her sister. "I'll behave," she said, putting a hand on her sister's shoulder. "I promise. You have enough to worry about."

Melanie couldn't help but notice the grimace that made its way across her sister's face. The Empires were practically guaranteed to make the playoffs and, according to the most persistent whispers, they could win it all. Other rumors talked about how Smythe was seriously considering crossing the Hudson to join the Empires once his makeshift, one-year deal with the Palisades was done.

Emily nodded, and relaxed her shoulders enough to meet Melanie's approval. "Thank you," she said. "See you in three hours?"

Melanie grinned and patted her sister's shoulder. "Three hours. Right." And then, before Emily could comment further, Melanie left the room.

Three hours. Three hours in normal people-speak meant literally one hundred and eighty minutes. In Emily-speak, three hours was less than that. Much less. Directly depending on her stress levels. And that was the kind of thing that drove Melanie the craziest.

"Fucking hell, Em," she shouted in response to the incessant knocking at her bedroom door, trying, yet again, to fasten the clasps of the tiny bra she had to wear with the dress she'd chosen. "Are you kidding? Really?"

"Are you even close to being ready Mel?"

Melanie could tell from the sound of her sister's voice the three hours they were supposed to devote to getting ready hadn't done anything to calm Emily down. "I'm on my way," she said, honestly. "But if you want to come and sit down…"

"In this dress?" her sister wailed from the other side of the door. "You're kidding me. You're absolutely fucking kidding me."

"Come *in* already," Melanie insisted. "If you need me to look, I can't see through the door."

Seconds later the annoying little bra dangled from her hands, as she watched the spectacle unfolding in front of her. Emily, confined by a slinky, skin-tight dress, entered the room at a speed even a turtle would consider too slow. "You're kidding, right?"

Emily sighed. "It was so cute, you know?"

"Cute," Melanie pronounced. "But really dumb."

"Speaking of dumb," Emily interjected. "What's with that thing dangling from your hand?"

"Oh, this?" Melanie looked down at the annoying piece of lingerie. "Having trouble with getting it on."

"Go without," Emily pronounced. "Your dress would so work without it."

Melanie looked down at her dress, its tight bodice and beautiful beadwork, as it lay on the bed. Then she looked down at her chest. "No," she said, shaking her head sadly. She knew her luck all too well. "Without some kind of protection, the girls'll find a way to come out to join the party."

Emily nodded, and Melanie could see the sympathy in her sister's eyes. "Yeah."

Then it was her turn to give her sister a critical eye. "So they're going to put you on a flatbed? Or is Mark going to carry you?"

She was rewarded with Emily's sudden burst of laughter, followed by a deep breath and a change of expression that reminded Melanie of a fish. "Dear God," her sister groaned. "Why am I wearing this dress?"

"Change." Melanie gestured towards her closet. "And if you don't have anything else, you can borrow one of mine." From the look in Emily's eyes, Melanie knew she'd been had. She shook her head and then glared in her sister's direction. That was when she noticed Emily hadn't moved very far from the closet. What Mel had initially deemed movement hampered by the dress, was in fact, deliberate strategy on her sister's part. "Fine." she said, a put upon sigh escaping her lips. "Just because I love you, you can borrow a dress. But, Em? Don't spend that much money on a disaster you know you won't be able to wear."

"I love you too, Mel," Emily replied, grinning happily as she flung open the closet door.

Melanie loved her sister, but there were time she wanted to kill her. She hoped this was not a sign of how the evening was going to go. Because if it was, she wished she could stay at home under the covers.

*****

When he got back from Razor's, Chris saw that Semenov had already left for the evening, so a last minute pep talk from someone who knew how to stay out of the spotlight wasn't an option. Instead, he walked into his bedroom and headed to his closet. The tux he'd bought for one of his sister's benefit concerts but never wore was within easy reach. He put his hand on the hanger and—

His thoughts froze at the sound of the ringing of the phone. He didn't want to answer, but he had a feeling who might be calling him this evening. He waited, hedging his bets, debating whether he wanted to answer, then deciding he didn't.

"Hey big bro," his sister's voice boomed from out of the answering machine speaker. "Wanted to see how you were doing before the crazy night of…"

Electing to answer the living room phone, as opposed to the one in his room, needing to work off some more nervous energy, he raced down the stairs and reached the land line just in time.

"Kayleigh," he said, grabbing the receiver and cutting off the ancient answering machine mid-recording. "Hey. How are you?"

"Okay," his baby sister answered, exhaustion evident in her voice. Playing for the New York Philharmonia was difficult, but his sister was talented and had a kick-ass work ethic. "Busy. Practice then performance on Thursday. Wanted to see how you were doing tonight, y'know."

He nodded, then started pacing around the living room. "Yeah. Fine. Getting ready."

"I should probably let you go, but I should also tell you that you're awesome and you'll be fine. Leave the assholes out of this and be

215

yourself." She paused, and he could hear the classical music in the background. "The people who matter will love you for who you are. Ignore the bullshit, Chris. Be yourself."

"Love you too Kay," he replied, knowing that his sister meant well. "Don't work too hard. See you on Sunday?"

"Absolutely. Usual time?"

He nodded, then remembered she couldn't see him. "Yep. Can't wait for those popovers."

"You'll do fine tonight," she repeated, and then with a click she was gone, leaving him hoping her nervous phone call wasn't a sign of disaster to come. Because if it was, he probably should just stay home, despite the fact he'd probably get in more trouble than if he went.

CHAPTER TWO

As the rented town car pulled up to the building where the event was going to take place, Melanie took a deep breath. This wasn't going to be difficult. This was going to be fine. And sure enough, as Emily and M-F got out of the car, the Empire State building could have fallen down behind them and nobody would have noticed her. Which was a relief.

"Having fun yet?"

Melanie grinned at the sight of Arnie Dawes. He was her mother's childhood friend, yet neither of her parents had decided to support him, his team or Emily this evening. But she didn't care. Less parents, more fun. "Yes," she said, letting the older man embrace her. "I am having fun. You must be having a blast."

Arnie nodded, his eyes gaining a slight but sudden sheen. "All my life I wanted to own a hockey team. And this is their second year." He smiled, reached for his handkerchief and wiped his eyes. "My Jennifer would have been so proud of this…"

She nodded at the mention of his late wife. "Absolutely. She would have loved this."

"She would have loved it more if you were having fun, Melanie. You were her favorite."

Melanie couldn't help but laugh. "I'm not inside yet. But I'll have fun, Uncle Arnie. I promise."

Satisfied, Arnie nodded. "All right. Now let's party!"

And with that, she followed the team owner into the building, happily incognito for the first time in her life.

*****

"Christopher!"

The booming voice of the team owner was hard for him to ignore; and why would he? Arnie Dawes was a wonderful man who treated the Empires like gold. Chris had absolutely no illusions that he would be playing in New York if this man hadn't demanded it. "Mr. Dawes," he replied, as he headed over to the older gentleman. "Thank you so much for tonight."

Dawes smirked and patted Chris on the shoulder. "Thank you for bringing your spirit to the team. We wouldn't be where we are without you." Then he looked him over once again. "Though I almost didn't recognize you."

It was now Chris's turn to smirk. Dawes noticed the blue streaks enough to miss them? "Formal event, sir," he replied. "Had to look my best."

Dawes shook his head. "Let nobody tell you different, kid. You look your best when you're being yourself."

He didn't want to argue with the team owner—he'd be out on his ass if he did that—but he had to at least explain himself. "To be honest, sir," he said, feeling weary. "Trouble happens when I'm being myself."

"That's where you're wrong, Christopher." Dawes gave him a kindly smile, one that looked as if it was usually reserved for the criminally stupid or insane. "Trouble happens when people don't think before they react. Trouble happens when people don't understand." Dawes paused, and Chris suddenly felt the weight of the world on his shoulders. "And as far as I'm concerned, that is, and can *never* be your fault. No matter what other people say."

What the hell was the team owner telling him? Was there trouble brewing in the upper levels of management? Did he want to know? Not really. But he wanted to ask anyway. "No matter who those people are?"

Dawes shook his head, his eyes twinkling. "Don't push it, kid. Just be yourself and everything else will follow."

Confronted with the obvious support of the team owner, and the genuine pride in the man's eyes, Chris felt humbled in a way that he hadn't before. "Thank you for your faith in me, sir."

"You deserve it kid." Another pat on the shoulder from Dawes and then a grin, the moment over. "Come on," the owner boomed. "Let's go mingle."

And on the heels of his team owner, Chris headed into the crowd, ready to enjoy the evening.

*****

The crush of people reminded Melanie of a scene out of one of her books, except the formal attire people wore was a little… different, and the gambling wasn't done in a 'hell', but rather a large, open room covered in marble, luxurious carpeting and beautiful, glittering chandeliers.

The Empires had outdone themselves this year, and the charity they supported would benefit. She had to remember to send the PR people at her publisher a note about partnering with the organization at some point around the release of her new book. She let her thoughts continue to drift, concentrating on the promotional push she'd have to deal with as she headed into the gaming area.

A sudden cool sensation on her back jolted her mind back to reality. She shivered, all the while attempting to reach for the stole she'd worn on top of her cute strapless dress. The problem was that sometime between coming into the ballroom and now, she'd given it to her sister.

"I'm sorry..."

From the pronunciation, the speaker was obviously Canadian and, with a beautiful, deep voice like that, *had* to be male. She turned around to face him. He was tall, which meant she had to look up in order to see his face.

But when she did see his face, she was captured by his smile. It dazzled her and halted the breath in her throat. The sarcastic reply that came to her lips stopped too. She was supposed to be on good behavior, which meant no sarcasm. "It's fine," she managed in an attempt to sound graceful.

"Did it spill?" he asked, sounding just a little bit nervous himself. "I mean..."

"No." She shook her head, and felt her dark hair swirl and settle on her shoulders. "I felt a chill, but not something spilling down my back."

He nodded, and focused a beautiful pair of grey eyes on her. "Well how about a glass of something warm then? Would that help?"

Why did he offer to get her a drink? Did he want something from her? "You...I mean..." She shook her head again. "Don't take it personally, I'm just wondering why."

He smiled, and she liked the dimple his smile revealed. "Consider it chivalry," he said, complete with a bow. "I'm the reason you're suddenly freezing. Let me fix the problem."

She was wary, almost too cynical for her own good, but she wasn't stupid. Hot guy offers to buy her a drink? Why not? "Fine. Let me run to the bathroom and I'll meet you back over by the main bar."

"All right," he replied. "See you soon?"

"Yes."

*****

Chris was behaving. Really. Okay. He was trying to. After leaving Mr. Dawes' company, he'd smiled at tons of fans, said hello to a bunch more, talked to people who were terrified, in awe and somewhere in between the two, helped Miller deal blackjack and shuffled at a poker table, much to the delight of the fans there.

But in the back of his mind, he knew he couldn't be too…much. In order to make good on the promise to Michaels, he had to hide a little bit of himself. Al had taken care of the physical—the blue streaks were gone for the night. It was up to him to take care of the emotional, and he'd been doing a pretty good job.

But then he'd managed to bump his drink against the back of a hot chick's dress. Not that he'd deliberately done it, but if he'd actually been planning, he would have chosen someone like her. Dammit, she was cute. And maybe a cute girl was just what he needed. Maybe….

No. He had to concentrate. This season demanded all of his concentration. There was potential for something, and no he was *not* going to think about the cup. Maybe after everything was over, he might be able to investigate some hot chick's ass. No. Not now. Not in the middle of the kind of season where everything seemed to click.

Speaking of potential, the sound of a gathering crowd broke through his thoughts; footsteps on marble, the deep intake of breath and the silence. He felt himself head towards the building commotion, almost as if driven by an outside force. His stomach clenched, the reflexive concern that he'd somehow caused the problem eating through his bones. Shit. At least with the blue streaks, people would recognize him for the brash, bold persona he usually played, but like this? He felt like the wannabe-academic-farmboy he was underneath it all. Dammit.

He found himself stopping just outside the main group, watching carefully, not pushing. "What happened?" he asked someone.

"Some chick tripped on the stairs coming down from the bathroom, and gave everybody a show."

*****

So a guy with a cute ass and gorgeous eyes, not to mention a beautiful accent, wanted to buy her a drink because he thought he'd made her feel uncomfortable? These were all benefits of being on good behavior. Unfortunately, she decided, as she stared at her unfamiliar, unadorned reflection in the bathroom mirror, this sweet, subdued guy probably wouldn't be able to deal with all of her foibles. She wanted to be herself, her real self, with a guy who'd get it, at least once. Sighing, she realized that wasn't going to happen anytime soon, so she reapplied her lipstick until it looked about as right as she could make it, then took a deep breath and headed out the door.

She needed to be careful, but confident. Good behavior did not mean doormat, or the dormouse that was afraid of everything. It just meant no screaming dragon bitch all over the place. She could do that. She could be gracious and graceful. Including while going down the gorgeous flight of stairs that separated the bathrooms from the rest of the ball room. And descending those stairs made Mel feel as if she were in a Marilyn Monroe movie or the corresponding Madonna video. It was perfect, glamorous, with the uncharacteristically comfortable pair of Jimmy Choo's…

She knew the moment her heel came out from under her, catching the stairs, that this was going to hurt. Falling on her ass, in this gorgeous dress. *Dammit.* Of course.

If she was making a public appearance as the infamous spokeswoman for romance novels she'd become, wearing her trademark corset and kick ass boots, she'd know how to deal with this. She'd be able to brazen it out, make some pithy remark and everything would be fine. But in an elegant cocktail dress, in an even more elegant location, she was clueless. Fish out of water, daughter of a famous critic and even more famous journalist. Confused as to where she belonged and desperately wanting to hide.

Then she looked down. Just as she'd predicted, the girls had joined the party. Despite the fact she'd worn a bra underneath her dress. *Ohshitohshitoshit.*

She scrambled, wishing for the stole…something… anything to hide herself with. Her stomach twisted with concern, with *dear God this was going to be all over the place and she was just…*

"Hey lady…I'd play with those melons any day…"

"You can't," she said as she pulled the front of her dress up, standing tall, and glaring at the son of a bitch who'd been drooling at something he had no right to lust over. "You're too busy playing with your own."

The sudden hush that fell over the crowd made her swallow, reminding her all too quickly that she'd broken the night's one commandment. Except she'd been defending herself against someone she knew wouldn't stop. Unfortunately, she recognized the type— the slobbering jock who believed he deserved the world, worthy of attention from the peons who populated the rest of civilization. The good in all of this is that she was just the sort of girl to remind him that not everybody was going to come at his beck and call. That gave her the courage to stand at her full height, full of pride and glaring at every single person in that entire group who contributed to the fact she felt two inches tall.

*****

"You can't because you're too busy playing with your own…"

The tone of the woman's voice and the words she used echoed in his head. They were familiar. From where? He racked his brain. And then he remembered…

"Yeah," she'd said, her voice calm, joking and relaxed, "cock, ass, cunt. They're words. They're easy words to write, easy words to say. They can have their place in a romance novel. But the more important words, the ones that mean the most no matter how many times you write 'fuck me', are three little words. And if you don't get them right, all the big cocks in the world won't save you."

"And what are those?" The radio shock jock seemed confident. "Fuck me in the ass?"

She laughed, this time bigger, throatier. "Four words, and though that might be in some, they're not the ones I was talking about. You ready?"

"Ready."

"They're the crux of every single romance novel, and if they don't work, the whole book is shit. They're I. Love. *You*."

Melanie. Emily-the-blogger's big sister. In that dress, without the corset and the boots, he hadn't recognized her and was going to buy her a drink. She and her ass were cute but she was *'The Girl in the*

Lace Corset'—too loud for someone who was trying to hide, to be incognito for once in his life. He couldn't be anywhere near her cute little ass and keep his place on the team. He just couldn't.

"Silly little bitch, spending too much time writing about balls like mine than actually scoring."

Fuck. With a shock, he recognized the voice of Chuck 'Alsto' Allston. Womanizer, screwball, sonofabitch and all-round asshole. Nobody on the team liked him, not even Miller, and he was the man's defense partner. And yet there Alsto was, at the bottom of the stairs, taunting *her*.

This could get dangerous because neither of them would back down. She'd goad him, he'd continue because *god* forbid he get bested by a girl and, clearly, she had no tolerance for assholes. Who knew where that would lead. Nowhere good, that was for damn sure. He had to do something.

So, he took a deep breath and started to make his way through the crowd. "Put your cucumber back where it belongs Alsto," he shouted. "And leave the lady alone."

*****

"Put your cucumber back where it belongs, Alsto and leave the lady alone."

The crowd parted in a mix of astonishment and awe at the loud booming voice. Mel found herself wondering who, aside from *her*, would say something like that? She couldn't see a damn thing beyond the people at the foot of the stairs and the asshole's stunned face, a problem chalked up to her height deficiency.

But as the presumed speaker came closer, Melanie recognized a pair of gorgeous grey eyes, a build that was tight, with the promise of a twelve pack beneath his tuxedo shirt. He was the hottie she was supposed to meet at the bar. But instead of a slightly shy smile, there was a brashness to his expression, a dangerous light in his eyes that made him look familiar despite the fact that his dark hair was only one color.

"Emerson. What do you think about the so called 'Avery rule' and the clarification of goalie screening?"

"I think the league was right in doing what it needed to. There's screening and then there's modern dance. Not that there isn't a place for modern dance, but it definitely doesn't belong in the middle of a hockey game."

"Emerson? Emerson? Were you complaining about anti-Semitism in the NHL back in November when you talked about a lack of matzoh Ball soup in Orange County?

A laugh, a sigh. A look in his eyes like there he was again. "Anybody who knows me, knew that I really wanted a bowl of matzoh ball soup. I wasn't feeling well and it's become a comfort food for this Regina farm boy when he's sick. But at the same time, prejudice is something we all have to deal with, because you can't sweep it under a rug. Nor can you prioritize which is more important. Whether it's against someone's race, sex or something you can't see, like religion or sexual orientation, it has to stop." A big sigh of relief and a shake of his head. "But all the same, I'm glad to be back here in the Big Apple."

Chris 'Emo' Emerson. Hot, known more for his off-ice antics than the fact he was heading for a thirty goal season and on a scoring streak to boot. He'd come to rescue her. Shit.

She had to think fast. "You really…"

"All right," Uncle Arnie interjected, interrupting it all. "There's nothing to see, nothing to do here. Go back and play and enjoy

226

yourselves." As the crowd began to disband, he turned to Emerson. "Get her out of here, will you?"

Unfortunately, in a situation like that, she knew he couldn't say no. "It'll be my pleasure," he said, as he gestured towards the coat room. And, as if she had any choice in the matter, she smiled at him, rolled her eyes at Uncle Arnie and left the room.

*****

"You really don't have to."

It wasn't exactly the first thing he'd expected to hear from the hot chick, Melanie, a.k.a. Emily-the-blogger's sister, once they'd gotten into the safety and relative quiet of the cloak room. But all the same, he raised an eyebrow. "I don't have to what?"

"Take me anywhere. I can just go home. Really." She blushed. "You did enough. I can deal with this on my own."

He shrugged. "I never doubted your ability to deal..."

"Once you figured out who *I* was."

He rolled his eyes. "Fine. Whatever. But, if I had to guess, we wouldn't be having this conversation, had you not figured out who *I* was."

The shock went across her face in a wave. "What do you mean?"

"Well," he replied. "Before all of this happened, you were meeting me for a drink. Afterwards, you're running as far from me as you can get." He considered the irony as the words came out of his mouth. Quiet was not what she and her cute little ass would bring him. And now, as she was telling him she wasn't interested, saving him from the trouble of the noise and the cameras, he was trying to get her to come with him? He was simply certifiable.

"That would be after my uncle, your team owner, practically forced the issue. Last thing I need is a pity drink."

She was conflicted. Emotions seemed to alter the planes of her face in a way that reminded him of one of his brother's early attempts at a mural. Colors all over the place. Anger, embarrassment, nerves, and even a little bit of hope. He shrugged. Despite how bad she was for him, he understood. And he'd bet that he'd be able to find his way around the path she'd been walking. He shrugged. "Well here's the deal. I need a drink, and I owe you one. No pressure." Hands up palms out, as though he wanted to squeeze her ass. "You come with me, I buy you that drink. You don't, well then we'll have to do it another time."

"But," she interjected, sighing. "That really assumes you actually owe me a drink. Really. No harm, no foul. I'm fine, no worries. It's okay."

"Okay," he said, trying to behave, to be good, to act like a normal guy for once. "Fine. Whatever. I'd like to buy you a drink whether you think I owe you one or not. I like you. And…well, the rest is up to you."

He turned, and clear on his course, headed towards the door.

"Wait."

He stopped, waiting, wondering.

"No funny business?"

He would have laughed, except he knew she was serious. The sarcasm waiting in the wings got swallowed down. "All I'm doing is going for a drink. I'd prefer if you came with me, but I've got no problems going by myself." Whether he actually would go and have a drink by himself was debatable, but she didn't need to know what.

And she nodded. "Fine. I want you to know. I'm not going out of obligation, or a sense I think you owe me a drink. I just...want one and I don't want to drink by myself."

He'd take that. He'd really take that. "So come on. Let's go." Then he offered her his hand. Miracle of miracles, she took it.

CHAPTER THREE

Melanie held his hand, but she felt like she was jumping off a cliff instead of holding something that would keep her afloat. "I just want peace," she said, staring down at the shoes that had caused her so much trouble. "Really. I just want…to go away and hide for a while."

When she looked back up, he was looking back at her. And that half joking, half indulgent expression was gone. Instead, there was something else, and she wondered if there was more to him. If there was something inside him that really could understand her.

"Yeah. I know."

And it wasn't rude, or as if he was repeating himself. His words sounded weary, bereft of the façade he'd worn in front of everybody that night. This was the version of Chris Emerson who she wanted to have a drink with, the one who'd managed to get her to agree to meet him at the bar in the middle of the insanity. So she nodded, smiled, not full on flat out glow, but a real one.

He nodded back, a small smile of his own meeting hers, as he led her to an underground garage. "I left my car here," he explained, opening the passenger side door of an expensive German car that looked like a sedan had swallowed an ATV. "If you don't mind me driving…"

She shook her head. "Not really. I haven't driven in Manhattan in years." And then, as she let him close the door behind her, she thought about it further.

"Even more importantly," she said, as he got into the car on the driver's side. "I haven't driven at all in about as long, so it's fine either way."

"Now before we head out," he began, his voice soft and clear, "I'm taking you seriously."

What did he say? Had he not been taking her seriously before then? Did the sudden change of mind require a declaration? Fucking asshole.

"Hold up, let me finish before you let loose the firing squad."

His eyes met hers, and she took a calming breath. "Okay."

"So you want to hide for a while, have some peace, right?"

She nodded. "That's right." Then she paused, adjusting her seat belt, waiting for him to continue. "That's what you're taking me seriously on?"

"Yeah." He ran his hands through his hair before turning towards her, focusing over the gear shift. "But I'm taking you somewhere special, somewhere private, so you have to promise me…well you'll just relax and enjoy yourself. Just be yourself, is all I ask."

She smirked at him. "Leave the corset at the doorstep?"

He shook his head, which surprised her. "Just be yourself. You don't have to feel like you're on good behavior or that you're 'on'. I want you to be *you* tonight. Because? Fair warning? I'll be *me*."

231

She hoped, she prayed that he meant it. Because more than anything else in the world, she wanted someone to *get* her. And maybe, possibly, there might be a chance he could.

*****

She looked comfortable sitting in his car, Chris thought as he drove down through the windy and traffic-filled streets of the city. He probably shouldn't feel comfortable as he drove, but he'd been one of those weirdoes who had to have a car in Manhattan and so he'd learned to just deal with the crazy. He'd also driven this way so many times, he could do it in his sleep.

More importantly, there was space in his special parking lot, located two blocks away from Razor's Ink. He'd be able to tip the guy extra to keep the car overnight and pick it up the next day. Life was good, and contrary to what most people said, Manhattan was really a collection of small towns disguised as a big city.

"All right," he said. "We'll walk the rest of the way," and found himself smiling at her horrified expression. It was, in fact, February, and he had to remind himself that not only was she unused to Regina winters the way he was, she also wasn't wearing very much. "It's not far. Block or two from here."

She nodded, apparently willing to trust him that far. "Okay."

"And," he added, as he got out of the car and went to open her door. "If you need another layer, I've got my coat and a jacket I don't need."

She raised an eyebrow and he couldn't help but smirk back. "I'm from Saskatchewan," he replied. "This is nothing." He offered a hand and helped her out of the car. "Not to mention your clothing is less winter friendly than mine is."

232

That got a laugh out of her. A throaty, strong, beautiful laugh, only slightly obscured by the beeping of the car as he locked it and set the alarm. "I'll give you the FWS," she said.

It was his turn to raise an eyebrow, and he did so as they started to walk down the small, cobblestoned street. "FWS?"

"Freeze Warning System." She shrugged. "In case of freezing, before my teeth start to chatter, I'll let you know."

"Thank you," he replied. They fell into a companionable silence, and he put his arm around her. She didn't pull away, but she did look at him.

"Ice," he replied. And it was true; he'd seen the telltale signs of black ice on the cobblestones, and on the sidewalk. "I'm probably better equipped to deal with ice."

Once again, he was rewarded with the sounds of her laugh, but this time, she leaned against him as she did so. "What, you have blades on your dress shoes?"

"What?" he wondered, confused as they continued along the street.

She shook her head, and he felt the softness of her hair against his jawbone. "I have a close friend who's a really good skater, but you wouldn't know it because without blades on the bottom of her feet, she falls at the first signs of ice."

He laughed, grinned and pointed. "Well we don't have to worry about falling, at least not now."

Her eyes were focused, full of questions. "Why?"

He gestured towards the wooden door with his free hand. "Because we're here. Welcome to The Elk" And without looking at the expression on her face, he pushed it open.

CHAPTER FOUR

Melanie looked through the door, seeing the stone walls, wooden floors and polished bar. She wasn't sure what to expect of a place where 'Emo' Emerson would come to find a bit of relaxation, but then again, he'd probably be surprised what qualified to her as a calming spot.

"Christopher!"

A guy who looked to Mel like he was in his early forties, with a bald head and focused eyes, headed towards them. "What are you doing here tonight? You did the books already…and I thought you had that crazy shindig earlier?"

Did the books…?

But Chris shook his head; apparently he wasn't going to elaborate. "Yeah, well, Bruce, y'know, totally crazy-ass. Didn't stay for long."

"What?" A young woman with bright eyes came into the room. "You got your sorry arse in trouble already? Duuude." She shook her head, put her arm around the bald headed guy and looked at them. Despite herself, Melanie found herself relaxing. "And in trouble with her?"

He shrugged his shoulders, and she could see the humor in the young woman's eyes. "Y'know how it goes, Sousa" he replied. "Woman who can kick some serious arse charges into battle like a gladiator, only her opponent isn't necessarily prepared to fight a gladiator. Soo, I can't help myself and well…"

"You in trouble?" The older guy, Bruce, focused on her before turning back to him. She wondered what Chris had done to earn his watchful eye. "Though from the both of your expressions, you need a drink. What is it? On the house."

"Tequila shots. Three for each."

She bit her lip and looked at Chris, then at the small group of people watching them. "I don't like tequila," she said softly.

"Then what do you want?"

"Lemon drops."

Bruce stared at her. The woman, Sousa, gazed at her with frank appreciation.

"What the hell's a lemon drop?" Bruce asked, all New Yorker in his anger.

Sousa rolled her eyes. "She wants vodka, sugar and lemons. She'll match him as he goes with his salt and tequila."

Bruce shook his head. "I don't believe this shit. Sucking sugar with a goddam vodka shot. Next she'll be drinking fucking diet coke with Crown."

"Well, it's what the lady wants, man." Chris said, quiet, clear, and just very relaxed. She liked that.

"So," Sousa interjected, "go grab a corner and Bruce'll bring your bottles, glasses, shakers and citrus fruits to you. Come on. Shoo."

"Shall we?" Chris asked her, a smile even in his eyes.

And considering she felt like grinning from ear to ear, she nodded. "We shall."

*****

Chris showed her to a wooden table in the corner, smiling at the expression on her face. "So what do you think?"

"This is awesome," she replied, with a look of amazement that warmed his heart. "How did you find this place?"

"Sousa's my sister's best friend from high school. This was her brother's dream, and she was a bored first year financial analyst when he died. So she went through with it." And then he stopped talking, tapping his hand against the table. What was it that made him want to confess his secrets? What about her was it?

But instead of shock, there was understanding in her eyes. "One of my college buddies, he did the same for his sister. He went to medical school, and his sister died during the middle of it. She'd been off saving the world for some humanitarian organization. He decided it was more important to save the world than to go into private practice, so he went off and joined Doctors Without Borders as soon as he could. He's been running around ever since."

He smiled at her, wondering if there was anything he could say to that, but was stopped by Bruce's arrival. The older man put the two bottles, six shot glasses, a bowl of sugar, a salt shaker, lemon slices and lime slices in front of them. "Enjoy," he said. "And don't drink too much."

He smiled back at his friend. "Thanks, man."

"You're welcome."

And like that, Bruce was gone, leaving him with Melanie. And she looked adorable, happy, a bit of expectation in her smile.

"So?"

He grinned up at her, reaching to separate the different items Bruce had delivered. "I still don't understand how you drink this," he said, looking up at her, shaking his head. "I mean…well." His hand encompassed the sugar and the lemon.

"Tequila is disgusting," she replied. And she was cute saying it.

"No," he replied, staring at the bottle of vodka he'd placed near the sugar and her lemons. "You're doing vodka shots. *That* is disgusting."

"Gin shots are disgusting." She shook her head, and went about the business of putting together her shot, pouring the vodka and licking her thumb in a way that made him hard before putting on the sugar. "Bottoms up," she said. Then she downed the vodka in her glass and sucked on the lemon wedge in front of her. He tried not to think about what those same lips would feel like on his cock. "Lemon drops are not disgusting."

He tried to ignore her as he put his own shot together. Then he found himself concentrating on the burn of the tequila before focusing on the fact she'd said she'd had gin shots. "You're crazy," he exclaimed, before sucking on his lime. "Where the hell did you drink gin shots?"

"Went to a conference in college," she began, her laugh getting throaty, her eyes looking off to some faraway place. "Friends took me to this bar and ordered gin shots. I was so excited to be able to drink legally in college when I was a sophomore that I said yes…and then I realized I was drinking gin. It was awful."

He laughed, then looked closely at her. She'd gone to an American university, and there weren't many, if any places she could've had a legal drink while there. He had to know, so he asked. "Where were you…I mean where did you make this unfortunate mistake?"

"This bar called…Montaigne, I think?" She looked puzzled, even as he got excited. "Yes. Montaigne. It was in Montreal. Such an amazing city."

He grinned. "Spent three psychotic years there myself," he answered. "Went to McGill for three years, so I know all too well about Montaigne, and the green beer at Peel pub."

"Oh my God!" It was excitement, not shock or surprise that altered her expression, and that made him happy. "That's so cool. I wish I'd spent more time there. What did you study at McGill?"

"Economics," he said as he poured himself another shot. "Debated between a business degree and an economics degree, but went for the pure economics as opposed to the BCom."

"So what…brought you here after only three years?"

"Played a really kick butt season with the hockey team, we had a CIAU championship and a scout came to visit me. He said you're burning yourself out here, not doing what you could be." He shook his head at the memory and drank the shot he'd poured. The tequila burned his throat, but he took a breath and held on before continuing. "Over a really good shawarma sandwich at this awesome hole-in-the-wall on Crescent, he told me that if I wanted to be an economist, that was great, but if I wanted to play hockey, now was the time."

"And the rest is history?"

He nodded, smiling. "Yeah. It is."

*****

One hour turned to two, shots were drank, both his and hers, before Chris dragged her to another place he knew to get some food. "You're gonna love this," he'd told her, excitement in his eyes. "Something about this food soaks up the alcohol the best."

She nodded, let it happen, even as her heels languished in a bag in favor of the boots she'd bought on the street. They walked through the cobblestone streets of the village, to a place that had a blue flag with tons of fleur de lis hanging down from a dowel above the front door. She'd seen British places, French places, even drank at the Scottish bar on 46th street, but never saw anything like 'La Poutinerie'.

"What is this?"

He grinned, and reached to lift her jaw closed. "This," he said, "is where you can find the best smoked meat in the city. One of the guys on one of the other local teams missed it so much he stole his grandmother's recipe and threw his lot in with someone who knew the business."

"That's so cool," she said, as he shouldered open the door.

"Emerson!" An older man grinned in his direction. "I thought you did the books…."

This place too? How many more people would say that?

He shrugged in her direction. "The business guy got too involved in other things, and…well."

"A guy from Western Canada couldn't resist the siren call of a Quebecker in trouble." Then the older man turned to Melanie. "So you're with him tonight?"

He smiled, putting his arm around her. She was glad; it felt comfortable. "Yeah. We're enjoying the city on a beautiful night."

"Well," the older man replied, and if Mel listened closely, she could hear hint of a French accent in his voice. "Come sit down, there's a table. The usual?"

He nodded. "You want the best smoked meat this side of the Canadian border, and to share a poutine?"

Melanie nodded back. She'd had a vague memory of something that might have been called 'poutine' from her brief stay in Montreal, but she'd been too chicken to try it then. Tonight, however, was supposed to be fun, so she'd let the chips—or fries in this case—fall as they would. "Yes. Whatever it is, it sounds great."

He grinned and guided her to a table, pulled out the chair and gestured. "Mademoiselle?"

"Oh," she batted her eyelashes, playing along in the moment as she sat down in her chair. Simpering was not her style, but she could try. "You are too kind, monsieur."

He laughed; she liked the sound. Maybe it was the time she was spending with him, but he was really starting to grow on her. But she had to know. "You can't not do the economics too?"

He blushed. For the first time that night, he blushed. "Yeah." He looked down then back up at her, a shyness that he hadn't shown before all over his face. "I can't help myself. And I enjoy it…helping people. I have the training, well, not really, but I have the aptitude." He stopped and *looked* at her "You don't think that's crazy. And I can't believe I told you."

She shook her head. "I think that's awesome. It's amazing. And I'm glad you told me."

He almost shuddered. "I don't tell people. I don't…this isn't… what I show anybody." Then he closed up, turned away before looking back at her. As she was about to yell in protest, he took her hand and squeezed it, showing no signs of letting go. It was comfortable, and she liked it.

That same feeling warmed her stomach with the arrival of the food. Plates filled high with sandwiches, and an amazing smell that came from a dish their waiter put at the center of the table.

"Bon appétit."

"Merci bien, Martin."

His French accent was amazing, and his eyes twinkled as the older man slapped him on the shoulder. "Un petit chou?"

"Cauliflower?" Mel found herself interjecting. "Um…"

"The crazy Quebeckers," Chris replied, embarrassment coloring his cheeks again. "They use the term 'little cauliflower' to mean 'significant other.'"

"Aaaah." She nodded, then looked down at her fingers. *Significant other?* Him? Yet? Um. Not really.

"Sorry you asked?"

The surprise, and maybe hurt, in his eyes was shocking. She hadn't expected her reaction to being called his girlfriend only hours after meeting him, to mean that much. "No," she replied. "Not really. Just, well. Yeah." Because really? This was too fast. Whether it was the alcohol, the companionship, the lust she felt deep down at the pit of her stomach, or the fact that he understood her? She didn't care. It was moving too quickly for her tastes.

*****

Chris could do this. He was surprised how easily he could be calm with her. Yeah, it would be difficult, but fuck, he hadn't…this hadn't happened to him in ages. He hadn't found someone who made him feel like this in a very long time. And she looked bright, happy, gorgeous.

Nervous. Even as they brought the poutine and the plates piled high with smoked meat sandwiches, he could see the fear in her expression. "Hey," he said, putting his hand out to cover hers. "It's just a snack. We're fine. Right?"

She nodded, and he could see her shoulders relax. "Right. Sorry." And then she looked at him, as if she could see right through him. "You *really* don't bring people here."

He shook his head. He had to be honest. "No, not really. I mean they're public places and people go. But not with me. They're my places. People who I trust own them. Which means, you know, for five minutes I can relax." He took a bite of his sandwich and enjoyed the taste of the meat and the bread on his tongue, then swallowed. "I hope you've been able to as well."

She suddenly covered her mouth; she'd taken a bite of the poutine and the cheese was dangling from her lips. He wanted to use his tongue to take it off, but he didn't think she'd react well. Instead, he smiled, let her eat and concentrated on his own food.

But his fascination with the cheese dangling from her lips continued, and so he resorted to taking a long swallow of the glass of ice water Martin had put on the table for him. No luck.

"This," she interjected, as he took a bite of his sandwich, "is so good. Oh my god."

He smiled around his sandwich. "Glad you like it. One of my favorite things."

"Tequila shots and hockey on ice, cheese fries with gravy and smoked meat on rye."

"Saskatchewan winters that melt into spring," he sang, happily yet badly. "These are a few of my favorite things."

She shook her head and laughed. "This is awesome."

"Yeah," he replied. "This is pretty great."

And it really was. Through the ride in the hired car she called because he'd driven them down and afterwards, as they walked, hands entwined, in the cool night air to her apartment.

"You know," she said as they headed into the building, "I had a good time."

He nodded. "I did too." And then he looked at her. "I want to do it again." His heart stopped beating in the moments he waited for the answer. He hoped, didn't want to push, just hoped. Wished. Maybe...

"Me too," she said, her voice barely louder than a whisper.

He grinned and put his hands on her shoulders. She didn't move away, didn't stiffen. "A kiss?" he asked.

"Yeah."

His lips touched hers and, all of a sudden, it went from soft and sweet to boiling in sixty seconds. Her tongue met his. She opened to him. He lost all control, taking her in, hands down her back, hers up his. The sudden feeling, the sudden *need* burst through his brain. All sense of propriety was gone, all sense of time was gone, all sense of who he was supposed to be flew out the window. There was only her, her lips on his, and the fact he didn't want the moment to end. Ever.

But it did. She pulled back, leaving him wanting…something. He closed his eyes, trying to bring himself back from oblivion. But the expression on her face when she broke the kiss, however, brought him back down to earth really quickly. He didn't know what he'd do if she denied the way it felt.

*****

Melanie was incredulous, surprised. Like this wasn't serious, couldn't be serious with a man like him. And yet… Her heart was pounding against her chest, and she felt lost now that she'd broken the kiss. "This isn't real," she said, trying to make sense of the situation.

He shook his head. "Nope. Imaginary. A moment out of time. Take your pick…"

His words were dripping with sarcasm and she bristled. "This doesn't happen to me," she responded, the words stark against the moment. "It doesn't," she insisted.

"No. Only in those bodice rippers you write."

She rolled her eyes. "Yes. And I'm sure you prefer to spend your time fucking some puck bunny…who just happens to be somebody else's sloppy seconds."

"Jeez." He stopped, his eyes wide, his hands dropping from her shoulders. "I was just kidding."

She glared at him. "Well, so was I."

"You didn't have to be so nasty about it. You know better."

She raised an eyebrow. "And so should you. If you don't want stupid stereotypical bullshit thrown at you, don't throw it at me."

He didn't step away, didn't hide behind the 'it's not the same.' Simply nodded. "I'm sorry," he said, his voice solemn, his eyes not meeting hers. "No excuse would make that make sense."

She nodded. "Okay. I'll take that. Because, well…" She trailed off because the intensity of his gaze almost knocked her over.

"Yeah," he said, filling in the silent space with words. "Because this is real."

She grinned back at him, even as she noticed that the first few rays of sun were coming through the lobby window. "It's also getting real late."

"Late…early, same difference." And then he swallowed, as if he'd realized something was wrong. Really wrong. "I have to go if I'm going to."

She nodded, and felt…weird about it. This was nice, but she wasn't going to…no. "I think you should," she said. "Not that…"

"Your number," he replied. "Or some way of getting into contact with you."

She grinned at him, and tapped his nose. "You're smart," she replied. "You'll figure it out." Then, she turned and walked away.

CHAPTER FIVE

Chris had slept in. Of course he had. He'd gotten to bed at an hour he sometimes woke up at, so the sleeping in wasn't a surprise. But he was surprised to arrive at Popovers after a mad crosstown dash, breathless and hair frozen from the fact he'd stepped outside with it wet, to discover his perpetually late for brunch sister, standing in front of the restaurant and smiling up at him.

"You're late," Kay said, her blue eyes wide. "For the first time ever."

He looked at his boots, embarrassed, not sure how to explain to the one person who…

"Oh stop it, Chris. Really." Kay rolled her eyes and wrapped her arm around him. "Be a good big brother, buck it up and take me to brunch."

And the smart guy he was, he helped her inside and followed the hostess to their usual table.

"So what's going on," he asked once they'd settled down.

"Practice, conductor's an idiot, life is busy, I'm exhausted, blah, blah, blah." And then she focused on him. He hated how his little sister could see right through him. "But you were late this morning. And there were festivities last night."

He gave her points for being careful. They were known quantities at this place, but, well, there were tabloids everywhere. "Yes," he confirmed. "There were festivities last night. But how do you know I'm not just hung over."

Once again his sister rolled her eyes. "Because I'm your little sister. I *know* when you're hung over. And this isn't hung over brother. This is *'I had an adventure last night'* brother, and so you're going to spill."

And so, once their coffee had been poured, and their meals had been ordered, he told her.

*****

Sunday brunch was usually fun. Mel and her sister would go to some crazy place, look inside the window, view the menu, and then head to their favorite little diner in the middle of midtown. Except this morning would be an inquisition.

"You tapped him on the nose? And then let him leave without your information?"

Melanie sighed. Her sister didn't even wait until their regular waiter had refilled their coffee. "Yeah. I know. But…"

"No buts. That was dumb. After that spark, that tension, that awesomeness last night, you seriously need to be shot."

Instead of replying, she looked deeper into her menu. Ignoring Emily would work for a little…maybe.

"How do you finish a night like that with a tap on the nose? I mean really." Emily paused, and Mel recognized the look in her eyes.

"Unless this was an aborted one night stand, at which point the tap on the nose was even dumber."

"I was being playful," she replied. "I mean I just…well…"

"You lost your nerve," Emily replied, staring right at her. "He was right there, totally into you, totally there. Did I mention totally into *you*, and you acted…"

She took a swallow of the coffee in her mug, then tried not to spit out the unsweetened/un-milked taste of it. "I mean," she managed. "I don't know. I wanted to be playful, you know…keep…"

"Tapping someone on the nose is *not* playful. It's immature, dumb and well, stupid."

"So what would you have done?" Melanie asked. "I mean…to have kept the mystery. To be a little fun and playful."

"Not tapped him on the nose," Emily replied. "Now let's order. I'm hungry."

Which was a clear sign the discussion was over, leaving Mel to wonder about what she was going to do next.

*****

Kayleigh hadn't responded after Chris had finished telling her what had happened to make him so exhausted…and late. In fact, his sister seemed perfectly happy to discuss everything else but his adventure with Melanie. Their parents, their brother, her new instructor and the way the conductor treated the rest of the orchestra.

She even asked him about how practice was going, and how things had been otherwise. Not one word about Melanie. Until they walked outside the restaurant and into the bitter cold. "She's insane, but then again, brother dear, so are you."

He shrugged as he walked beside her. "Yeah, well. I try not to be insane most of the time."

"This time doesn't make sense, though." She paused, standing close enough to the edge of the sidewalk where she wouldn't be in anybody's way. "I'm not sure how to read her. She's very...well..."

She sighed, then turned away from him. The fact that his sister proceeded to look everywhere else but at him was not the best of signs. In fact, it made him feel something awful deep in the pit of his stomach. And there wasn't anything worse than the look in her eyes when she finally met his again.

"She's...weird," Kay said, shaking her head. "All that chemistry and she *tapped* your nose and then headed out?? I just don't know about these things."

He nodded, upset that she wasn't able to give him any advice or insight. But being the good big brother he was, he let her guide him down the street towards the subway she needed.

"But," she continued as she reached up to rub his cheek, "I can see from your expression that she's something. Just don't let yourself fall for her too easily. She might not deal so well. She might not be there with you."

He nodded. "Thank you. Really." He appreciated her advice, despite it not helping him understand the situation.

"Of course," she said into the silence, "you know that still means I wish you luck with her."

"Let's hope so. I think I'm going to need it." And then, after a quick hug, Kayleigh headed down into the subway, leaving him to wonder how he was going to find Melanie again. Unfortunately, he had absolutely no idea how. But there had to be a way.

Determined, he turned around and walking back to the brownstone. One thing he knew for sure was that he wasn't going to ask her sister.

That was lame. His goal was to make her realize he was serious about them—that he wasn't just going to let their spark go. He had until Tuesday morning to see her one more time before he went on the road, and by god he was going to do it.

When he reached the brownstone, he took his keys out of his pocket and opened the door. "Hello?" he yelled as he walked inside. No response, which meant his roommate was gone, and he was on his own.

He took off his jacket, trying to figure out a way to find her without doing something that would be too public, like twitter, or too weird, like showing up on her doorstep with flowers. What was a non-intrusive way to get in touch with her?

Suddenly, he knew what he was looking for. Of course! He made a beeline for the kitchen and the huge boxes of books that were waiting for the library shelves to be delivered. He got down on his hands and knees in front of the closest box and started searching. He knew his roommate had most of his collection stored on his phone's reading app, but he had to have one of the books in paper in one of the boxes.

Finally, after turning the kitchen into a tornado of books, he found one. He didn't even pause, just paged through the title in search of the information he wanted. And once he found one, he grinned and headed off to send the all-important email.

*****

To: Melanie@MelanieGould.com
From: cemerson@empiremail.com
Dear Madam,
I have recently come into my title, but I have garnered myself a scandalous reputation which makes it impossible for me to find a wife.

I enjoy wearing cravats and drinking ale, as well as taking part in contests of speed and skill. I wonder if you might be of some assistance.

Yours,

The Dangerous Duke

Melanie couldn't stop laughing. Actually, more importantly, she didn't *want* to stop laughing. The email she'd received while revising the draft of the book due in two weeks made her want to fall over despite her deadline.

"What the hell?"

Emily's voice, then her footsteps broke through her brain enough to make her think to a degree. But Mel couldn't stop laughing her ass off.

Footsteps turned to incessant pounding on the door. "Mel?"

Emily was relentless, but Mel still couldn't stop laughing. She'd stop for a few moments, then stare back at the email and start laughing all over again. Oh dear god, she was hopeless. Scratch that. Beyond hopeless.

The door swung open, and Emily stepped into her room. "Come on, girlfriend. Spill!"

"He…" she couldn't speak, even as her sister stood in front of her, arms folded, eyes intent, "he…"

Yes, Emily's expression was incredulous, but Mel still couldn't bring herself to not laugh for more than five seconds at a time. The words wanted to come out, but she was so happy, so unexpectedly giddy that they were blocked.

"Oh fucking hell."

Mel heard Emily's cursing, and then, after deciding it was probably the easiest way things were going to get done, moved out of the way to allow her sister a clear view of the screen. "Here you go."

Her sister immediately sat down on the recently vacated desk chair and stared intently at the screen before bursting out into laughter herself, making Mel feel slightly vindicated. "Oh my god," Emily said after she'd calmed down slightly. "Holy crapwad."

When she turned around, Mel saw the expression on her sister's face, judging it as not to be played with. "You have no excuse," she said as she stood up from the chair and gestured towards the empty seat. "I'm going to be gone tomorrow night. The apartment is yours. Now tell him."

And so she did, holding her breath until he replied. Thankfully, he said he'd come over. Now, she had to plan.

Chapter Six

Chris's day had been…interesting. Practice, then home, then… here. Downstairs, in the carpeted lobby, waiting for Melanie. He smiled, sat down on one of the large, comfortable chairs and tried to take a deep breath. She said she'd be waiting and unfortunately he was early. He turned towards the paintings that had been hung up around the entryway, trying to focus on something.

"So," her voice rang in his ear. "Here to finish what we started?"

He laughed, turned back around toward where she stood and looked into her eyes. He liked what he saw there much better than the paintings. "Heeey there," he said, standing up to embrace her, enjoying the way she relaxed in his arms.

"You know," she murmured, "if we stay like this we're not going to get upstairs."

He grinned. "You're right." He took her hand with the one that wasn't around her shoulders, and nodded at her. "Lead on," he said, letting her lead him to the elevator.

"So," he asked her once the elevator doors closed. "What do you want to do?"

"You like stew?" she asked.

"Yeah." And she looked so cute, so nervous, with a dark stain on her shirt, he wouldn't have refused her even if he didn't. "Awesome on a night like this."

"It is." She smiled back, sheepishly. "Good. I'm glad. It's the one thing I can cook. So I did."

He thought better of asking her more about her cooking and instead, let her lead him into the apartment.

*****

Mel decided that inviting Chris over for dinner had been the *worst* idea ever. What had she been thinking? She'd *cooked* for fuck's sake. And right now, if she was honest with herself, she'd admit to being terrified. She wanted to drink, and lose herself in the alcohol and... well...

He squeezed her hand, halting her thoughts and reminding her he was there. "It's all right," he said, his voice covering her like a caress. "It's just us. Nothing else. I'm not going to bite...not unless...well anyway." He shook his head, and he was so cute in that moment, she wanted to jump him. "We're just here. It's fine, yah?"

Melting all over him would probably be a bad idea, but really, who actually cared? He was in her apartment and probably didn't notice she was wearing mismatched socks and had gotten stew on her shirt.... which hadn't exactly been her plan.

She nodded. "All right. I'll go change...make yourself comfortable..."

He shrugged his shoulders. "Whatever's easier for you is fine with me. As far as I'm concerned, you look beautiful just the way you are."

A line if she'd ever heard one. "What? Where…"

"I have a younger sister," he replied, grinning in a way that made her feel even more mushy inside. "I watched, paid attention and learned."

"You," she said, grinning at him, relaxed in a way she hadn't been until then, "are dangerous."

He laughed. It was a gorgeous, husky laugh. Dear god, she was in trouble.

*****

A few hours later, she'd fallen asleep in his arms. Sated, happy and comfortable, cuddled up in a blanket on the floor. The stew had been wonderful, they'd watched a few movies on the TV. He looked down at her, so peaceful, so…

"Hey," she murmured, looking up at him, focusing. "What happened…"

"You let your guard down," he replied grinning back at her, before reaching up to tap her on the nose.

She giggled. "Is that so?"

"'Fraid so. Only one thing we can do to fix that."

She raised an eyebrow, but she didn't pull away. A good sign. "And what's that?"

Focusing on her, on the way she looked, he leaned down and pressed his lips to hers and just let go. Let her feel him, open up to him, respond, her hands through his hair, his hands moving down her back, cupping her ass as she sat up, as if she wanted more. He felt her hands reaching for his shirt, then the cool air that caressed his back.

"Mmmm," she murmured against his jaw, "this feels so good…"

And it did, the way her hands found all the right spots on his back, then his ass.

"I think we're wearing too much clothing," he whispered, as he pulled on her shirt.

"You know," she replied before she kissed him, "I think we are."

"Think we should fix that."

In a tangle of limbs, a blaze of heat, jeans and shirts hit the floor. Mismatched socks were lovingly caressed off her feet. He looked at her as she stood practically naked in front of him, not being able to resist her. "Do you want to take this slow?" he asked.

"No," she replied, staring at him. "I want you. Badly." A slight smirk, a sudden redness to her cheeks. "Now."

He leaned in to kiss her again, his hands gravitating to her bra, fingers finding purchase on the little hook and eye, taking it apart, freeing the beautiful mounds of flesh that he'd been fantasizing about since he'd seen her on Vegas night. He couldn't help himself. Once the bra had joined the rest of the clothing, he reached out for those breasts, kneading and caressing them, seeing her expression as it changed from slight desire to pleasure.

"Two can play at that game." As if making her actions match her words, she kneeled in front of him, unceremoniously lowered his boxers, exposing his cock. And without another word, he felt her tongue, her mouth, licking, persistent, sucking. He breathed in, trying not to cum all over her, as she showed him exactly what he'd wanted since he saw her sucking on that lemon back at 'The Elk.' "Oh god." He groaned.

Like a hurricane, the intense pleasure and pressure was about to do his head in. And yet he rode through the orgasm. "Fuck...."

She swallowed him down, then looked up at him. He smiled and she pulled him to the floor, letting him collapse on her shoulder for a little while. "Mmmm."

"I take it you liked that, hmm?"

"Liked?" he replied, half asleep, as she ran her fingers through his hair. "Don't think there are enough words in my head right now to describe how what I thought of that."

"Now," she said, sometime later, whether it was a few minutes or a few hours he wasn't sure, "to be rather unoriginal and quote a famous movie, Take me to bed, or lose me forever."

He laughed, recognizing the quote, then decided that it was a pretty agreeable proposition. So he bent down and lifted her into his arms.

*****

The fact Chris had to ask her where her bedroom was didn't cool his ardor, and the fact she half-wondered if she'd remembered to clean up after her attempts to change didn't cool hers. Nor did the last minute thought that she had, in fact, put the box of condoms Emily had reminded her to buy this morning on the bedside table. He carried her over the threshold and grinned, and she felt something wonderful at the pit of her stomach at being the object of his grey eyes' intense focus.

His hands felt so good on her ass and, as he slowly let her down on the bed, she wondered why he didn't follow her onto the mattress. The sudden dip at the end of the mattress was her answer.

A brief glance down at him and she saw his eyes were focused, heated.

"Payback," he growled.

And before she could consider what that meant, she felt his hands on her thighs, felt him open her legs, his breath between them. And then his tongue penetrated her cunt and began to move inside her. She felt the way his lips moved expertly on the lips of her cunt, all the while his tongue danced through her innermost parts. Movement, massage, his tongue and lips expertly wielded. Constant, motion, not letting up, the sucking and the motion inside. She didn't want it to end and then…sudden tightness. She held on and she fought, but ….oooh. The orgasm overwhelmed her, and the words she was so wonderful at using left her completely.

Yet the sight of his expression left her wanting more Specifically, his cock. "Come to me baby."

The fact she'd managed a genuine sex kitten purr straight out of a 1960's movie made her giggle as Chris moved just a little faster, the sound of the foil packet ripping. His hands settled on her shoulders after he'd put on the condom, his knees holding his body in position as she came up to meet him.

"Hello babe." A whisper as she felt his cock penetrate her very wet cunt, slowly and easily, filling her up completely.

"Mmm. So what do you have for me?"

She put her hands on his shoulders, and she let herself go as he began to move, bucking his hips, swaying slowly then faster, slowing down again as if he knew he was torturing her. "What the hell…"

"Hmm…" His voice was breathless. "Maybe…I…should stop?"

"No…Don't. Please." She was so impatient, so ready, she wanted to strangle him; instead, she dug her nails into his shoulders. "Dammit…"

"Fine…" He leaned down to kiss her neck, which was a very poor substitute for the motion of his hips, but it worked for then and there. And then he started to move his hips, back and forth, slowly then faster, faster still. She swore she could feel every stroke of his cock as he moved inside of her. Every torturous inch drove her wild. Until she reached orgasm.

But so much more than just an *orgasm*. It was a perfect moment of friction beyond friction, of tightness, of holding on and not wanting to let go.

"Oh Chris…oh my god…." And that was…so much. She looked at him and he smiled, pulled out of her, took off the condom and pulled her close. And for the second time that night, she snuggled into his hold. This time, however, she knew she was going to fall asleep and she let herself.

CHAPTER SEVEN

Sports Beat: New York Empires 3 Carolina Typhoons 0
Finishing up their recent road trip, Empires goalie Alex Semenov was spectacular, stopping 50 shots and extending his shut-out streak. ...Marcus Mitchell led the defense in minutes played... Chris Emerson scored a goal, had an assist and fought with Carolina Captain Joel Montrose, after Montrose attempted to shove him into the boards, shoulder first.

@Emo27: love roadtrips but love coming home best. New York is awesome...

Melanie_Gould DM @Emo27: heeey was going to call you. This is easier while I work. Welcome back!

Emo27 DM @Melanie_Gould: Thanks. It's been a pretty crazy trip. You saw the Carolina game?

Melanie_Gould DM @Emo27: Oy. *g* That must have been crazy. Shoulder okay?

Emo27 DM @Melanie_Gould: Eh. How's the book
Melanie_Gould DM @Emo27: Eh. I'm hungry.
Emo27 DM @Melanie_Gould: Pizza?
Melanie_Gould DM @Emo27: Yessss…

"I come bearing pizza," he said, as he came into the apartment.

"Yum!" She grinned as she closed the door behind him. "No writer on deadline would refuse pizza." Of course she couldn't help but watch him as he closed the door. He did look gorgeous, wearing jeans, sneakers, a hoodie and a parka he hadn't bothered to zip. "Rocking the rugged look?" she asked, heading past him and scrambling to gather plates and glasses and placing them on the kitchen table.

He nodded, smiling slightly, his lips quirked.

Adorable, she decided as she ran back into the kitchen to collect a pitcher of water, the diet coke that was her deadline companion and some garlic powder. They joined the pizza, the plates and glasses, which he'd set out, along with napkins that he presumably had *folded*. Adorable and helpful.

"I guessed," she said sheepishly, gesturing wildly at the table's nonalcoholic contents. "I wasn't sure…"

He shook his head. "Thank you," he replied. "But no. Not drinking tonight." He paused and then looked down, slightly self-conscious once again, as if he thought she'd judge him for what he was about to say. "I don't usually drink during the season. Vegas Night was an exception to the rule."

Surprised? Yes. Judge? No. "Aaaah. Okay."

"Yeah, well," he gestured to the table. "I guess I'm full of multiple contradictions. But there's pizza to be had, and well, we should eat."

She nodded. Especially since she wasn't letting him stay long because she had to get back to work. "It's probably better hot," she returned, smiling as he opened the box, unleashing a cloud of amazing smells. And the simple fact the pizza was half extra cheese, half pepperoni.

"Wasn't sure if you ate pepperoni," he interjected, focusing on her expression. 'Figured it was better to assume you didn't."

"I do," she replied. "We grew up kosher, but…"

"You're Jewish?"

She nodded. She'd heard rumors about his feelings towards Jewish people, ones that didn't really jive with the fact she'd seen his closest friend on the team at High Holiday services every year, or any public statements he'd made. But as she'd gotten to know, rumors didn't usually end up being true when they were about Chris. And yet she still had to ask. "That a problem?"

"Is the fact that I'm not a problem?"

"Whatever is going on between us, you're doing with me, now, not my faith. When it should get important is when you decide what you feel about the fact that my faith is a part of me, that it's important to me." She shrugged as she removed a slice of pepperoni pizza from the box and took a healthy bite. "Whatever you are is important to you that same way."

He blinked. "What?"

He looked so adorably confused that she had to smile. "As long as you don't have issues with me being Jewish, I have no problem with the fact that you're not."

She saw his shoulders relax in relief as he took a big bite of his pizza, and found herself watching the cheese as it unraveled like a ball of yarn. He looked cute, irresistible and so she leaned out and bit

261

the cheese closest to his mouth, sucking it towards her mouth, leaning towards him as she sucked.

She caught the anticipation in his expression and sucked more of the cheese, following the path until her lips met his. Then she let go, her lips on his, her tongue brushing his amidst the taste of the pizza.

*****

"That tasted good," he said, as they came up for air. "You look adorable and taste good. Even on deadline."

She giggled. She looked hot, even in a well-loved sweatshirt from an American university he didn't recognize, and sweatpants that hugged her ass. Her hair hung down, framing her face, and he felt this sudden impulse to kiss her again.

"Plans this week?" she asked, busting him and his lack of concentration.

He shook his head, tried to concentrate. His shoulder apparently had not liked the fact he carried a pizza across town. "This week… Off day tomorrow, early practice Monday and then we head off on Tuesday. Games the rest of the week. You?"

"Book," she replied, as if it were the worst thing in the world. "I need to get it done by the time you guys leave. So Em can read it on the plane or something."

He nodded, wondered, considered. "Would you be able to come to a party with me, on Monday?"

She raised an eyebrow and he wished that she hadn't been so surprised. "So what kind of party? What kind of people?"

"Few of the guys…wives and girlfriends only. Guys I trust…"

Another eyebrow. Confusion? Wonder? Annoyance? "Wives and girlfriends?" she asked, smirking.

He nodded, took a drink of the water in his glass. "Yeah. Wives and girlfriends."

"Me?"

He grinned and leaned in closer. "Yeah," he murmured. "You." And then he kissed her, letting her tongue invade his mouth. She tasted of pizza and diet coke and an indefinable essence. "So?"

She grinned. "Yeah."

He was a very lucky guy. There was pizza and Mel. And he had them both.

CHAPTER EIGHT

Damn his fucking shoulder. It hurt. Chris had tried to sleep in a bit, but it didn't work. The shoulder was still killing him, and if the text he'd gotten from Al hadn't been clear enough, he'd have to haul his ass to Razors as soon as he could manage it. He had a lot to do, which included seeing how Mel was doing on her quest to finish the book before her deadline. All of that meant there'd be no time for physical therapy before heading out.

He nodded, braced himself and then headed into the shower, forcing himself to move quickly. Extra heat on the shoulder, careful as he ran through the shower one-handed. Not wanting to jar it before he covered it with his favorite no-time ointment. A bit of an improvised massage before reaching into his emergency first aid case and pulling out a patch, placing it on top of the pain-filled spot. He hoped it would hold. He prayed it would hold. He also prayed it wouldn't smell too bad. Then he changed into a pair of black jeans, a grey polo, thick socks, a pair of black boots with their famously heavy tread and a black fleece.

He opened his door, intending to head downstairs, but he found himself assaulted by the amazing smells coming from the kitchen. His roommate was either trying out a new recipe, or, more specifically, cooking lunch for someone. And if it was the latter, then he was glad he had plans. Early plans. Plans that involved getting out of the way and staying that way for a while.

He sighed, grabbed his wallet and headed downstairs. Drawn by the delicious smells that signified cooking, he popped his head into the kitchen as he grabbed his keys. "Hey man," he said to his roommate, noticing the baking stuff as well as the cooking stuff covering a lot of the available counter space. "What's...?" And then he heard the doorbell ring.

"Could you get that?"

He nodded. "Sure," he replied, leaving the kitchen, heading towards the door and going through the steps to open it. Only to brace himself when he saw that Nathalie, one of the physical therapists was on the other side. This was *interesting*. His roommate was *cooking* for Nat. He liked the idea. "Hey, Nathalie. Come on in. He's in the kitchen."

"Thanks."

He grinned, taking her coat and hanging it on the closest clear hanging post. Then he led her into the kitchen, hoping he'd get major points for his poker face. Because, yeah, his roommate was going all out in order to cook lunch for Nathalie. And not just cook. From the looks of things, there was going to be baking involved, which as far as his roommate was concerned, was tantamount to screaming commitment of a sort off the rooftops. Very, verry *interesting*.

He was half ready to inform Semenov that he should maybe get out of the refrigerator and greet his lunch guest, but he'd turned and faced them, but more specifically faced Nathalie.

"Hi," his roommate said, brandishing a bowl of strawberries. "Glad you could make it."

She was fidgeting, nervous, and he couldn't help but see the slightly hopeful expression on Semenov's face. Hmm.

"I can't stay long," she said out of nowhere, clearly hesitant. "My grandmother called this morning and wanted to have lunch. I told her I was busy, but she insisted on an early dinner."

The tone in her voice and her absolute and utter inability to stop fidgeting clearly meant she was two seconds from bolting. He also recognized the expression on her face from spending years with a younger sister. Kayleigh had a similar expression, and it never meant anything good. He had to do *something* before shit went south. "He's been in here cooking all morning," he said, gesturing towards his roommate. "You have to eat some of it."

There was the smile. Just like Kayleigh. She was still nervous, but she'd be okay in the end. Semenov would owe him. Not really. But still.

"Great game Friday." she said.

"What the hell is that smell?" Semenov interjected, stopping him mid comment. And then he saw recognition in his roommate's eyes. There was no stopping him. *Fuck.* "You've got that shit on again, don't you? Get out of my kitchen with that smell. You'll ruin my food."

"Hey, now," he said, wagging a finger at his roommate, trying to get him off the scent—literally—while beginning to edge out of the room. Nathalie was looking for a distraction and he was dammed if he was going to provide it. "Don't knock the Miracle ointment. The stuff is awesome in a pinch and I have no time to do anything else today."

"You got hurt Friday?" Nathalie interjected, having followed him out of the kitchen, a hand on the *other arm* and the inevitable realization in her eyes. *Fuck.* "What's bothering you?"

"Chris...."

He caught his roommate's eye, then looked to Nathalie. She wasn't stopping, wouldn't let him leave without trouble. Trouble that would fuck up the rest of the afternoon. For everybody involved.

Resigned to the inevitable, he dumped the fleece on the floor and pointed to the annoying spot in question, just beyond his reach at the back of his shoulder. "There. I can't even reach it but the muscle is spasming. Needed a mirror to get the patch on."

"Let me see."

Shit. She was doctoring him so that she didn't have to face Semenov. This was not happening. He had to leave. Now. "Nat, I don't think..."

"Show me. Now."

At the insistent cue that wouldn't quit, he rolled up the sleeve of his polo, taking care not to lift the left shoulder in the process. And once again, her hand was warm and on his shoulder. He had to admit it was much better than the patch, even though the guilt was killing him. She was here to relax on a Sunday. Not doctor his lazy ass up.

"Just relax," she said as if she could feel his guilt somehow. And then he remembered that the stressing made him tense. Course she could feel that. Which made him try to calm down a little.

"Feels like a pretty solid knot back here. Let me see what I can do."

He closed his eyes, tried to keep himself calm, wondering what Mel was up to. Thinking of Mel, and her sexy grin, the way she moved her ass...

And as the heat began to soothe his shoulder, he found himself relaxing that much more. He focused elsewhere, on a waterfall or something like that. Thoughts of Mel could lead him to disaster or some sort of embarrassment. Like a very obvious and raging hard on that his roommate would think applied to Nathalie.

And then, there it was. A temperature that didn't make him want to fall over from the pain or anything else. It was perfect.

"That hurt?"

Hurt? Fuck no. "No," he replied. "It feels great. Your hands are really warm."

"Is the muscle relaxing? Any more spasms?"

"That's helping a lot." He sighed in relief and genuine gratitude. "Thanks." Which was, in his estimation, the perfect cue for her to continue exactly what she was doing. He was lucky, and his shoulder felt absolutely perfect for the last few seconds before she stepped away.

"Thanks, Nat," he said once again. "That really worked out the kink."

"No problem," she returned. He couldn't help noticing she seemed more comfortable, maybe because she was doing something she knew she could. Kay was like that too.

"But you should come into the Center tomorrow and have it worked on a little more. And put a hot pack on it tonight to keep the muscle from seizing up again."

"Will do." A reprieve. He turned towards his roommate, and there was something in Semenov's expression he'd deal with later. "I have something I need to do so I'll see you guys later. Enjoy lunch." And then, with a wave, he headed towards the door, and on his mission of mercy.

*****

Emo27 DM @Melanie_Gould: How's the book?

Melanie_Gould DM @Emo27: deadline sucks. How's the shoulder?

Emo27 DM @Melanie_Gould: it sucks, but I got some heat on it now. You going to be able to get away tonight?

Melanie_Gould DM @Emo27: *sigh* I wish. If you want me to play with your boys tomorrow, I gotta work tonight…might be able to meet you later if I get my pages done. What are you up to?

Emo27 DM @Melanie_Gould: checking books @ a place in the village. Late lunch/early dinner after?

Melanie_Gould DM @Emo27: text me. Will let you know either way.

True to his word, Chris headed out to Razor's to fix what Al needed doing, and when he got there, he took a moment to breathe. The smell of the ink coming out of the tattoo rooms. The joking in the barber chairs, a few dudes laughing and grinning at the stuff they had on TV.

"Christopher, thank you God!" Al boomed as he came outside, shaking his head. "You know that fucking son of a bitch…"

He sighed, shook his head and clapped his hand on Al's shoulder. "I'm here, dude. I can fix this. Come on." He gestured towards the office and started heading back there. "Get me a cup of coffee and I'll clean this mess up in no time."

"Heey…"

The familiar drawl butted into the conversation, and he turned around to recognize M-F Smythe. "Jersey boy," he replied with a grin. "What brings you here?"

"I got an appointment with Marco," Smythe returned, that Oklahoma accent of his messed up as ever. And they said *he* talked funny. "We have a few off days so I'm finally finishing one he started. You?"

"Taking care of some stuff," he replied, hedging. Smythe dated Mel's sister, but the man didn't have to know he was at the shop to deal with a financial crisis. "I'm supposed to be texting Mel when I'm done."

"Yep," Smythe replied, nodding. "I'm meeting Emily and we're going to Darcy's. You should come, with or without Mel."

He knew Darcy's. It was the pub next door. It was cozy and convenient. "Maybe," he replied, aware of how much of an emergency would prompt Al to call him down to fix the books. "Don't know how long I'm going to be. You should probably…"

"Em wants to talk to you." Smythe shrugged. Something was up but Chris wasn't really in the mood to figure it out. "Maybe I do too."

It could still be anything. Official? Unofficial? Family? Who the fuck knew. "Inquisition or official?" he asked, deciding it would be better to get it out in the open as opposed to letting it go over and over in his head.

"I think," Smythe replied, looking down to stare at his shoes in a way that made Chris curious, "maybe a little bit of both."

That was it. He'd go. Mostly because he couldn't stop himself; the temptation to figure out what the hell Smythe had to talk about was too great. "All right," he said. "I gotta finish up here, but if I'm not ready to go when you are, I'll meet you guys."

"Good." With that, Smythe followed one of the junior tattooists into one of the ink rooms and shut the door behind them, leaving him no excuse but to go bury his nose in the Al's latest financial question.

*****

E_GouldNYE DM@Melanie_Gould: you should come.

Melanie_Gould DM@E_GouldNYE: d.e.a.d.l.i.n.e not to mention I'm supposed to go to some party tomorrow. Can't go to the party if I don't get my pages done. If I'm out tonight, I can't get pages done.

E_GouldNYE DM@Melanie_Gould: u need to come. mf wants to talk about stuff and need u to be there…

Melanie_Gould DM@E_GouldNYE: so you're using me as a shield?

E_GouldNYE DM@MelanieGould: no. just an added benefit. U need to be interrogated by family.

Melanie_Gould DM@E_GouldNYE: you expect me to leave my work willingly to be interrogated by rebelboy?

E_GouldNYE DM@Melanie_Gould: come on. Besides. *He* wants to see you.

Even though she knew she could see Chris with or without the added interrogation, Melanie decided to humor her sister. Not to mention she'd made the night's goal, which probably explained the pain in her fingers and her annoyingly dry eyes.

She deserved a reward.

And that meant a very extended taxi ride—subway would take too long—all the way down to the village, and a breathless half walk/half run following the direction pointed to by the icon on her phone's handy-dandy map. Nervous and excited to see him again, she tried to breathe and calm herself down in some way as she walked into the pub. The last thing she needed was to pass out at his feet.

Unfortunately, as she began to look along the bar and at the people seated at the tables organized across the dining room, she found that didn't recognize anybody. She wondered if she'd beaten them all to the pub, at least until she heard footsteps pounding in her direction. She turned towards them and saw her sister. Emily was dressed in clothes that suggested she'd taken a trip into the office—heels, a pair of black pants and a white collared shirt—yet her expression was far from businesslike. In fact, if Mel was a betting woman, she'd say that something was definitely going on.

"You made it! Really. So happy you came."

Yep, something was going on. Her sister had either been drinking or doing some other thing she'd rather not consider. She opted for the easier to handle option. "How much have you had to drink?"

Emily shook her head. "Not a thing. Not a drop. I'm high on life and the possibilities, you know?"

Mel rolled her eyes, unconvinced. "And? What happened?" Emily shrugged, and Mel wasn't sure what was going through her sister's head. "Okaaay...."

"Well...you'll see what's happening when they get here."

Used to her sister's cryptic issues, Mel threw up her hands. "Whatever. I'll just take this and run with it, as you're apparently doing."

Emily nodded. "Good. Just...really good."

Unfortunately, nothing scared Mel more than that.

*****

It had taken Chris the better part of four hours to fix the mess made by the fact one of the junior barbers hadn't remembered to pass in his most recent set of receipts. Not to mention the ones he had passed in were full of dye. It took him a matter of minutes to understand Al's screaming on the other end of the phone.

But once his emergency patch job was done, he left Al's office, attempting to stretch his left arm without straining his right shoulder, reminding himself he needed to put more ointment on it, as he headed into Razor's main room. And there, sitting patiently on the couch, was Smythe.

"I take it this is a neutral zone?"

Chris laughed. "You think they'd let people wanting to stir up shit in here?"

Smythe nodded as he got to his feet. Asshole was a bit taller than him, even more so in cowboy boots no self-respecting Saskie would wear anywhere, even if they were doing farm related stuff. "Right. So can we talk?"

He shrugged, and gestured towards the office he'd stolen from an ever grateful Al. "This way. Probably the type of shit'd be better with the door closed."

Smythe nodded. "Yeah."

Once the door was closed, and they were sitting down, Chris drummed his fingers on the desk. "So what's up?"

"I want to drill," he replied. "You and I. Just quiet like. Maybe, testing some stuff."

Chris raised an eyebrow, but he'd suspected something like this once Smythe said he wanted to *talk*. Even as the rumors got bigger that the Palisades weren't going to trade the guy, it didn't mean that Smythe himself wasn't investigating other options for next season. The man was a top centerman, long reach, strong on assists. Empires could really use a guy like him next season. "Thinking about crossing the pond?"

Smythe crossed his arms and sat back in his chair. "Figure we can play, see how it goes. If I can play with you, then there's a possibility. Shit, we're practically family."

That's when the discussion changed from hockey to the inquisition. "Aaah, yes. Would you like to tar and feather me or boil me in oil?"

Smythe raised an eyebrow. "Fucking hell, boy. Can't you be serious for once?"

Chris sighed. "Well, nobody expects the Oklahoman inquisition, but if you're serious…"

Smythe tried not to laugh, he respected the man for it. But that didn't stop the freight train of discussion. "You just better not be playing around with her," Smythe began. "Mel seems like she's all tooth and nail, but she's making Em freak the fuck out because half the time she doesn't know what she's doing. And when Em freaks out…"

Now it was the 'rolling of the eyes' time. "You get to kick my ass?"

"Abso-fucking-lutely."

He shook his head, but he just had to grin. "I'll totally drill with you, but ass kicking leaves you on your own."

Smythe nodded. "Good," he said as he got to his feet. "Now, let's go eat."

"Sounds like a good idea," Chris returned, even though he knew there was going to be much more to dinner than just the food. And none of it would be good.

*****

It didn't take long for Melanie to discover what Emily was alluding to. Her sister and Mark…MF—whatever his name was—dropped their little bombshell not long after the foursome sat down to dinner.

"So," Emily interjected, "what are you doing tomorrow?"

"Um," Mel managed to swallow the bite of the burger she'd taken before she replied. "When tomorrow? We're busy tomorrow night, but…well…"

"So," Emily continued, as Mel hoped she wouldn't say anything to freak Chris out. "Mark and I are meeting Dad tomorrow for a late lunch. We were hoping you'd…you know…invite Mom to a late lunch. You and Chris…."

She raised an eyebrow, trying not to focus on Chris's expression. Their parents had a contentious relationship when it came to their daughters. It was the one thing that could bring a couple that had been together for thirty years to blows. And it was better to bring their mother to lunch than their father. Once she'd gotten herself together, she turned to Chris, who smiled indulgently. "Sure."

Emily smiled. "Awesome. Arnie's been talking and you know, Mom's been curious to…well…"

Mel rolled her eyes, swirling a fry in the ketchup. "So why did you not warn me before now? Or why didn't she?"

"You were on deadline and so I did you the favor of keeping her nose off the scent. Now, well, it's time for Mark and I to sit with Dad, and you need to sit with Mom."

Which, she decided, as long as Chris agreed, would be okay. Of course, she'd owe him. Big time. And she'd happily settle up. Later.

*****

Dinner finished without further incident, leaving Chris free to ponder what had actually happened. He'd been shanghaied into a lunch with her mother. But Mel had seemed so freaked out about the idea that he didn't mind so much.

"I'm so sorry," she managed as she put her head on his right shoulder and he'd found himself glad he hadn't injured that one.

They'd arranged for a car to take them back to her apartment, thankful Smythe and Emily headed back to Jersey. "I really didn't mean for you to have to deal with my mom….my parents even, not yet. And I can't even have you upstairs tonight because I'm behind and I..."

"Hey," he said. He ran a hand through her hair, trying to calm her down in some way. "It's fine. Really." He smiled and kissed her cheek. "It could be worse you know."

She turned, and looked at him, rolling her eyes as if she couldn't think of anything. "Mmmm?"

He laughed. "I suspect you're better at drawing crazy scenarios than I am," he replied. "The ones that go through my head either involve numbers or hockey players."

She nodded, and he saw the blush rise in her cheeks. "I actually am kind of bad at that. I'm...I overanalyze most things like a complete moron. And half the time, my sister tells me that I'm overreacting to something that half the universe doesn't see."

He nodded, grinning back at her. "I guess numbers could be interesting. You know, watching them as they get into fights over debt allowances and things like that..."

This got her to laugh. "They end up in the penalty box?"

He shrugged, then focused on her. "Only if they push the debt over the available capital..."

The sound of her laugh pushed a smile onto his face, made him relax, made him grin, made him look at her in complete awe. So he did the only thing he could possibly think of. He kissed her. Let go, there, in the car, a driver she knew in the front seat. Not paying attention to a damn thing except the feel of her lips, the way her hands moved right to his ass, the way he couldn't sit next to her as her tongue made moves in his mouth without getting hard, and how easily he lost control around her.

He moved his hand around the front of her to her skirt, pushed inside...tight fingers on her stockings, the way she didn't let go, didn't pull back but pushed forward, meeting his fingers with hers, shoving up the skirt, exposing the nylons beneath.

"Oh god…" Her words were raspy, swallowed as if she was reaching for air. "Oh god."

"Mmmm. You make me lose control," he murmured as his fingers found purchase underneath the nylons and the cute cotton bikini panties she wore underneath. "Mm…"

He placed his finger in the space between her panties and her legs, then carefully and easily brought his finger home. He followed the rhythm of her breathing, followed her focus, moving faster and slower with her cues. "Ohgodohgodohgod."

"You like…"

"Very much…yessss…."

He grinned like a Cheshire cat as he watched her fall apart. "Good."

Then he carefully pulled up her stockings and smoothed down her skirt. Once she was put back together, he leaned over and kissed her. "Think of me, mmm?"

She laughed and leaned towards him, touching his nose with the tip of her index finger. "I don't think you should read the book I'm writing now," she replied. "I think you might find things…"

He shrugged, grinning back at her. "I can only suspect…"

"I can't stop thinking about you," she returned, her voice breathy and gorgeous. "But then again…"

He laughed as she got out of the car, shaking her ass just so that he'd see it. Dear god, he was going to die with a hard on.

CHAPTER NINE

Melanie woke to the ringing of the phone. Which would have been fine except it was much earlier than she'd planned to get up. She'd spent half the night writing to make up for the time she'd miss during the rest of the next day, and the time she'd taken off for the dinner the night before. Once she got to bed, her dreams had been wet, full of the many positions in which she'd fuck a Duke who'd been on the wrong side of the scandal sheets, who looked very much like Chris, if he were wearing a thin black cravat and nothing else. Which meant she'd not gotten very much rest.

"Hello," she said as she picked up the phone, still barely making any effort to move from her bed.

"Melanie Jane," her mother said, sounding rather sanctimonious. "Where are we going for lunch?"

Mel sighed, finding herself suddenly sitting up straight in bed, her forehead resting on the palm of her hand. "I just found out we were going," she replied as she decided this conversation required caffeine of a sort. "I didn't realize I was supposed to make the reservations."

"That's all right, dear. Knowing you'd be so last minute about things, I made a reservation at this charming Greek restaurant in Brooklyn. The reservation is for 1:30. You are bringing that fellow of yours?"

She searched for Zen, calm…something that would give her a degree of peace. It was probably impossible at this point, but she struggled with it anyway. "Yes, Mom. I'm dragging the guy that might be something in my life to lunch with you in Brooklyn. Today."

"Might be something in your life? Melanie," her mother sighed, her voice filled with the strange mix of patronizing and caring that she used when she received answers she didn't quite like. "Melanie, really. You have to stop being so…insecure about relationships. I'm your mother. Arnie has spoken to me, and the fact your sister is *not* talking to me about this tells me all I need to know. Now you're in one, Melanie. I would suggest you stop denying it."

She sighed. "We haven't characterized it yet. We're enjoying it, but I'm not sure what it is yet, and I'm not going to tell you before I've decided what it is myself. I'm looking forward to lunch though," she replied, as she got out of bed and padded to the kitchen. "Besides. You're meeting him earlier than I would have chosen, so consider that a victory."

"And I should drop the subject. Fine," her mother replied, grudgingly. "I will see you then."

Then her mother hung up the phone, leaving her speechless and in desperate need of both coffee and time to breathe.

*****

After a quick morning skate, a work out and a session with Nathalie during which the events of the previous day were *not* discussed, Chris headed out of the training center intending to drive back to Manhattan with enough time to spare before he had to meet Mel. Unfortunately, intentions went directly to hell as Coach Michaels met him in the hallway halfway between the locker room and the parking lot.

"Walk with me," he said, an expression on his face which made Chris nervous.

"Sure, Coach." Because what the fuck else could he say?

Michaels nodded. "I have to say," he began, his tone still ominous, "that I'm rather impressed with how head down you've been as of late."

"Thank you." But he knew as surely as the sun rose, the worst was yet to come.

"I have my ears out, Emo. Right now you're skating a streak and that's fucking awesome. But there's shit beneath the surface with you and if it erupts, fucking..."

His coach had turned the color of a tomato, and yet still, in that moment, the man paused in a surprising show of control to take a breath.

"All I'm saying is that if what I'm hearing about you and the 'Girl in the Lace Corset' ends up ripped all over the tabloids and overshadows the great work this team is doing, you're riding the fucking bench, streak or no streak. Don't think I won't."

He then clapped Chris on the *wrong* shoulder, and only with a dose of herculean control of his own did he not show any sign of pain.

"Enjoy the day off, Emo, but not too much. See you tomorrow."

And with that, Coach headed off towards his office as if nothing had happened, leaving him with a forty minute drive to replay the fucking conversation in his head. Lovely.

Not.

*****

"What's wrong?" The question sat in the air, untouched, unanswered, as if by ignoring it Chris could make it go away. He'd been stewing about *something* since he arrived to pick her up and it hadn't let up when they got in the car they'd hired to take them to Brooklyn.

The fact that he proceeded not to say anything about it to her drove Mel absolutely batty. Maybe she was insane for focusing on it, maybe she was overthinking the sudden change in his mood. For all she knew, he was angrier than he'd shown about being dragged to this lunch.

But there they were, walking through Brooklyn, past pizza joint after pizza joint, searching for the Greek restaurant her mom had chosen. She let Chris's hand go for the second it took to reach under her coat and readjust the skirt she knew continued to make its way around her waist. "I'm sorry for dragging you out like this," she murmured. "If you want to head back, I'll meet you at the party."

"And tell your mum what?" he replied, a surprising amount of anger in his voice despite its low volume. "That I got sick? That…"

"Fine," she spat back, cutting him off. "You were distracted. I thought it was because of the lunch. Clearly I was wrong…"

"My coach is an idiot and the season is insane. Lunch with your mom is *clearly* not the biggest of my troubles."

"And I'm dealing with an editor who gave me a huge, single spaced revision letter on my last book. I'm stressed as all get out for this deadline. I get the crazy. Believe you me. I get the crazy and I get the pressure. I was the one who said you didn't have to go in the first place, remember? Because *clearly* you don't."

Waiting for Chris to answer, or not, was one of the hardest things she had to do. She could barely breathe.

"Yeah. I'm sorry." He took her hand and the warm sensation of how his fingers felt around hers made her smile. "Coach pulled... well suffice to say I got a lecture this morning. The eyes everywhere lecture, the one about if we hit the papers, I get trouble..."

She nodded, suddenly feeling about five inches tall. Her editors gave her shit, but not about whom she appeared with or what she did in public. "I'm sorry." Because what else could she say? "Do you want to cool it...or...?"

He shook his head vehemently and she loved the conviction in his eyes. "And if we were in a more private space, I'd show you how much I didn't want to cool it." He had pulled her close, his breath tickling her ear as they stopped in front of a restaurant with a blue and white flag filled with stripes and a cross. "Besides, I think it's time for lunch."

She grinned, nodded and followed her...boyfriend into the restaurant.

*****

Chris guided her into the restaurant, his hand carefully on the small of her back. He wished he could do or say something that would relax the tension he felt underneath her coat, but he didn't want to risk anything. Not there, not then. He was courting trouble and he didn't want to make it worse. Especially because someone was waving at them. Not widely, like they were flagging down an airplane, but just enough that it was obvious.

"My mom," Mel whispered, her lips brushing against his ear. "No worries."

And suddenly, he'd relaxed. His heart had stopped pounding and he could breathe again.

"So," Mel's mother said with a grin on her face, as they sat down after dispensing with their coats. "This is what Arnie thought of when he sent the two of you out together that night." A knowing expression, like he'd seen on his own mother's face, crossed hers. "I see it too. Now," she said, suddenly commanding, imperious. "Let's have lunch."

Much to his relief, they did. And it was fine.

CHAPTER TEN

"Well," Mel wondered as she sank against the seat of the town car Chris had insisted they call. "How was it? Are you okay?"

"Fine, actually." He looked closer at her and she tried to figure out what was going on in that head of his. "She was really nice."

"She was on good behavior," she replied, laughing. "She knew this wasn't the way I wanted her to meet you."

He shook his head and put his arm around her. "It's fine. It was fine. She took it easy, which is perfectly fine. My mum's a piranha. Dad's worse."

She nodded and snuggled into him. "Sorta the same with mine. That's why my dad wasn't there. They…well…in situations like this, they like to see us separately because my mom and dad each have issues with the way the other treats us." A sigh. "It's a complex relationship but they do it."

"Parents are complex people. I'll tell you about mine later." And then she looked up to see him glancing out the window. "Cause I think we're about here."

She nodded and sucked in a breath as the town car pulled over. "So anything you need to tell me? Any bit of disaster I need to be prepared for?"

"They're good guys," he replied as he got out of the car. "Really."

And then the blush spread across his face, his eyes taking on an expression that reminded her of an animal that had been caught in a trap, like he'd just remembered who he was talking to. Someone with very clear and obvious knowledge of how nasty and asshole-ish some of his teammates could be. She didn't make a big deal about it. She didn't have to.

"Well," he began again, focusing once more on her as opposed to her feet. "Most of them are. And the ones having the party are guys I trust."

That made it okay. She could deal with it. She hoped. And dinner, despite the fact she really wasn't hungry, was pretty good. She found herself at a table with Alex Semenov and his girlfriend Nathalie— who was a *reader* and rather cool. But she and Chris tried to make conversation with everybody and she liked how he tried to make the conversation that much more bearable in general for everybody.

Yet once she found herself in a room with the rest of the girlfriends, she wanted to slit her wrists. She put herself in a corner next to Marcus Mitchell's girlfriend Annalise and Nathalie and tried to ignore the rest of them, but it was impossible. The babble, the chatter was mostly inane, delivered in the high pitched voices of people who spent their lives sucking down helium for fun.

"I was in page six yesterday!" squealed one of the girls. "I think they're going to make me a regular feature!"

The worlds made Mel's blood run cold. Oh shit. Dumb was okay. Attention seeking was not and, as the conversation turned to one girlfriend's quest to convince MTV that she was the perfect lockout replacement for a show about a basketball player and his wife, she left the room, making a comment about needing a drink that didn't even ring true to her own ears.

Unfortunately, when she got back, complete with a glass of water, the conversation had changed, but not for the better. Dumb was okay, attention seeking was bad, but mean was worse. With voices that reminded her of nails running across a chalkboard, they focused on their target. Annalise.

"Marcus dates models and actresses," the inflatable doll said. "What did you say you do?"

It took every ounce of herculean strength she had to keep herself from getting up and punching someone. But Annalise, as uncomfortable as she was, could handle this. She would step in if she had to, but losing her head at the beginning wouldn't do anybody any good.

"I didn't," Annalise answered, calm and strong in a way Mel wouldn't be able to when she felt this annoyed. Mel couldn't help but admire her. "I work for the caterer who did the event."

"Doing?"

That was it. Mel had had enough. She crossed the room, allowing her heels to hit the floor, making her actions and movements clear. When she made it to the other side, she pushed herself back into the seat on the couch next to Annalise that she'd vacated when she left the room.

"Hey, ladies, we're trying to have a good time," Nathalie, Alex Semenov's girlfriend said. "What's with the inquisition?"

"Yeah," she found herself interjecting. "Can we please talk about something else?"

The Barbie doll shrugged her shoulders. "Just trying to find out more about our new friend."

Mel felt like she needed a towel just to wipe up the puddle of sarcasm that landed at the stupid woman's feet. Once more, the urge to punch someone made her blood boil. She settled on a glare, knowing the last thing she wanted was to get into a physical fight with one of these idiots.

"After all," the Barbie doll continued, "Marcus is one of the stars of the Empires. He has a reputation to uphold."

"What reputation?"

Annalise's words left her mouth faster than Mel could stop her. Because that question… That question? It begged for the kind of trouble Mel didn't feel up to stopping.

"One that doesn't include dating waitresses."

The stricken look on Annalise's face was more than Mel could stand. Thankfully Nathalie intervened, but the Barbie doll didn't take the hint and shut up. "You'll never keep him. Never."

"And you're involved in this how?" Mel found herself saying as Annalise ran from the room in tears. "Like it matters to you who someone else dates, unless you're jealous he won't look at you twice?"

"And who are you with, you silly skank?"

She laughed. Loudly, and shook her head. "You really don't want to get into this with me," she said, sadly. Trying to behave did *not* include punching this stupid woman. "Because I've done this before, with people much more prepared for a battle of wits than you are. You just have to learn to watch yourself."

And then, before she lost her own battle, she got up and left the room. In search of air, in search of something that wasn't going to get her in trouble.

*****

At the sight of the expression on Marcus Mitchell's face as he left the kitchen mid-discussion, Chris could tell something had happened.

But what? The only thing he was sure of is that Mel would be in the middle of it. He waited a few minutes, listened for the heavy tread of Miller's footsteps, and then headed out of the kitchen to get some answers.

What he found, three steps outside the kitchen was Nathalie. "What happened?" he wondered, trying to play it somewhat cool.

"You'll have to ask Melanie," she replied before heading past him and into the kitchen.

He nodded, then started walking towards the living room in search of Mel, sure that she'd need something. Luckily it only took a few more steps towards the living room to find her.

"I'm going to kill them," she said, looking as if she was about to explode. Without pausing, he took her hand and led her into the closest room, which happened to be the bathroom, before closing the door behind them. Once assured of privacy, he put his arms around her, and let her put her head on his shoulder. "Okay. So we've remembered that murder is illegal. So who's doing what?"

"They were awful and I wanted to kill every single one of them to bits for being complete morons," she whispered, sounding on the verge of…something. And knowing Melanie, it would be split odds between kicking someone's ass and crying.

He nodded, rubbing her back. "Mmmm. Attention seeking, gold digging or other?"

"Much of the first two," she said. "But that I could deal with. I can ignore that. I did, actually." She looked up at him, and he saw the need for approval in her eyes.

"I know you did." He paused, trying to figure out which way to go next. "So what put you over the edge?"

288

"They were mean. Awful. Terrible. God. I wanted to rip their eyes out."

What broke his heart was that her head was still buried in his sweater, as if sniffing it would give her strength. "Shh, honey," he said. "It's over. Tell me what happened to you and we'll see what we can do to kick some ass."

She sniffed and looked up at him. "No...not that, not me, though I'm not sure how to take the fact you thought it was."

He chuckled, taking the opportunity to brush some strands of hair out of her eyes. "Take it as I want to play superman, not that I don't think you're capable of kicking ass on your own." He paused and smiled. "Some battles are best fought together."

"Mmmm..."

A noise filled with more skepticism he hadn't yet heard. She hadn't said a word and it was still dripping with doubt. "Now come on," he offered, trying to sound encouraging as opposed to threatening. "Spill, Melanie Jane Gould. You're still upset, and it's something we can fix. Together. Doesn't have to be your burden alone. "

She nodded, sighed deeply, her expression looking as if she'd come to some sort of decision. "So, yeah. The girl who's dating Marcus Mitchell. Her name's Annalise, right?"

He paused, thought about it. "Yep. Annalise. He seems really happy, and I'm kinda glad..."

"Right. Well those stupid god-awful bitches were all over her." A pained expression flitted across her face. "I tried to do something, to take them off the track, but they'd decided they'd scented blood and that was it. I swear...they're so catty and petty...I expected that, but I didn't expect mean." ·

This time, he could feel the head back on his shoulder before it even got there. "Shhh," he murmured. "I'm sorry. I'm sorry you had to see that."

"What the…"

He shook his head, fully aware she'd misinterpreted his words. "I'm sorry that they pulled that shit. I'd thought better of them, but apparently they're about as classless as… well." He smirked, and found himself relaxing at the playful expression in her eyes.

"Yeah."

And then he dropped a kiss on her forehead; he'd rip her clothes off later. "You think about what you want to do, and we'll do it. I promise."

She smiled, squeezed his hand. "Maybe we should leave the bathroom first?"

"I think I can manage that one." And just to prove her right, he reached around her to open the door and, with one hand in hers, he let her lead him into the hall.

*****

As they stepped out of the bathroom, she couldn't help but grin at the way Chris's hand felt on her ass. It was nice. Just, in fact, as nice as the way his other hand felt in hers. They complemented each other, and she was glad for that in the insanity this party was becoming. Yet despite herself, she felt he needed to be with his teammates a bit more without her acting as a needy appendage. Because truth be told, she wasn't needy and didn't like to feel that way.

Especially at the laughing from Chris's teammates as they stood in line for the bathroom.

"Had to be Emerson," one said.

"Must be a tiger in there."

"Thankfully," he joked back as he squeezed her hand. "I picked the door with the lady."

She couldn't help but snicker at the literary reference. From the lascivious looks on his teammate's expressions, they probably didn't get it. But he played along all the same, and she loved him for it.

And yet even as the guys were joking behind her, Mel caught a glimpse of Annalise and Marcus as they left. She squeezed Chris's hand before letting it go, walking past the group in order to intercept them before they left the apartment. She must have pushed past a bunch of people to get to them but she managed it.

"Hey," she said when she finally reached them. They both turned towards her, but it was Annalise whose expression she focused on. She was clearly still upset. The last thing Mel wanted was to upset her further, so she chose her words carefully. "Don't let them get to you. They're just jealous because the only thing they've got going for them is their looks, and plastic surgery won't help forever. "

"Thanks."

She was rewarded with a slight smile from Annalise.

"Of course," Mel replied, smiling back, and reaching out to touch her arm before heading back inside.

Two steps inside, she saw Chris, watching her with a grin on his face. "You," he said, "were awesome. Just what she needed."

*****

Melanie managed to stay at the party until she'd been called on to "testify" to the bad behavior exhibited by the stupid bimbos. Then she'd lost her stomach and despite the fact Chris had been having a good time with his teammates, he hadn't wasted a second before getting her out of there into the town car where they were now sitting. She really appreciated the fact he hadn't questioned her, not even for a second. And, she decided, she liked his ass.

"You were amazing…"

"I am so proud of you…"

She grinned at him. "Great minds think alike," she said. "I'm actually…"

"Horny?" he ventured.

She saw the look in his eyes and found herself considering the possibility and seeing potential in the moment. "I might be," she returned, reaching out to brush his neck with her fingertips. "If given the proper enticement."

And just as she finished speaking, he leaned towards her, stealing her words, twining his tongue with hers, his mouth meeting her own, his hands caressing her ass, bringing her closer till she was almost straddling him in the back seat.

"I want it," she managed, her voice practically a purr. As his hands moved further and further up her thighs, she was thrilled she'd decided to wear a skirt, albeit one that misbehaved. And yet as she felt his hands on her upper thighs…

"Careful…tights," she managed.

"Damn," he half growled, his hands pausing at her hips, then slowly making their way up to her waist. Slowly, being the operative word.

She didn't want him to stop, wanted him to keep touching her, wishing he'd explore her clit with his hands. She wanted to forget her name.

"Don't stop!" she yelled. "Pull them down…"

"I think," he said in her ear. "I think we're at your place."

She felt like an idiot. "Ummm…well…does this guy…"

He raised an eyebrow. "He drives Semenov and I to practice every once in a while. He won't say anything."

"Okay. Okay. Okay." She took a deep breath. "Okay."

"Trust me," he said, pulling her close to him. "I never would have… let myself go if I wasn't completely safe. Sure that you would be safe." He paused and she saw the question in his expression. "Upstairs?"

She nodded, grinning. "Upstairs."

*****

Their clothes didn't last more than five minutes after they had gotten upstairs and into Mel's apartment. She'd kissed him and that was it. Against the living room wall, their fingers grabbed and pulled off any article of clothing that was in reach. And then, as they stood stark naked and horny in the middle of the room, she gave him a look that nearly incinerated him on the spot. Then her cute little ass headed towards the bedroom. "Come and get me, stud," she called over her shoulder.

He ran after her, following her into the bedroom, making some crazy primeval growl as she jumped onto the bed, falling on top of it.

He found himself focusing on that nice ass of hers. And in an instant, he knew what he wanted to do. He reached out, grabbing her hips and pulling that cute butt towards him. "You're mine," he said as he kneeled on the bed. She was ready and dammit, he wanted inside those slick folds. With one smooth stroke, he entered her from behind, eliciting a gorgeously beautiful sigh from her lips. Feeling the wetness of her clit, he reached down to her outer folds, hoping he'd be able to give her something as he turned into the two minute wonder.

"More!" she shouted as she grabbed onto the headboard. "I want to feel you…."

And so he pumped, thrusting his hips. He was in so deep he couldn't tell where he ended and she began. He was about to lose it, and he felt her tightening around him like a glove. The edge was so close… he tried to hold on, but he couldn't. He let go, and pushed over the boundary line.

"Chrissssssssssss!" she shouted. "Oh dear god."

The sound of her letting that pleasure wash over her cut the silence in the apartment.

He watched her as he pulled out of her, focusing on how she fell against the pillows. She was adorable, she was his and she was there, soft and comfortable in his arms. And until his phone rang early the next morning, he wasn't letting her go.

CHAPTER ELEVEN

After Mel had woken up from the post-book coma, she found herself glued to the streaming video on her computer screen, watching the Empires games as live as she could get them. Once his games were over and he was back in his hotel room, she and Chris would talk, Skype, text or talk, win or lose. They joked about her cover art for the book that was coming out and how he'd managed to avoid getting hit by the flurry of hats that came his way despite the fact he was playing an away game. But nothing could compare to seeing him.

Which meant the first night he was back in New York, they had dinner at Darcy's. It was safe—since Chris had agreed to start doing the pub's books—comfortable and rather delicious. But after her burger, she looked at the dessert menu and decided she wanted something else. "I want a cupcake," she said, grinning up at Chris. "And I saw a few places nearby."

He nodded, signaled for the waitress. "Can we have the check, Caro?"

As the waitress returned with the check and they did their traditional stare down, before he rolled his eyes and paid, Mel realized beyond all else, she felt happy. Warm. Comfortable. Loved.

"You ready?" he asked, excitement in his eyes.

She nodded. "Absolutely."

Together, they walked hand in hand out of the restaurant. "Feels good, doesn't it?" she asked.

"Yeah," he said as pulled her closer and kissed her cheek. "It does."

She giggled, and gave herself up to the moment, the feeling of walking down the cobblestone streets with him, towards the place she'd seen. Tiny shop, glass window, familiar joker in the window. "Here," she said as she pulled him into the shop.

"Whoa." He grinned, but followed her lead all the same. "A woman who knows what she wants. I like that muchly."

"Like?" she wondered, her eyebrow raised as she gestured towards a display case filled with cupcakes of all sorts. "A woman who brings you this, and all you can say is like?"

This coaxed a full-bodied laugh out of him. "I might have a few other 'l' words to contribute to the discussion," he returned, once he'd stopped laughing. "I mean there's lemon, lickable…."

She rolled her eyes and grinned at the people behind the counter. "One lovely squiggle and one…something for the lummox over there." She turned towards Chris. "What do you want?"

And in the middle of the silence, she stared in the direction of the lights that were coming through the glass and blinding her.

They'd been found.

She tried to breathe, tried to calm down but she failed miserably. Chris's angry expression left as suddenly as it came, then his arms wrapped around her, pulling her towards him "Okay," he whispered. "Okay. We'll get out of this. I promise."

"Yes. Yes," she managed. "We'll go when I nod."

Then he turned back around, placed a twenty on the counter and focused on her. "Ready when you are, love."

She was so nervous that she almost didn't catch it. But it was there, and despite everything, those casual words hurt her heart the most.

*****

He grabbed her hand, watching her. At her nod, they broke out of the store, leaving their cupcakes behind. Forget the fucking icing, they needed safety from the disaster waiting outside. They busted through the barricades, the swarms of people in front of them. He knew these streets like the back of his hand, and kicked himself for not being smart enough to drive down.

He heard her breath, coming in quick gasps, and felt her hand tighten around his. They ducked around a corner, letting her breathe for a second. "The Elk isn't that far from here," he replied.

"Dammit," she said, her words lost in the tears she was fighting. "All I wanted was a fucking cupcake. I'm sorry…"

He shook his head. He needed to cut off that argument immediately. "Not your fault."

A small grim smile altered the planes of her face before he saw her take a deep breath and begin to pull herself together. "Let's go," she pronounced.

They ran through a few more alleyways, then opened a back door Bruce always kept unlocked in case of emergencies.

"Fucking hell," Bruce said as he and Mel came through into the kitchen. "You two alright? You need anything?"

As Chris was about to answer, he saw Sousa running into the back. "You guys need to get out of here," Sousa said, her words quick. "Kay just called…you're all over the place and they're trying to bust in here. Fuck knows what happened. But Al…Razor's Al, put the word out. He said the guys by him'll take you somewhere. Fucking hell."

Mel looked at him, fear and worry on her face. "There's one place I can think of."

And as she took out her phone, Chris held his breath. He focused on his Melanie as she dialed a number and spoke into the phone. And when she put the phone back into her pocket, she met his eyes.

"Uncle Arnie said to come to him from wherever we are."

He nodded. Now that their destination was set, they were ready. They had to go. And fast.

CHAPTER TWELVE

The safety of Arnie Dawes's apartment was something she hadn't expected, but Melanie grabbed onto it with both hands. "Thank you so much," she replied. "I mean…"

"Of course, my dear," Uncle Arnie said, smiling as he ushered them both into his study, closing the door behind them. He gestured to the couch and Chris guided her towards it, concern in his eyes. She must have looked awful to make him look like that.

"You can do whatever you both need," Arnie said, as he continued to pace in front of the couch. "But I think the best thing would be to lay low for a while. And because the paparazzi seem to be on to you two, you won't find any peace in the city or the surrounding areas. I can get you an airplane, a car and security."

She looked at Chris and he seemed so lost, it hurt.

"Yeah," he said. He squeezed her hand and stood up, leaving her alone on the couch to pace. "I think that's a good idea." And then he paused. "I'm not sure how far we need to go."

She watched Arnie's expression change from concerned to happily surprised. "Just across the border would be enough," he said as he reached out to clap Chris on the shoulder. "I'm not suggesting the other side of the world."

Chris shook his head, and sighed. "Yeah," he said as he took his phone out of his pocket, a smile on his lips despite the desolation in his eyes. "I should probably make some calls."

She nodded, looked up at him. "Yeah. I'm sorry…"

He stopped pacing and bent down in front of her. His sudden focus scared her. "This is not your fault," he said as he ran a hand through her hair. "And I don't want you blaming yourself. No matter what happens. Not your fault." And then he kissed her, his focus changing from her mind to her mouth, his lips burning hers, his tongue invading, catching her almost unaware."

And when he broke the kiss, he smiled at her in a way that made her insides melt.

"Not more in front of your uncle, Mel. But you needed that, and well," he blushed. "I did too. Now I have an idea of where we can go."

"Where?" She focused on him, saw the nervousness in his expression and knew this was going to be difficult.

"North of the border." he replied. "In Canada, but I have to figure out exactly where."

*****

Chris braced himself. It was going to be complicated. But dear god he had to do it, and so with Mel and his team owner looking at him, he dialed the long distance, international number and waited. Ring. Ring.

"Chris, what the heck is going on? Kayleigh called us, to warn us? You and this girl…caught by the paparazzi. What exactly have you done?"

300

"Mom, I…" He swallowed back the pending explosion. He couldn't lose his mind like this, in front of both Mel and Arnie Dawes. His mother was freaking out. "The girl I'm with might be it. And she needs me."

He took a breath, tried to take the words back, but the look on Mel's face didn't say scared, so it was okay.

"For fuck's sake, JoAnn," his father interjected before he could say anything more. "The boy's been tortured enough. So has the girl."

"Graham…"

The sound of his father's voice as he made his presence known might have been enough to knock him senseless if he hadn't already been sitting down.

"Now Christopher, you may think we don't notice what you've done for the family, your siblings over the years, but we do. And what your mother is *trying* to say is that we can't help you unless we know what you need."

"I need a hideaway," he began, getting to the heart of the matter. He'd react to the nuclear fallout of the discussion later. "Bryson's using the cottage?"

"Don't even go there," his father said ruefully. "Your older brother's in one of his moods." Then he paused.

He knew his older brother's *moods*, and hoped this installment wasn't too serious. Just as he was about to ask, he heard his father's voice.

"What about your grandfather Leroux's place?"

"We never did anything with it," his mother interjected. "It's still in his name. Up in Ontario."

And after little while, he hung up the phone, arrangements having been made. Then he looked at Mel and Mr. Dawes, both of whom stared at him with such faith. "We're going to Ontario."

CHAPTER THIRTEEN

Melanie was terrified. Chris had bailed them out. Arnie had bailed them out. Emily had bailed them out, making some sort of magic with both the Public Relations people at her publisher and the Empires. Even Pierre, a relative of the guy who owned the Poutine shop bailed them out! Pierre picked up the keys, aired out the cottage they'd be staying in and met them at the airport. And she, who had done nothing, sat there on the plane, shaking like a leaf, as the song said.

"Shhh," Chris murmured in her ear. "It's okay."

"I don't *do* this," she replied. "I'm not like this. I'm stronger…I don't…" And then the tears came, racing out of her eyes like someone had turned on a faucet. "I don't sit on the sidelines as things fall apart around me. I take charge," she managed between the incessant bawling.

"Just because you're not taking charge for once doesn't mean you're not strong, Mel," Chris replied, his voice soothing in her ears. "There's so much you handle, so many situations where I would have

302

blundered, still would, and you walk right through them with a smile on your face. This time's mine."

He paused, and she felt as he ran his fingers through her hair. She liked the way it felt.

"And by the way, love, just because I'm not losing it doesn't mean I'm not freaking out."

She tried to remember that as they snuggled in the cottage in front a blazing fire. They talked, laughed and shared so much of their stories. It felt so comfortable. And yet.

And yet through the course of his storytelling, she noticed a common thread. Nobody really, extensively, had ever taken care of him. And that, she decided, needed to change.

*****

It was early, just starting to get light outside. Chris couldn't sleep anymore, and so he kissed Mel's shoulder and carefully got out of bed, throwing on a pair of sweatpants and a sweatshirt he'd casually left on the floor of the bedroom they were sharing. Yanking on a pair of boots, he headed outside to the Jacuzzi Pierre assured him still worked. He needed a soak.

The air was chilly, biting but perfect. He took a deep breath, and soaked in how pure it was. God this was good. Bad circumstances but good all the same; a getaway from *everything* with Mel by his side. But soon life would intrude. He headed over to the Jacuzzi, pressed the button and, within moments, Pierre's prognosis proved true as the bubbling began.

After waiting for a while he undressed, letting the air briefly hit his skin before he practically took a leap into the bubbling tub and settled in for a soak. It was wonderful.

*****

Melanie woke up when she rolled over and didn't collide with the large body of the guy who was sharing her bed. She stretched, sated, wondering where Chris had gone. She missed him. Wanted him. And decided she needed to go and get him.

She got out of bed, covered her body with the nearest blanket and headed into the kitchen. She'd take a look, she decided before going back to sleep, or not.

Stepping into the kitchen, she didn't see him moving around, but she caught sight of something outside, on the porch. The Jacuzzi.

Grinning at the prospect and the possibilities she could envision, she ran back to the bedroom. Then she grabbed a condom, ran back to the kitchen and opened the sliding door that separated the kitchen from the porch. And after taking a deep, bracing breath, she stepped through.

Quick footsteps took her to the Jacuzzi. Despite the fact she was moving quickly, she still was freezing her ass off. "Holy fuck, it's cold!" she exclaimed. She put the wrapped condom in her teeth, electing to keep her hands free enough to clutch the flimsy blanket to her naked body.

"It's March in rural Ontario. Of course it's fucking freezing," Chris replied, grinning at her, as he stood up from the tub. He was hard, big and ready. "Want to warm up? I'm all ready for you."

"I thought you'd never ask," she returned, grinning back at him after Chris had taken the condom.

As she dropped the sheet and sank into the tub, she watched Chris put on the condom and found herself, once again, rather thrilled at the size of his cock.

"Let's get warm," he said as he sank into the tub, the warm, bubbling water making her hot.

This time, she grabbed his good shoulder and, as they floated in the center of the tub, put her legs around his waist. "This way," she purred as she sheathed him. Holding him tightly, there was motion, friction deep within, his cock rubbing against her inner walls, the water bubbling around them pulling them closer. Pulling, pushing, closer, faster, harder, his breath against her, her heart flying…

And then they fell over the edge, together, not wanting this moment to end.

She felt his hands massaging, touching. This was perfect, this was simply perfect. He was so…*god*. She knew this would end, knew they'd have to go back to New York and she'd have to let him go. Because as the new book came out, she would become the public loudmouth 'Girl in the Lace Corset' once more, and he didn't deserve to lose his career because of her. He didn't deserve to be forced into her shadows. And that's what broke her heart.

But that would be later. Now, she luxuriated in his arms. She wouldn't let him go until he got called to join the team, and not one minute before that.

CHAPTER FOURTEEN

The Call came early in the morning. Melanie was put on a plane to New York, and no amount of discussion would convince her otherwise. In the end, he couldn't argue with her need to edit any more than she could argue with his need to meet his team. And because she wouldn't consider that kind of thing, he had to respect her wishes.

But that departure wasn't the only thing on his mind. In fact, Chris arrived at the team hotel in Toronto with a nasty feeling in the pit of his stomach that had nothing to do with Mel. The message left on his voicemail was unexpectedly ominous. And so he was looking for Assistant Coach Jim MacArthur, who everybody on the team called 'Mac', instead of Coach Michaels himself as he headed into the lobby.

"Coach wants to see you," Mac said as soon as they spotted each other.

He nodded, taking the folder with the check-in information and the room key. Same information, different hotel, he noted as he paged through it, grinning. Then he focused on the fact he'd been instructed to see his coach. "Everything okay?"

He knew Mac wasn't exactly going to elaborate, but he figured he should probably ask him anyway.

"Good luck, Emerson."

The usually stoic Mac had an expression he couldn't decipher, which once again, was bad news. "Thanks, Mac," he replied, smiling back despite the churning in his stomach, hefting his bag as he headed to the room number the coach had written on a slip of paper.

The feeling of dread didn't go away, even as he rode the elevator up to the meeting room and his destiny. His feet sank into the carpeted floor as he tried to mentally prepare himself for what was going to happen…for what he knew awaited him on the other side of the door. And when he got to the right one, he knocked.

"It's open, Emerson."

The tone of his coach's voice sounded ominous, the fact he didn't use the nickname he'd been saddled with made things feel worse. But he opened the door all the same, revealing a large living room suite, the coach sitting at a table.

"Come on in," he said, "and close the door."

He did, not saying a word, instead finding a seat across from the coach on a wood backed chair.

"You knew this was coming," the coach began. "I told you it was coming. Streak or no streak. You dress, but you're not playing, and if you, the media, anybody, bothers me about it, it will take you longer to touch the ice. That shit will put your *season* in jeopardy."

He nodded. He couldn't speak, there were no words he could use to answer, other than, "Yes Coach."

"Don't fuckin' yes me to death, Emerson. Your ass is mine to do with as I see fit. Hell, I can make you hang up a Canada Sucks flag every day if I goddam want to."

Coach's face was red but Chris didn't focus on it. Instead, he tried to keep his mind blank. He had to keep his cool and say nothing, do nothing if he wanted to keep his career. And so, somehow, he got through the rest of the meeting, let himself into the room he was sharing with Semenov and fell asleep to the sound of a cooking show.

*****

Melanie was alone in her apartment, staring at the television, her book done for now. Emily, her beta reader, had taken a red-eye to Toronto. Spin control the Empires called it. Her publicist had called her, wondering if there was anything she wanted, but she declined, deciding that all she really needed that night was the ability to bathe in chocolate.

Because ever since she'd gotten back from the cottage, she'd been bombarded with images and accounts of the mistake she'd made, and how she'd drawn Chris into it as well. The press had gone psychotic, the romance blogs were having a field day, the sports blogs were going on the romance blogs… It was just a mess and she wanted to hide.

But the television was off. She couldn't watch him play tonight. It hurt too much.

And then her phone started to buzz. She grabbed it, noticing the symbol for a new text in the corner. Three simple words. "They benched him." She started to cry.

*****

Chris had to keep his cool. Losing it in public was not going to help anything, least of all his already shit relationship with his coach. But both Miller and Semenov made a point of clapping him on the shoulder as they headed out onto the ice each night, in a visible show of support. Through Toronto, Ottawa and Montreal, and he still didn't play.

It got worse when he got back to New York. Worried calls from Kayleigh and his parents mixed with increased silence from Mel. He ignored the papers and the news channels, concentrating instead on the mess Darcy's previous management had made of that restaurant's books. He practiced and worked out as if he was going to get ice time. But it didn't happen. The season was starting to wrap up. And it was going to leave him behind.

*****

Emily had the nasty habit of interrupting Melanie at the worst possible moments. She was concentrating on the final edits of the now completed 'The Dangerous Duke' before she sent it to her agent. Not that it wasn't serious, but if she were being honest with herself, she'd admit that she was burying herself in edits instead of having to talk to Chris.

"So what are you going to do?"

"I don't know," she replied, sighing. Unfortunately, she did know what needed to be done. She just didn't know how or when she'd bring herself to do it.

"Whatever it is," Emily said, "you should do it soon, because it isn't fair to leave him hanging."

And as he remained a 'healthy scratch' in New Jersey and on the Island, she knew she had to do something.

*****

Chris didn't know how to react when Melanie finally contacted him. "God." He'd said as he organized the papers on the table he'd commandeered at Darcy's. He wondered what she wanted, though she seemed ominous. Her words, her tone. His stomach fell. *Fuck.* And of course she looked gorgeous, but he could see the circles under her eyes when she came in and let him guide her to a table in the back.

"Your own maître d'?" she asked, a grin on her face, though it was a small one.

"There's a lot here to go through," he replied, running a hand through his hair. "I haven't even breached the surface. It's been a mess for a while." And then a shrug. "It comes with privileges."

"Damn well it should." Then she laughed, and then sighed, staring at him.

He wished she wouldn't be so serious, so focused on him. "Did you finish?" he asked. "I know you've been working…"

She nodded. "Yeah. Thanks. I…well it's been hard." And then as if she'd changed her mind, she shook her head, all traces of her exhaustion gone. "But I'm sorry."

He raised an eyebrow. "For? Excuse me? Mel, I…" He broke off because once he put his hand on the table, she immediately removed hers. As if she couldn't bear to touch him.

"I'll be right back."

She ran off, leaving him sitting at the table, alone, wondering what he should do, full of words, full of sarcasm with no clue how to deal with any of it. Dammit. He was…trying to make something serious and there he was, looking like a complete moron. He held his breath and did the only thing he could. He waited.

*****

Melanie threw cold water on her face, as she stood in the bathroom, slowly losing her mind. She wasn't ready. She couldn't do this. But she had to. He deserved to be taken care of at least once in his life, and if she was going to break her own heart in the process, let it be for that kind of good cause.

Resolve. And so she took another deep breath, walked out of the bathroom and headed towards their table.

"Hey…" he said, concern in his eyes once she sat back down. "You know you matter…I mean really matter to me."

"I wish it didn't matter this much," she said, staring at the woodwork beyond. Anywhere but at him, anywhere but into his eyes. "I…can't do this, Chris. No. Not anymore. Not to you, not to me…"

"But Mel, you…you get me and…"

She shook her head, and this time, she let him see the tears that had refused to fall since they'd been on an airplane on the way to Ontario. "No. I want to, I really want to. And in a different world, we'd be perfect. So perfect, that this would be it for me, that you would be it." She stood up once again, swallowed and brushed his cheek with trembling fingers. "But life isn't perfect, not when you need to be low profile and I won't be able to hide once the new book comes out. And I won't cause your life to go upside down because I'm selfish. So this is goodbye." So before she lost her nerve, she left the table, the restaurant and walked onto the street outside. Against the bitter cold, she stood and waved her arm in the air, hoping a taxi would take her away from the misery threatening to overwhelm her.

CHAPTER FIFTEEN

One Week Later

His skates cut through the ice on the Tarrytown reservoir as easily as they did on the ice in Brooklyn. It was chilly, cold down to his bones. Reminded him of home in a way most things in New York had no chance of doing. Usually he didn't need that, but dealing with something like this, he did. He needed to be able to think in a way that running the city streets, or even in Central Park, never inspired him to.

The wind blew through his hair, his heart pounded against his chest. She'd left him. *Left him. For his own good*, she'd said. Fuck *'his own good'*. At least what she thought was his own good. He could go back to school if they sent him down, or released him, either of which would be easier than the continued benching. Go back to Montreal and finish the year he had left at McGill, then maybe get a PhD in economics, or an MBA and make the financial planning/accounting/advising stuff he'd been doing his real job. He wasn't without options.

Michaels was the only game in town, but he didn't have to play. Maybe he'd go somewhere else. He'd see. But he needed Mel to understand that she was more important to him than hockey. More importantly, he needed to remind her that he wasn't a one trick pony. He had more to recommend himself than a career in professional sports.

*****

Melanie was looking over the email from her agent. He'd pulled together all the travel commitments the publisher wanted, all the media tours they'd booked in conjunction with the new book—the one she'd written last year. When she was not dealing with a broken heart.

She recognized the usual mix of blogs, cities across the country, a few TV and radio shows along with some new things. And an event scheduled next week with an organization she didn't recognize.

She blinked and called her agent's office; he answered her questions better over the phone than in any other method. "What's this 'Empire Bridge Foundation'? What do they do?"

"That's the one you asked about last month—the one that got the proceeds from that casino night you went to. Your publisher's PR people loved the idea and organized some kind of 'Skating with the Authors' for the kids and more importantly, their mothers. You were on deadline, but I set it up so that you can decide within the next few days if you want to do it. You're not on the list officially but if you want, you'll be a surprise guest."

"Thanks," she replied. After a few more bits of conversation, she hung up the phone. What was she going to do?

*****

It was a summons from Arnie Dawes that brought him into Fort Greene after the morning practice session. He wasn't sure what to expect, but he had to go. A summons from your team owner conquered all.

"Mr. Dawes, sir?" he called, as he entered into the team owner's office. "Is everything—"

"She's upset. What happened?"

He laughed ruefully, as he sat in a chair across the oak desk.

But the team owner tapped his fingers against the desk, focusing on him behind a pair of wire rimmed spectacles. "So? What happened?"

"She ended it," he began, deciding there was no other way than to be honest about the situation. "She said it was for my own good."

"And because the ownership group has decided to let Michaels hang himself, I'm assuming you haven't been included on the 'Skate with the Authors' event that Empire Bridge is doing Friday?"

He shook his head, knowing that he was in a very weird position. He didn't want to whine to the owner but this was a very particular situation. And he had no choice. Especially since the man had just thrown him a rather large bone. "Nope."

Dawes nodded, once again tapping his fingers against the desk. "Hmm. Very interesting situation this is," he said, as he took a sip from the Empires mug that sat on his desk. "Just be prepared to go to that event on Friday, Christopher. We need you."

He nodded, clear that the meeting was over, and left the room. He still didn't know what to do, nor did he know what Dawes expected of him.

*****

"I will kill you," Emily said, as she came into Melanie's room the next morning. "If you don't do this thing on Friday."

It took Mel a minute to realize what Emily was talking about, partially because she was still catching up on the sleep she'd missed over the past few days. "Why? Why is it so important that I be there?"

"Because." Emily sighed as she plopped down on top of the bed where Mel had happily been lying. "Because you're not a coward. Because these women need to see you. Because they deserve to smile. Because you need to think of someone other than yourself."

Melanie rolled her eyes. "It's too early to be on the sanctimonious trip. You need to give me more concrete answers."

"It's never too early to try and appeal to your good nature, your charitable personality. Besides." Emily stretched out on the bed, forcing Mel to curl up. "You're the one who started this. From what I hear, your agent talked to the PR people at your publisher and this is what they cooked up. So you need to do it."

"And what do I say if I see him?"

Emily sighed once more, making Mel feel like she was about three years old. "Say what you need to *if* you see Chris, the big huge *if* playing a central role here. We're dealing with someone who's in chateau bow-wow for reasons that Michaels won't really elaborate to the press. I don't think the man is going to send him to something like this."

"But then there's Uncle Arnie," Mel interjected. "Arnie will."

"Who knows what Uncle Arnie's going to do. It all depends on what's going on in general, what he's in the mood for. All I think," Emily replied, "is that you need to go and be the 'Girl in the Lace Corset'. Whatever happens, happens. And, if you decide to fix what you broke—and don't think I don't know what happened—then that will fall into place too."

Mel nodded, well aware that she had no choice but to attend the event. She didn't know what would happen, but she'd deal.

Chapter Sixteen

The first part of Friday's event was fun. Chatting, signing over hot cocoa and tea, skating with the kids and their mothers on the ice before the kids went off with a group of the Empire players that didn't include Chris Emerson. Then the real conversation started.

That was fun too. She let herself go a little, spoke about why she loved writing about Duchesses, about women raised to be powerful and how well they were able to use the power they had to make Regency society better. At least, she told the group who asked her, that's what she thought. Other writers could have their Dukes, but she liked her Countesses and Duchesses, and the men they loved.

"Why the regency?" someone asked. "Aren't there any other periods that intrigue you? Regency is boring."

"Regency is home," she replied. "It's what I grew up reading, what I studied in College and in Grad school as a result. I love the period, love using what I learned in the books that I write. Not that I give all the details because they'd be boring in the end, but the details that I learned through my course of study have been turned into some of the best books I've written."

The comfortable chatter that followed made Melanie very happy. Unfortunately, it was the calm before the storm.

"So," interjected the young woman who was in charge of the event, "we're going to have a fun competition we like to call 'Skating With the Authors.' Each author will be paired with a hockey player, and it's up to each one of you to skate with your hockey player to a win."

A pause and one of the boards opened up, revealing someone standing in skates. And familiar blue streaks in his hair…

Mel's stomach twisted. Not in a good way.

"And because we've got more authors than hockey players, we'd like to add one more to our list. Please give a great Empire Bridge welcome to a man we'd like to see more of on the ice, our very own Number twenty-seven, Chris Emerson."

Oh great, Melanie thought to herself. This, would be fun.

Not.

*****

Some of the guys and some of the authors weren't having any fun. They were talking, not skating at all, treating this like they'd been chosen for torture. And that didn't make Chris very happy. The author/ hockey player combinations were being watched by women who spent most of their time with a terminally ill child. These women deserved to have a good time. And they deserved to grin along with people who were clearly enjoying themselves.

And so he came out onto the ice, searching for Mel, who was leaning against the boards, giving tips to some of the other authors. Girl could skate.

"Come on, miss," he said grinning, bowing over her hand. "Let's show them how it's done."

She looked at him, as if she was having trouble figuring out what he was looking for, what he wanted. And then she nodded. "All right."

A slow, languid song with the potential to kick butt started to play over the arena's speakers and, as the famous country singer began his refrain against the guitars, he took Mel's hands, watching as she skated and swayed to the music. But she wasn't moving the way he wanted her to.

"Hips," he said, grinning at her, his hands moving to those parts of her body, leaving hers to grasp his shoulders. "Come on," he encouraged as he moved her hips, first one then the other. "Leave it to me."

She blushed; he could feel the embarrassment rolling off of her like waves. Felt it dissipate into the air as the guys cheered her on.

"You can do it!"

"They're watching."

He nodded, not really sure what he was agreeing to, even as the authors joined the guys with whistles, and for the first time, not really caring.

"They can *see*."

It wasn't exactly a whine, but it was close. And so he took her hands back, satisfied she was loose on the ice despite her nerves, and skated her around a little bit more. "So," he murmured. "Let's give them a show. Because I'm not going anywhere anytime soon. This is real, Mel, and I'm not letting go."

"I…"

"Shhh," he replied, moving, leaning in and kissing her cheek as her hips swayed to the beat of the song. "You leaving," he whispered into her ear as he pulled her close, "totally not for my own good. Because, here's the thing." He took her hand, and skated backwards, then pulled her in close again, just like some of those pairs skaters did.

"There's more to me than hockey. Not that you don't know that, but what I'm telling you is that I'm in purgatory right now. I'm not playing and don't have you. You need to be out, loud and proud in the public with your books, and that's awesome. I can sit back and do financial planning. I'm cool with that. Because if I don't have you, nothing else really matters."

And as the singer continued to sing about the cool memories he'd had with the woman he missed the most despite whatever else he was doing, he skated with Mel. Gave her breathing room, let her think about what she wanted. Because in his mind, it was very clear. What he wanted was her.

*****

She wanted to say yes. Oh dear God she wanted to say yes. "What about your coach?"

"Coach benched me," he whispered. "I don't give a shit about what that asshole says. And I genuinely mean it."

"But here…"

"Arnie. He knew I wanted to see you. So he pulled rank and here I am."

She nodded. That meant her family…her mom and sister, approved. No wonder Em was so concerned about her not making it. "You sure you want this? Because what if…"

"Stop it," he said, reaching down to pull a tendril of hair out of her face. "Stop over-thinking, don't imagine any crazy potential scenarios. And kiss me."

Being the romantic she was, she did, to a crowd that cheered her on.

*****

After the event ended and they'd changed into more comfortable clothing, she'd agreed to go to 'The Elk' to celebrate the fact she'd agreed to consider their relationship again. "I'm not sure," she'd said, focusing on him. They'd just gotten into Manhattan and she was half on his lap, half on the seat, slightly negating the blunt force of her words.

He nodded slowly. "Really?"

"Really. Because you say you don't give a shit about your coach, but what if something happens? What if you end up regretting me because it hampers the rest of your career?"

"Ah, Mel," he said, grinning at her, kissing her cheek. "Let me show you the ways I won't regret you." He reached into his pocket with one hand and pulled her close with the other.

"Oh, that way?" she asked, sauce and humor in her voice.

He grinned back even as he pulled out his phone. "Maybe later. But now," he said as he used his thumb to navigate the spreadsheets he linked through his home screen, "I want to show you this."

She nodded and took the phone, and as he watched her looking at the rather impressive evidence of what he'd been doing with his money and his free time over the years he'd been playing hockey, he felt nervous. She'd seen the results up close and personal but had never actually looked at the hard data.

"Wow," she said. "This is…amazing."

He smiled, yet before he could answer, he heard the sound his phone made to indicate he had a new text. He looked at her and then, as she nodded, took back the phone to see if it was something he had

to deal with immediately. And as he caught a glimpse of the text, he gasped. "Oh shit. I have to go to back to Fort Greene. Coach…"

"I'll come with you," she said, his gladiatrix, his fighter.

"I love you," he replied. And even though they didn't say anything until they pulled back up the complex they'd left not long ago, he knew everything was going to be fine, no matter what happened.

*****

When Chris got up to the coach's office, Michaels was talking with the GM, a former player for one of the other New York area teams. He waited as patiently as he could, letting them talk and trying to breathe.

"So what happened?" asked Arnie Dawes, as he walked into the room. "Did you and my Melanie figure it out this afternoon?"

He smiled at the man who'd been wonderful to him and Melanie throughout the insanity that had been their lives for the last few weeks. "Actually, we did, I think, Mr. Dawes. We'll be all right."

Dawes was just about to reply, when through the silence Coach Michaels made an interesting sound.

"What the fuck?" The coach interjected. "I was just going to tell you that you were ready to come back and play, you fucking moron. Dammit Emerson, don't you realize that sluts like that corset girl are trouble? Fucking hell. You need to focus, maybe have a fuck buddy every once in a while, but not that stupid little bitch who can't keep her own damn nose out of fucking trouble, least of all yours. Back on the bench. Maybe down to Stratford."

"Peter, really?" The GM shook his head, staring at Dawes in silent accord. "You benched him, and though we disagreed with your choices, you are the coach."

"But," Dawes interjected, "when you continue to bench a player for no good reason and stopped his goal scoring streak…"

And as Dawes and the GM continued to list Michaels' faults, Chris found himself flabbergasted.

"Not to mention," Dawes pronounced, "you called my niece a slut. You're gone."

"She's your niece?" Michaels muttered as he left the room.

"Yes," Dawes replied. "She's my best friend's daughter. Now get the fuck out of here before I call the cops."

And if nothing else was going to surprise the shit out of Chris, it was that. Well, he hedged, either that or the look on Mac's face when he was called into the office.

*****

Melanie found herself pacing back and forth in the lobby of the Empires' headquarters. She got up from the chair she'd been sitting in, paced and then sat back down. She couldn't concentrate. Dammit.

What the hell was going on up there? What was happening? Why…

She checked her watch, and it looked like time was standing still. She couldn't believe this, couldn't understand why this was *taking so long*. Dammit.

She found herself partially wishing that she hadn't come, then decided that was insane. She needed to be there with him, needed to help him deal with whatever happened. And when the elevator doors opened, she lost her breath as she saw Uncle Arnie and Chris heading towards her.

"So, so, so? What happened? What happened?"

"Well," he said as he put his arms around her. "You know all those things that I'd been planning to do if this meeting went south?"